Break *Me*

- USA TODAY BESTSELLING AUTHORS -

MJ FIELDS

AND CHELSEA CAMARON

Break Me is a work of fiction. Names, places, and incidents either are products of the author's imagination or are used fictitiously. Any resemblance to actual events, locales, or persons, living or dead, is entirely coincidental.

Thank You

This book contains mature content not suitable for those under the age of 18. Involves strong language and sexual situations. All parties portrayed in sexual situations are adults over the age of 18.

This is a work of fiction. All names, characters, places and events portrayed in this book either are from the author's imagination or are used fictitiously. Any similarity to real persons, living or dead, establishments, events, or location is purely coincidental and not intended by the author. Please do not take offense to the content, as it is FICTION.

Break Me

All The Rest - Twizted
How To Live Alone - Evan Ross, T.I.
Sorry Not Sorry - Bryson Tiller
Let's Get Lost - G-Easy, Devon Baldwin
Hollow - Tori Kelly, Big Sean
Overdose - Alessia
All Eyes on You - Meek Miller
Free - Ryn
Shine - Years & Years

Other Books By MJ and Chelsea

The Caldwell Brothers

Redemption Road

Break Me

To break the chains that bind me, I must first acknowledge I am damaged. To change the patterns started long before me, I must first find the power from within to hold back. To be the man I want to be, I must break down the man I am today.

-Jason "Cobra" Stanley

Jason 'Cobra' Stanley is an underground fighter. Born to an asshole grown into an asshole, his life has been one hit taken, one hit given. The cycle needs to end now, but he can't sort it out.

He trains to contain his power, yet when he's home with the woman he claims to love there is a rage that builds inside. He doesn't mean to lose control. He doesn't mean to harm her, but he does time and time again.

Sorrow only builds the walls higher and fuels the isolation and rage in his mind.

The more he pushes, the more he pulls away. Lost once

to Jagger Caldwell, Jason feels like he's losing more than a fight, he's lost himself.

Lorraine Bosch is an ER nurse who prides herself in remaining calm in all the chaos of her job. Life hasn't been roses and sunshine for a little girl who was raised by the firm hand of her father. They say little girls find themselves in love with men like the ones who raised them.

Cobra takes one hit too many to the head and finds himself under the care of Lorraine. She's only with him for a short time, but her blonde hair shines like a halo in his fuzzy mind.

She's his saving grace. What happens when a visibly broken man finds his chance at getting it right? Can two people with similar pasts truly break the cycle of violence?

Dedication

This book is for everyone. Your past does not define your future. Fight to move forward and let nothing and no one stand in your way. Nobody can beat you down. You have the fight inside to overcome all obstacles in your path.

Foreword

The book in front of you may be one of the most rage-inducing books you ever encounter. The book you are about to read is unlike any common contemporary romance. It has triggers, many triggers. In writing this story, our intention was not to upset, enrage, or encourage any person. Our thought process in writing this book was one simple theme: redemption.

Jason "Cobra" Stanley is an anti-hero. He's not the man you love and swoon over. This is his story of breaking the cycles of his past. We do not condone the behaviors found in this book, but the reality is there are relationships like this. People are struggling with the fight inside to break the cycles of abuse in their history. There are women over-coming traumas and learning to love and trust again.

Please read with an open mind and heart. Please know we do not accept or agree with violence in relationships of any kind. Please read with the warning this book is trigger filled and we hope by the end of it, we have given you a story of redemption road … a path not paved and unclear, but one that comes to an end with a happily ever after.

Much love,
MJ Fields and Chelsea Camaron

Prologue

Fifteen years earlier

"How dare you shame me!" The backhand comes before I can brace for it.

The burn, the sting, the copper taste of my own blood fills my mouth as the next blow comes crashing down. By now, I should expect this. By now, I should know better. By now, I should give him back what he gives and give it harder. But I don't.

There is some warped, twisted part of me that feels like I have earned his punishment even when I can't explain what I did or even what he thinks I did. Some days, I could be given the blows simply because it rained and his designer suit got wet.

"How can people believe I'm able to run a city when I don't have control of my own house?" His voice booms, making each word thunder in my aching head. "Everything we do is under scrutiny."

I should say something. I should fight back. I should do

anything to get away, to find a reprieve. I don't. Instead, I numb my mind and let him hit me.

My face is swelling, and I think I may have a chipped tooth, but I don't cry. I don't make one sound. I learned as a young boy that the less I say, the less I move, the quicker it ends.

I can't remember a time in my life when everything I did wasn't under a microscope. I can't remember a time in my life when I did not make him angry to the point of rage. The more he reacts, the more he loves me. My mom has told me that more times than I can count.

At first, I told myself it was me. If I were a better boy, smarter, stronger, he wouldn't have to punish me. Later, I told myself it was him, and I simply needed to get by until I could get out. I dreaded summer vacation from school. It meant more time home and more time to fuck up. The only thing that kept me going was telling myself I would break the cycle.

At fifteen, I found my outlet in the gym. When the rage inside would build so deep I could feel it pulse through my very veins, I needed somewhere to get it all out. The heavy bag takes every punch and kick I give, and then it waits for more. The octagon of the underground fights has been my escape since I was nineteen. I take the hits I need to and lay out the motherfuckers when the time is right. Finally, I found a place I don't have to hold back.

By day, I'm Jason Stanley, son to Mayor Stanley. I grew up behind the gates of an upper-class suburb of Detroit. Politics and presentation are everything. By day, I work in the voter registration office of the city. By day, I am a college-educated, entitled prick. By day, I walk with my head held high and know I'm untouchable . . . except by him.

The man who made me, the man who molded me, the

man who I disappoint at every turn, James Jason Stanley, my father, accepts nothing less than perfection, and I fail every day. He rules the city with laws and police officers at his back. He rules his home with an iron fist.

I'm out of his reign of terror now. Missy, my girlfriend, and I have our own place. She is a twelve on a scale of one to ten. With tits, ass, and so much sass, she pushes my buttons and keeps my dick hard. She needed a deeper commitment than just fucking, so we moved into this condo together. It's not large, but it's far from small. I give her freedom with my bank account to decorate it however she likes. Thank fuck, she doesn't put up a bunch of dust collectors and frilly stuff. I could give a shit about décor; I just need a place to fuck her when I want, how I want, and without anyone to answer to.

"I saw you today." The brunette in my life walks in. That's Missy: no regular greeting, just balls to the wall, in my face.

"Well, hello to you, too." I give back her attitude.

"I saw you with her," she adds as she steps out of her sky-high heels and walks into the kitchen.

I raise an eyebrow in question. "Inform me; who exactly did you see me with?"

Pulling out a bottle of her favorite red wine, she sets a wineglass in front of her and pops the cork.

I stalk over to her, waiting for an answer.

"Renee Felicia—I saw you with her at lunch." She pours her wine and sips the liquid slowly. As she closes her eyes, I can feel the anger coming off her. It amps me up.

I feel my heart beat faster, my blood pump harder, and my eyes zero in on my target as the adrenaline fuels me. Just like before I enter a fight, the energy builds up inside me like I may explode.

"Renee Felicia, as in my father's secretary?" I ask,

knowing damn well I was with her today, but we did not have lunch. She was at the same sandwich bistro I was at. She had to get my father's sandwich just right, and she was already having a bad day. She asked my thoughts, I gave them and hoped he was in the mood for roast beef on rye; otherwise, Renee would have the afternoon from hell.

Setting the glass on our counter, she taps her professionally manicured nails against it. "Do not patronize me. Do not act like I'm crazy." She raises her voice with each word. "I saw you with her!"

"Baby." I come around the corner and into the kitchen. I need to diffuse the situation. I feel myself on the edge. She will push me, and it may be too far. "I helped her order my father's meal. That's it." She raises an eyebrow at me in irritation. "She's old enough to be my mother," I add, thinking that will explain everything. "My dad's an ass of epic proportions—you know this. Renee's had a shit time lately. I was trying to help her."

Missy doesn't speak. Before I can react, her hand is around the neck of the wineglass and it's in the air. The wineglass hits my face, the red liquid splashing into my eyes, burning and blurring my vision. The glass hits the tile floor and breaks, shards flying everywhere.

What the fuck is she thinking?

"Don't you baby me, Jay." She doesn't move, only glares. "I know all about the cougars in city hall. She probably sucked your cock in the bathroom before having your father for an afternoon snack."

Rage fills me. I step closer to her, and she steps back. Ignoring the pain in my feet as the glass slices into my skin with each step I make, I move until she's backed against the counter.

"Were you not on my dick this morning? Were you not on my dick for hours last night? I'm not fucking Superman. I love pussy, but, Missy, a man has to let his dick have a small break. That's why we get jobs and go to work."

"Yeah, and you probably fucked her wrinkled pussy in the bathroom for your lunch hour." Reaching down, she rubs her pussy through her pants. "Hope that cobweb-filled, old, stank pussy was worth giving up all this, because you aren't coming near it again for a long damn time." She taps her finger on her lip like she's thinking. "I'm sure I can find someone to take care of my needs."

She threw a glass of red wine on me. My feet are sliced and bleeding because of her. To top it off, she taunts me. Does she not realize she's poking a sleeping bear?

I step toward her, the glass cutting deeper into the bottoms of my feet. The pain only adds to my anger.

"Jagger gave it to me good in the past." She sucks on her finger. "I wonder if he could free up his schedule for another round."

I see red, and it's not from the liquid running down my face. My hand goes around her throat, and I push her into the back wall of our galley kitchen. She has nowhere to go as I pin her there.

"Bitch, if I wanted her on my cock, she'd be there. She's a damn cougar, sure, but she didn't have a piece of me. Before you come in here, spouting some crazy shit, you better have your facts straight." I release her neck, and she gasps for air as she runs her hands over the reddened skin. "As for someone else wanting your magic pussy, you should know there isn't another fucker out there who will put up with your crazy outside of a bedroom, so your pussy is all you're good for."

"I'll show you crazy, Jay." She scratches at my face, and I feel the burn as she cuts me.

I raise my right hand in the air and swing down. The only noise is the sound of me connecting with her.

I can't think anymore.

I can't see.

I can't hear beyond the roaring in my ears.

I feel pain.

I feel infuriated.

I feel betrayed.

I feel hurt.

I feel completely out of control.

It's like my brain leaves my body; I am watching someone else as she paws me, scratching, clawing. She screams as my hand comes down again. She keeps fighting me. She yells, but I can't understand her words as I reach up with two hands and grip her throat.

I need her to stop.

I need her to be quiet.

I need her to feel me.

I need her to feel my pain.

I need her to understand my emotions.

I love her. I hate her. I can't be without her.

My lips crash down on hers as I release her throat. She reaches up and pulls my hair, my ears, trying to get me to stop kissing her. It takes a moment, and then she relaxes against me and kisses me back.

My mind calms. My body relaxes. The tension between us moves from that of anger to sexual. All the emotions and passion take over, and we can't get enough of each other. This twisted game only fucks with my head more.

I told her the first time I put my hands on her that it wouldn't happen again. That time, I only grabbed her arm to stop her from leaving. She winced, and I immediately released her. Somehow, things changed, and she pushes and pushes until I crack now. She knows where it will lead, but she won't back off. She doesn't deserve this, but why can't she stop herself from pushing us there?

Every time, I'm left with regret. I'm left giving the apologies that are nothing more than words. As much as I don't want to put my hands on her, I can't seem to hold back. I can't break the cycle. I am weak. I am a bastard, born of a bastard, and I am destined to repeat my father's mistakes.

I hate myself. I hate what I do to her. I hate what we do to us.

I don't mean to hurt her. I don't mean to hurt us. I thought I could break the cycle. I was wrong. Can't she see I need her? Doesn't she see I love her? Can she understand this is all I know?

Chapter One

Getting ready for the day, I stand at the bathroom counter in only my green boxer briefs. I pick up the can of shaving cream, then squirt the white foam into my hand. Wiping it across my jaw and neck, I turn when the door opens.

Missy enters in her black silk lingerie. She moves to me and pushes me back, climbing onto the spare space of the countertop. She picks up my razor, leaning over and wetting it under the running water. Without hesitation, she slides the sharp metal down my face and neck. The only noise between us is the running water.

I cage her in with a hand on each side of her as she leans over to wash away the shaving foam and my facial fuzz. Eye to eye, I take in the woman who consumes me.

She's short, five foot three to my six-foot-two frame. Missy has ample breasts with an hourglass figure that bubbles out into the hips and thighs I love to grip as she rides me. Her tanned skin is flawless, as is her heart-shaped face that is full of pinup style seduction.

How did it start so amazingly and go to hell so fast?

I get hard as she sits in front of me, her chest rising and falling with every breath she takes. Her nipples poke out from the thin material. She licks her lips, and I want a taste.

Leaning in, I lick her lips. With our faces inches apart, she pulls the razor down my face again. Her legs wrap around my back, keeping me in place.

"What's on the agenda today, Mr. Stanley?" she whispers seductively.

I smile as she rinses the blade. "Meetings at nine and eleven, lunch with Tatiana, planning conference at two, and then I'll be at the gym till after dinner." I give her my day honestly.

With a smile, she brings the blade to my face. She starts at mid-cheek and comes down. At my jaw, she twists, and I feel the telltale burn of a cut.

"Lunch with Caldwell's woman?" The tone in her voice is pure evil, as was the cut I now sport on my chin.

I jerk back, her legs releasing me. "That's what I said, wasn't it?"

Her eyes flash from sexy to malicious. "Maybe I should give Jagger a call. He sure did give me good. I don't know why I ever came back to you." She reaches out to swipe at me with the razor, but I catch her wrist, stopping her.

"Are you fucking psycho? I could crush you, yet you cut me and try to do it again." I fight to contain my anger. "Why do you do this, Missy?"

"Don't you give me that shit, Jason!" she screeches, swinging out with her other arm, which I catch at the wrist, forcing me to step into her. "This is not on me!" I wonder how she can say that when I feel the trickle of blood move down my freshly shaved throat. "You put your hands on me," she continues yelling. "Then it's 'I'm sorry, baby,' and you do all the right things until you fuck up again."

I look in her cold, dark eyes and spout, "I fucking hate you."

She smiles. "Likewise," she taunts, which makes the rage build inside. "The Cobra, so deadly. Watch his strike . . . more like, watch his strikeout against Caldwell."

I wrench her arms behind her back, holding both her wrists in one hand. She drops my razor as I step into her space.

Inches away from her face, I inhale, smelling her soap and arousal. "You shouldn't play games with someone who has as much venom inside as me," I warn.

She laughs in my face. "What are you gonna do, hit me? We've done that dance before, Jason." She meets my stare. "More than once."

Shame washes over me. I said I wouldn't put a woman through what my mother and I endured.

Releasing her, I shove away and move to stand in front of the sink. I pick up my dropped razor, ignoring her, as I do a quick finish of my shave. I fight the fury inside me that wants nothing more than to break her.

Like she's broken me.

I won't do it.

Growling, I continue about my morning as she sits on our countertop, watching me.

"Legacy. Oh, the Caldwell legacy," she whispers, removing her top. "The way he handled me." She cups her breasts and tweaks her nipples. I watch from the corner of my eye as I try to clean up the cut on my jaw. "Your little mouse, Jagger Caldwell's little one, can't handle a man like that. It's only a matter of time before I can have another hit of the Hitmaker. He's a drug all his own." She slides her hand down her panties.

Ready to blow my top that Jagger Caldwell can turn her on with me standing right here, I move away from her and drop my boxers. I step into the shower as she moans out his name.

Where did the love go?

Once upon a time, I couldn't get enough of her. Now, I swear she lives to see just how deeply she can cut me.

The water beats down on my body as my muscles flex instinctively. Jagger fucking Caldwell, the man who came from nothing to be a legacy of everything I ever wanted to be and won't ever be.

I punch the subway tiles of my shower. My knuckles split, but I keep hitting. I won't touch her again.

Little mouse, Tatiana Rand, now Caldwell, was raised by a monster much like mine. The night I took away all her fears, I promised myself this would be a turning point for her and for me. I would only use the fights and the gym for my aggression.

The night I gave Tatiana's father everything he had coming to him and more, I told myself that was it. If Jagger Caldwell could be his mother's legacy of good in a world full of bad, then I could find a way, no matter how much Missy provoked me, not to put my hands on her.

It has become a sick and twisted game between us, one I'm not proud of. I have to learn control. Underneath it all, we are two people who once had an undeniable love and passion between us. I need to remember what started it all before I lose it all. I need us to go back to the place before it all got shot to hell.

Hit after hit, I pound away, knowing this is going to cost a mint to repair. When I have exhausted myself and my mind can't think beyond the burn in my knuckles, I stop. The soap is fire to my open skin as I wash up.

However, the physical pain is a welcome reprieve from the pain clawing inside of me.

After losing my fight with the unmoving wall of my shower, I get out and towel off, wiping the blood from my knuckles. I look at the soft, white towel now stained with my blood.

How many times have these towels been marred with the damages of Missy and me fighting? How many times has her blood been mixed with mine?

I can't even count anymore. Somehow, what was never supposed to happen, something that was never supposed to occur . . . I promised Missy I would never lose it no matter what she did. I would not overpower her. Yet, time and time again, she pushes, and I fall weak to my anger.

This ends now. No more push and pull, no more anger and love all entangled in a mix of bad magic.

Brushing my teeth, I listen for noises in the apartment. When I hear nothing, I make my way to our bedroom and get dressed for the day. As I knot my necktie, I step out into the living room to find Missy crying on the couch.

I look at the mess of a woman on our sofa. I look at what we've done to each other, what I've done to her. I can't help but blame myself, I'm the man. The once vibrant, smiling, confident seductress has been reduced to a puddle of tears and anger.

"Baby," I call out to her. Sad eyes meet mine. "Why do you push me? Push us?"

She turns away from me. "This is the only time you see me, Jay."

My chest aches, and I fight my instincts to get defensive. "Missy—"

"No, Jay. The only time you really see me is when I'm in your face. You're gonna leave here now, and the best part of your day will be lunch with Caldwell's woman.

That's messed up. I have never been the best part of anything for you." She sobs, and I immediately feel like a douchebag.

Going to her, I pick her up easily and sit down, pulling her into my lap as I hold her close.

"I love you, Missy. You."

"Tatiana has a piece of you."

I sigh because she does. Tatiana Rand Caldwell has a twisted, dark piece of me. I killed her tormentor, and I don't regret it one bit. She is in love with Jagger. We're friends, sort of. That's her boundary, and if I cross it, I lose the only person who can look into my dead eyes and find something good in me. I almost lost having anything with her when I tried to push for more.

"You have me, Missy." I kiss the top of her head.

"I want all of you, and I'll never have it."

How can I reply? She can't possibly want to see all of me, otherwise she wouldn't prod the dark within me. She doesn't help me to fight back my own demons. She doesn't make me a better man.

Saying nothing, I hold her until I have to get up to leave. As much as I hate for things to be like this, I can't be late for work. My job was given to me the day I earned my political science degree, and it came based on my last name alone. The only perk to being the son of James Stanley is having a solid career . . . not that it's the one I would choose for myself, but no one ever asked.

I leave her silently contemplating on our couch; I know that nothing will change, she'll be there when I come home and we'll be back at each other's throats all over again. On the drive to work, I try to think of a way for us to come back from our demise. And like all of the other times I've tried to grasp at a solution, I come up empty-handed. I have no answer.

My morning is like any other day at the office. Then lunch comes, and I happily escape, loosening my tie as I leave. The café Tatiana and I meet at isn't far, so I walk. I grab a table outside and wait. It's not long before the tall, skinny, raven-haired Russian makes her way to our table. She sits, and I know better than to hug her.

Caldwell and I will never be friends. My respect for Tatiana is what keeps me from pushing for anything more. I tried to at one point, but she shot me down. Even after I admitted what I did for her, Caldwell still won.

He will always be the better man and her champion. Still, I would rather have her as my friend than not have her in my life at all.

She started out as a toy in a game between me and Caldwell. In the end, she changed me from the inside out.

"Jason." She smiles softly. "How are you?"

"Getting by, mouse. Getting by." I look over her shoulder to meet the brown eyes of Jagger "Hitmaker" Caldwell. She notices where my eyes are and turns her head to smile over at her man. There is love in her eyes. She then turns back to me and twists her hands nervously.

"Sorry, Jason. Jagger and I do most things together."

I smirk and give a little taunting wave at my past enemy.

I guess the only way to describe us now is frenemies. We will never be close. He will never trust me, and he shouldn't. If I had a woman like Tatiana going to lunch with a man like me, knowing what the past holds between us, I would be sitting within earshot, too.

"I get it, mouse. He's got a good thing in you; he's not going to let that slip through his hands."

"Back to you, Jason. Your answer—getting by. Come on, you can't just get by. That's not living."

The waiter interrupts us to take our orders. It doesn't

take long for our food to arrive. Tatiana eats quietly before putting her fork down and staring at me.

"Tell me that came from a fight," she commands as she looks at my busted knuckles.

I shake my head.

She gasps, and I see fear flash in her eyes. I hate that look. I hate that she knows all my secrets and knows exactly what I'm capable of—the monster inside me that can't be held back. I told her everything the night I brought her back to my place after she was out looking for Jagger. I shouldn't have, but something about her had me sharing. Part of me did it to try to scare her, but the dynamic between us quickly shifted from me trying to mess with Caldwell into me wanting to have something real, a woman who knew what I was but believed I could change, even if that ended up only in our friendship.

She swallows hard. "How is Missy?" she asks on a whisper.

"When I left, she was pissed off, but physically, she's fine." I rub my jaw, feeling the cut from this morning.

I should probably explain to Tatiana that I didn't hit Missy, but I don't. In my mind, I beat the shit out of her. The only difference is, instead of it being her in front of me, I let it be the wall so I wouldn't destroy her. In my mind it was her, a blow for every damn comment she made about Caldwell.

Tatiana looks at me seriously. "Talk to me."

"There's nothing to tell you that I haven't already said before. I lose my cool with her."

I could whine and bitch that Missy pushes me, but in the end, I need to be accountable. I am the fucked-up son of a fucked-up man, and I can't help hurting those around me.

I look at the one woman who has been my only real

female friend ever. "Mouse, you should go. Have your life with Caldwell. I'm no good for you as a friend or a stranger." I drop my fork onto my plate, no longer having an appetite.

She reaches out and squeezes my hand. "You don't scare me. I see the good inside you."

I laugh sharply. "Tatiana, you see the good in everything. It's like in the Caldwell cocktail or some shit. Mouse, there's nothing good inside me. You should go."

Her dark eyes glass over in unshed tears. "Jason, fight back the darkness."

"I have, mouse. I have. She pushed and pushed, and I gave the punishment to the wall," I finally admit. "The thing is, my head was still there. My head was giving it to her."

"Do you ever stop to think you need a fresh start? You both have too much negativity shared between you, and maybe it's time to move on."

"I love her," I acknowledge, and I do. It's all fucked up and twisted, but once, there was love, deep, fierce love or something.

"Love isn't supposed to be painful."

This comes from the innocence of one who has never had her heart ripped to shreds. "If only I could agree with that . . ."

"Jason, I say this from a good place. You and Missy have a toxic relationship." I raise an eyebrow at her, but she keeps going. "Once, you saved me from a dangerous place. I'll never forget the freedom you've given me not to have to look over my shoulder. There is good in there. You and Missy, though . . . As my version of saving you, I beg you to let her go. This isn't healthy, and it's going to continue to hurt both of you."

I sigh yet don't speak. She's asking me to give up on the

one thing I have given my all to other than when I helped fix her situation at home.

Looking at my watch, I give her a quick goodbye, knowing I have an afternoon of work ahead of me.

I know she has my best interests at heart, but I don't want to just give up on Missy. We live together. This was supposed to be our life, our future, our time. But I know something has to change, too.

After a long day at work, my right-hand man, Brock, meets me at the gym. Before we can start a workout, his phone pings with a text. Location set—pop-up fight. He nods to me, and then we gather a bag of necessities before leaving the gym.

I need this: the release, the adrenaline, the blood pumping through my veins as my body fights for oxygen.

Chapter Two

Henry Ford Hospital emergency room has been extremely busy today. I swear it's a full moon. It's six o'clock, five hours after my shift was supposed to end, but there is no way I am getting out of here anytime soon.

All hope for leaving totally dies when a large, tanned man comes in through the ambulance entrance.

"I need some help here!" he yells, carrying the unconscious body of a barely dressed man who has been brutally beaten.

I grab the only spare gurney and rush down the hall toward them. Once he is on the bed, I yell for another nurse.

"He gonna be okay?" the man who brought him in asks.

"We will do everything we can. Have a seat in the waiting room. When we know something, we'll let you know," I tell him as we rush his friend to an examining room.

Later, when one of the staff goes out to the waiting

room to give an update and try to get the patient's name, the man who brought him in is long gone.

His injuries are pretty superficial, aside from the concussion. The bruising and cuts on his ribs and face are unbelievable. His hands are cut up, too.

When we cut his clothes off and I see the lean, ripped, muscular build of his tattooed and naked body, I am pretty sure my assumption about him is correct. He is a fighter. Not just a fighter, but an underground fighter. For a month now, we have seen an increase in patients coming in looking like this. From what I have been told, the fights always increase in the summer months.

Violence is senseless. At different times, it brings on different emotions from me: either fear or anger.

As I sit next to him, even with the assumption he is a fighter, I can't help wondering if he isn't a victim. Maybe he was out for a jog, and some random criminal jumped him. Maybe some person with no conscience or consideration for human life decided he didn't deserve his. Then I become angry. I am angry someone hurt him.

As I carefully clean the blood from his wounds, I sigh and whisper, "You're going to be okay. We're going to make sure of it. You're not alone."

After he is cleaned up, stabilized, and all vitals are solid, I sit next to him, making good on the promise that he won't be alone. The entire time, I tell him repeatedly that he will be okay.

After a while, his eyes begin to flutter and appear to be preparing to open. I quickly go out to the hall and grab a doctor.

I stand on the patient's left and the doctor on his right when his eyes open for the first time and he groans.

"Do you know where you are?" Dr. Bennett asks him. He is my favorite doctor here. He is good with everyone and has a great bedside manner, which many seriously lack. We also have a close personal relationship since his son dated my sister.

"Hell," he groans. "Kill the light."

Dr. Bennett gives me a wink, then looks back at the patient. "Can I ask you a few questions?"

"Not right now," he grumbles in a sleepy, deep rumble.

"Thank you for staying," Dr. Bennett tells me. "Things have quieted down out there. You should take off; it's way past the end of your shift."

"You sure? I don't mind," I say, looking from Dr. Bennett to the patient.

I love my job. It is my reason to get up every day. I swear, if they let me, I would live at the hospital. Helping save lives, fix breaks, clean wounds, ease pain, and comforting those in need are what make me feel something other than tragedy. It's odd, I suppose. Who finds comfort in crisis?

"Take off." He nods to the door. "Get some sleep, because who the hell knows what we're in for tomorrow."

"I have the afternoon shift; I'll be fine." I can't help looking at the patient, battered, beaten, but still breathing. There is no greater moment in my profession than when I see a patient's eyes open, since in all reality, it's never a given it will happen.

"Take off. I promise I can handle it," Dr. Bennett jokes.

I walk into the nurses' lounge and wash my hands before grabbing my purse and coat out of my locker. I make sure to fish my keys out before I leave the building.

I head out into the parking lot and make my way to my little white Ford Focus. It's not yet dark, and I am grateful for that. If I hurry, I can be home before the sun goes down.

Twenty minutes later, in a suburb outside of Rock City,

I pull down my street toward my house on a cul-de-sac in a once middle-class neighborhood where kids played in the streets until after dark, riding skateboards, playing basketball, riding bikes, or skipping rope.

Four years ago, that all changed. Now, as I drive slowly toward my two-story colonial, childhood home, I see security system signs in every yard, bars on windows, and no children playing outside. Yards are not immaculately landscaped anymore; there is debris in the gutters; and darkness seems to have settled over the house at the very end of the road.

I hit the garage door opener and race into the garage, quickly hitting the remote to close it behind me. I wait until it is completely closed, look around the well-lit garage, and see Boots, my gray cat with four white feet, sitting on the stairs, waiting for me.

I take a deep breath and get out, closing, then locking, the car door behind me.

"You happy to see me?" I ask as I stand in front of the entry door to the kitchen, allowing him to walk in a figure-eight pattern between my feet as he rubs against my legs. "That's a fine welcome home, Sir Boots."

I squat down and scratch under his chin, behind his ears, and then run my hand down his back a few times before standing up, grabbing the bat that sits by the door, and then punching in the code to unlock the house.

The lights automatically go on inside, and I take a deep breath and step in.

I scan the room as my heart beats against my chest, then close the door behind me. Without turning around, I lock the door, using the three dead bolts, and then punch in the code so that the security system's call center knows I am in for the night.

I walk around the kitchen to make sure each window is

locked before walking into the dining room, then across the hall to the family room, doing the same. I then peek my head in my parents' old room, seeing the closet doors are wide open and empty, as is the room.

After checking all their windows, I check the bathroom, making sure to look behind the shower curtain. Everything looks good.

"Come on, Boots." I call him to the bathroom.

He walks in and sits by the tub, licking his paws while I lock the door and dead-bolt it.

I undress fast, then start the shower. While waiting for it to heat up, I brush my teeth and wash my face. I use the toilet, close the lid, set a towel on top of it, and Boots jumps up and sits while I get in the shower.

I wash and condition my hair quickly, then shave my underarms and legs even more quickly. I scrub my body with a swiftness that I have grown accustomed to and am out of the shower in seven minutes flat. I then dress in the nightclothes I brought from my room this morning and towel off my hair before brushing it.

I take a deep breath, grab the bat, and unlock the door. I open it, holding my breath the entire time. When I walk out, I look ahead at the stairs. I hate the stairs, which is why the entire stairway is enclosed in plywood and secured with enough screws and nails that it would not go unnoticed if someone went up there without permission or a sledgehammer.

I grab an already prepared salad out of the fridge and a bottle of water. Then I look at the clock and start to feel anxiety rise. I grab another water bottle, knowing I need it for both of the cats' water dishes.

"Come on, buddy," I call to Boots as I walk to the doorway and punch in the code to the thick, steel door. As soon as I open it, Boots heads down the stairs, knowing the drill.

I step on the landing, close the door behind me, lock the three dead bolts, the chain lock, and the one on the doorknob, and then I walk down the stairs to the basement where Socks, Boots's brother, is waiting for us.

"Hey there, did you have a good day?" I ask as he stretches his back, then his front paws, and stands.

I grab the keys next to the door to my room downstairs and unlock it. The lights automatically come on, and once Boots is inside, I lock it—all three dead bolts, two chain-link locks, the doorknob—and finally feel like I can breathe.

I set the food and water on the small table that also acts as my desk and look around my twelve by twelve bedroom. There are no windows and one thick, steel door. The walls are bare, I can't look back on family pictures. I exist down here with just what we need to get by.

I bend down and pick up Socks. "We're going to be okay. We're going to make sure of it. We're not alone."

After a few minutes, I set him in the recliner near the bed with his brother and pick up the picture of my family. I run my finger over the frame, then the side of each of their cheeks and whisper, "I'm so sorry I was late."

Chapter Three

Blinking, the light burns my eyes, so I close them again. My body feels detached, and my mouth is dry.

Where am I?

The noise of a machine beeping has me blinking again. I see white. I damn sure know I'm not in heaven. I blink again as my mind races.

The cowbell dings from off on the side. We are in an abandoned parking garage.

I blow out a breath, and the cold Detroit air smokes out in front of me. My muscles are tight from the day and the temperature. I didn't warm up properly. I know better. I'm not a rookie, and this is a rookie mistake. The key to mixed martial arts or any street fight is stamina. Don't let your muscles or lungs give out before the final bell.

I hop from foot to foot in hopes to get my blood flowing. The graffiti on the cement walls seems to dance from the fires lit up inside barrel drums around the space. The place would normally reek of garbage, waste from the homeless fuckers, and rats. Luckily, it's all frozen, so I am thankful for the reprieve from the stench.

There is no octagon tonight, no ring, just a chalk line drawn on a cracked concrete floor. The crowd is sparse, and this isn't one of the usual locations. This wasn't arranged by the usual connections. Tonight is a risk and a gamble. Now that I'm in it, I'm beginning to wonder if this was a mistake.

I try to shut down my mind. I try to zone in. I need to get fight ready.

Instead, I think of Missy. I think of her message after lunch telling me she's going to find her way to Caldwell since I found my way to lunch with his wife. There was a time when her games with Jagger would work me up, but knowing what he has waiting for him at home, I know he's not giving that up for Missy.

I made a decision today. Missy and I are over. Tatiana was right; this is a toxic relationship for us both. I am not the man I want to be with her. I will never be a good man, but I can't continue risking her pushing my buttons.

My blood pumps harder as I let my adrenaline build. Mixed thoughts about my future only fuel my need to beat the shit out of someone. Tonight's fight isn't full of the usual onlookers. It doesn't have any fluff or fanfare. There is no announcer. There are no gloves, no tape, no headgear, and no protection of any kind.

Tonight is a street fight, winner takes all. No rules, no referee, just one man left standing to take home the money. There aren't rounds to take breaks and regroup. This is nonstop until it is done.

It's a bare-knuckles brawl with only Brock at my back.

It's not about the money for me; it's not about a title. Fighting for me is conquering and controlling. When I go round for round and pound for pound, it's about being in control of the physical punishments, both given and taken. It's conquering my opponent and conquering my past.

Every win is a win I never had as a child.

The mindset of a fucked-up boy grown into a fucked-up man. Break the cycle or break some noses . . . I'm better at the latter and wish I had been able to do the first.

My opponent stands in front of me—Chainz—all six foot six of him. The man is a beast. His olive skin shines in the firelight. He's lubed up, the smart fucker. I didn't, and this gives him the advantage. The tattoo of a chain winding up and down his right arm goes over his shoulder and wraps down his back and across his torso, going down his leg and ending at the top of his left foot.

Rumor has it, when he gets you in a lock, the grip is like he's wrapped a chain around you and is slowly pulling every bit of energy and life out of you.

Well, motherfucker, I'm Cobra, known for my quick strike and ability to move with speed. I have the movements to mesmerize and hypnotize like a snake dancing to a fife. He's going to have to catch me to wrap me in his chains.

The sideline's coordinator nods to me, nods to Chainz, and then we nod to each other. Then the cowbell rings.

We dance around each other. He's measuring me up as I do the same to him. I strike first, a jab with contact, and his head snaps back from the impact. He shakes it off as blood immediately pours from his nose. Then he glares at me as I glare right the fuck back.

I have no fear. I have nothing to lose on this cement tonight or any other night—except my need to come out on top. I will not let myself down.

We dance around each other again. He swings with a hook, and I move, making him miss. Dropping in, I take him out at the knees. He falls back and goes down hard.

We grapple, and I come out on top of him. Swing left, swing right, then I pound away.

My knuckles burn as my skin splits again from this morning. Pain shoots up my arms with each blow. I don't stop. I'm relentless.

"Cobra!" I hear Brock yell. "Drop!"

I can't react. A blunt object comes down on my head, and I am knocked off my man. The next blow comes down on my ribs. I can't breathe as the hits keep coming.

I hear Brock vaguely yelling. I hear the popping of gunshots, and then everything is silent.

The steady beeping of the machines, the bright lights . . . Things went bad. That's all I can gather.

I open my eyes again when I feel small fingertips on my wrist. What happened with the shots? Who hit me?

Inhaling, I'm in agony. Every breath feels like my chest is one size too small for my lungs. There's too much pressure, too much pain. I want to crawl back into the darkness.

The soft glow off her golden hair beams brightly. Her blue eyes meet mine, and I feel like I am in the hands of an angel. This can't be heaven, because the gates damn sure won't open for a demon like me. I don't know where I am or why, but I feel safe just from the look in her eyes.

"Calm down. Breathe easy," her soft voice soothes.

What the fuck is wrong with me? Was I shot?

The glow leaves me as she steps back. A man in a white coat with the name Sam Bennett, MD, on his chest stands over me. "You seem more alert now, so let's go over some things."

My head pounds, and the light is blinding. The blond nurse leaves my room. I am alone with the doctor. My ears are ringing, and I want this man to shut the fuck up, not go over some things.

"The gentleman who dropped you off exited before we could get your information. There is discharge paperwork for you to sign. With your hands being bandaged, someone from registration will be in here shortly to help you," he says, looking at the screen on his laptop. Registration doesn't need to come. I'm not staying. I'm not signing a damn thing. I'm not giving them any information for multiple reasons, the biggest one being the illegal fight in a ring. If word got out that I gave them that information, I would be signing my death certificate. The next one is that I am who I am, and who I am can't be laid up in a hospital after being in an illegal fight.

"Can you give me your name so I can at least update this until administration arrives?"

"Cobra," I say on a huff. No way am I giving him my real name. My father can't ever know I fight. My father can't know I tarnished his name and his upstanding leadership position in the community. I'm lucky he hasn't already found out and put an end to it . . . or an end to me.

The doc raises an eyebrow at me, but he doesn't push me further at the moment. He types away, and I can't help wondering what he is putting in the computer. Bottom line, I need to get the fuck out of here now.

"Given we had no contacts, we authorized emergency services access to your phone where they contacted the number you had listed as 'ICE' for in case of emergency," he rambles off.

Shit, is all I can think. I need to update that. When I put it in, I did it being a smartass. Knowing they used it, I fucked up. She doesn't need to be brought into this world anymore than she already has been.

"The woman who answered didn't seem to know who you were at first. However, after describing your tattoo, she figured it out and assured me she would have your family here for you today. However, she was evasive about your identity as well." He raises an eyebrow at me suspiciously.

Before I can figure out who would have been sent for me, I hear her screeching as she comes into the room. "You fucking piece of shit!" Missy wails as she storms over to me. "Tatiana Caldwell is your emergency contact!" Her hair is wild around her face, she isn't wearing makeup, and for the first time in the three years we have been together, she is out in public in sweats and a T-shirt. Missy is always put together, dressed in fifties glam . . . except for today, that is.

The doctor's pager goes off, and without a word, he bolts. Sitting up, I see my moment to escape.

Missy has a bag in her hand. I reach over for it. Looking at the gauze covering my hands, I begin to unravel them. Every movement is painful—from the top of my head down to my fucking big toe—but I have to get out of here and now.

Missy keeps pushing. "How is it you would consider her your contact? You fuck me, you live with me. Why her? What is she to you?"

I'm in no mood to give her the truth. She just wants to push my buttons . . . Well, two can play that game.

"Next of kin—that's who they say should be your ICE number. She's my next of kin."

"Have you lost your damned mind?"

I give her my best jackass smile. "Missy, I know you aren't going to understand this, but she and I were bred from the same kind of bastards."

Tossing the bag on the bed in front of me, I unzip it to find she has packed clean boxers, sweats, and a shirt. Perfect. I also find my phone is over on the window ledge of the hospital room. Brock must have my wallet and fight gear.

With my hands free of their confines, I get dressed. Every move is painful, but I can't let them know who I am. My determination drives me to get out while Missy continues ranting on and on.

"I don't even know why I'm here. To have her call me —her! You're a real piece of shit, Jay."

I look up at her as I get dressed. "You're right; I am. That's why I'm going to move out, and it's over between us. This isn't healthy."

Her eyes grow wide in hurt as she realizes I'm serious. I pull the tape off my wrist and slide out the needle of my IV. She stands immobile and unspeaking as I pull off the clip on my finger and pop off the heart monitors and blood pressure cuff. The machines start beeping like crazy, and I know I have to get moving before the nurses come in to fix it. I pull on my shirt and adjust my pants as I quickly slide into my shoes.

I groan in pain as I walk past her to the door. "Keep the condo. I'll help you cover the mortgage for the next three months. Then you're on your own. Get the shit in your name, I'll cover fees or closing costs. I'll be by for some stuff later, and next weekend I'll get the rest."

She opens and closes her mouth yet doesn't speak. I'm probably giving her too much, but frankly I need out before I do something I can't take back. I don't look back as I make my way out of the hospital with the hope I won't run into anyone.

Chapter Four

I sit in my black Chevy Impala with a cup of coffee, waiting with my notebook, waiting for him. He's first up of the five to watch.

The man: Adrian.

The house: 732 East River Drive.

The schedule: He leaves the house between seven and seven-fifteen in a suit and tie. He gets into his brown Volvo and doesn't buckle his seatbelt. I assume he is careless and believes he is untouchable.

I know that's not true. Everyone is touchable.

He is approximately five foot ten and bald. He has a round, clean-shaven face; beady brown eyes; and is mostly expressionless.

I stare at the picture taped next to the information before logging the time and turning the page. I wait for him to pull out of the driveway, knowing he hits the gym before he heads to his office.

Next . . .

The man: Jack.

The house: 8736 East Malloy Road.

The schedule: Eight a.m., he rushes out with two girls who are not twins. They are about seven years old, each blond and dressed in a little red and blue plaid skirt with blue cardigan. He loads them in the car, taking time to do so. I assume he is helping them with their safety belts. That's what a good father would do.

He is short, about five-six, with dark blond, buzzed hair. He is also clean shaven and wears a suit just like the last guy.

He takes his girls to Saint Anne's every morning, a private Catholic school, before heading to his office.

I jot down the time. It's exactly the same for the past two months.

Next . . .

The woman: Charlotte.

The house: 7930 Brown Avenue.

The schedule: At eight-thirty a.m., the garage door opens, and the sleek black BMW reverses out of the driveway and quickly onto the street. She's careless. She doesn't even look behind her half the time while she applies lipstick in the rearview instead of using it how it is intended. She throws it in drive and speeds away.

I follow her because she is far too worried about her makeup to notice she is being watched.

She pulls into her office parking lot and jumps out of her car with a black briefcase hanging off her shoulder and a cellphone stuck to her ear. She is wearing a navy skirt and matching blazer. She is thin and tall in her four-inch heels. Her dark hair is twisted up and away from her face perfectly.

I click a picture on my camera phone. This is the closest I have ever been to her. I will print it today and attach it to her page.

Next . . .

The man: Waters.

The house: 746 Wesley Drive.

The schedule . . .

"Shit," I mutter as I pull down Wesley Drive and see the white Lexus SUV pass me. I glance at him, hoping like hell he doesn't notice me.

His hair is slicked back, and he has dark sunglasses on.

"Eight fifty-five, eight fifty-five," I repeat over and over so I don't forget the time to log his departure.

I look at the clock. If I hurry, I can make the next one, and then tonight, when I am sitting in bed, I can try my damnedest to narrow down my list.

The man: Hill.

The house: 342 Standard Street.

The schedule . . .

It's nine-fifteen in the morning, and I am afraid I may have missed him. I put the car in park and hope I'm wrong. Five minutes later, I see him walk out the front door, still pushing his shirt into his pants. He is six feet tall, about two hundred fifty pounds, balding, and his skin is pockmarked.

Behind him is a much younger woman who is not his wife. She is wearing a big floppy sun hat and large black shades. If she's trying to go undetected, she is failing miserably.

A cab pulls up, and I see him hand her cash before she runs down the driveway in her six-inch stilettos and climbs in the cab.

He walks back inside, and a few minutes later, the garage door opens. He pulls out in his tan Jeep, clearly in a hurry and distracted, because he drives over the corner of the curb before peeling out and heading down the road.

I follow him and watch as he pulls into the parking lot of his office building. I drive past slowly and make my way to the parking area next to the public waterfront where I grab my book and my pen and write down the last two men's departure times.

I lean back and stretch as I look at the sunlight's reflection over the calm water of the Detroit River.

I wish it were as easy as it was back when I was a child with a fishing pole in hand, standing next to my dad, just staying there for hours and hours, waiting patiently for something to bite. This was his favorite place; he used to tell me that. And I was his favorite girl, because I would fish with him and my sister wouldn't.

He would take her to a museum or a concert in the park, but I wouldn't choose anyplace over this one. Not for a million dollars and a million cents; that's what I used to tell him.

"You're one of a kind, kiddo." He would wink at me.

"Two of a kind, Daddy." I would laugh in response.

"Oh, I forgot." He would wink again then tweak my nose. "Me and you."

I would laugh, and so would he.

No time to reminisce, I tell myself.

I grab the notebook and look through it. Four of the nine names have been scratched off my list of suspects since they haven't been in their positions long enough. Out of the ones I staked out today, Adrian, Charlotte, and Waters seem the most likely.

I put on my gloves then pull out the paper, tape, scissors, and newspapers. I take out the copy of the newspaper from the day it all happened and tape it to the top of a blank sheet of paper. I use the scissors to cut and trim out the letters and numbers I need, then tape them to it. I fold it up, then place it in the envelope already stamped, addressed, and ready to be mailed.

I do this three times. It will go to three people, and then I will sit and watch what happens next.

After dropping the envelopes into a post office box on the corner of a busy street, I drive away, hopeful that my vengeance will be delivered soon.

Chapter Five

After working my shift, I walk outside and quickly toward my vehicle. I hear a whistle, and the hair on the back of my neck immediately stands up. I quicken my pace.

"Hey." I hear a gruff voice call from behind me. "Hey, you! Stop."

I run to my car and jump in, locking it behind me. My hand shakes as I shove the key into the ignition. Then I hear a tap on the window as I start the car.

I am afraid to look, but when the knock is harder this time, I force myself to.

I immediately recognize the man, the patient from last night, the one who was beaten. He motions for me to roll down my window, and when I don't, he cocks his head to the side and looks confused.

I roll it down just enough that I can hear him, but not enough for him to be able to reach in.

"Name's Jason. I'm almost positive I owe you a thank-you for last night."

I nod and force a smile. "You're welcome."

His head cocks again, and he glances around then back at me. "You okay?"

"Of course," I answer.

"You sure about that? You took off running like you had a reason to. You took care of me, Nurse . . . ?"

"Lorraine," I answer in a whisper.

"All right, Lorraine." He nods then sighs. "Look, I owe you for sticking around last night—"

"I was just doing my job, Jason. Glad to help and glad you're okay."

"I owe you one, okay? If you ever need anything"—he pauses then pulls out a pen and tears off a piece of what I assume is his discharge paper and jots something down—"you call me."

When I don't reach up, he allows the paper to drop in through the gap in the window.

"Thanks."

He nods. "Like I said, I owe you."

When he steps back, I quickly put the car in drive and pull out of the parking lot as my heart beats nearly out of my chest.

I look at the clock. It's nearly midnight. I don't understand why he is being released so late. It frightens me, yet he was kind.

His name is Jason.

As soon as my front tires hit the paved driveway of my home, I press the garage door opener and race into the garage, quickly hitting the remote to close it behind me. As always, I wait until it is completely closed, look around the well-lit garage, and see Boots sitting on the stairs, waiting for me.

I take a deep breath and get out. Then I close the door behind me and lock it.

"You happy to see me?" I ask just like I do every time I

return home. Our routine is the same as I allow him to walk in a figure-eight pattern between my feet as he rubs against my legs. "That's a fine welcome home, Sir Boots. It never gets old."

I squat down and scratch under his chin, behind his ears, and then run my hand down his back a few times before standing up, grabbing the bat that sits by the door, and then punching in the code to unlock the house.

The lights automatically go on inside, and I take a deep breath and step in.

I scan the room as I close the door behind me. Without looking I lock the door, using the three dead bolts, and then punch in the code to the security system.

I walk around the kitchen to make sure each window is locked before checking the dining room then heading across the hall to the family room. I then peek my head in my parents' old room; the closet doors are wide open and empty, as is the room.

After inspecting all their windows, I head to the bathroom, making sure to look behind the shower curtain. Everything checks out.

"Come on, Boots." I call him to the bathroom.

He walks in, and then I lock the door, dead-bolting it.

I undress fast then start the shower. I brush my teeth, wash my face, use the toilet, close the lid, set a towel on top of it, and Boots jumps up and sits while I get in the shower.

I wash and condition my hair, shave my underarms, and then quickly shave my legs. I scrub my body with an accustomed swiftness and am out of the shower in seven minutes. Then I dress in the nightclothes that I brought in this morning, towel off my hair, and then brush it.

With a deep breath, I grab the bat and unlock the door. I open it then walk out, looking ahead at the stairs that I hate.

I grab two bottles of water from the kitchen then look at the clock, starting to feel that anxiety rise.

"Come on, Boots," I call to him as I walk to the doorway and punch in the code to the thick, steel door. As soon as I open it, Boots heads down the stairs.

I step on the landing, close the door behind me, lock it up tight, and walk down the stairs to the basement where Socks is waiting for us.

"Did you have a good day?" I ask as he does his normal stretch.

I take the keys next to the door to my room and unlock it. The lights automatically come on, and once the cats are inside, I lock the door.

I set the water on the small table. Then I bend down to pick Socks up.

"We're going to be okay. We're going to make sure of it. We're not alone. She's gonna help us. She's gonna figure out what happened, and then the whole street can play and laugh and maybe even sleep again."

I set him in the recliner near the bed with his brother then pick up the picture of my family. I run my finger over the frame then the side of each of their cheeks and whisper, "I won't let you down again. She's gonna help us."

It's morning. I know it. Not because the sunlight is peeking through the windows or because I can hear the birds awakening me with their chirping. I know it because the clock says so.

I swing my feet over the side of the twin bed then push my feet into my slippers. I quickly change into my clothes and run a brush through my hair. I grab the bat and the small basket of dirty clothes, unlock the door, and slowly walk out of the room.

I look around and let out my held breath. "Come on, scaredy-cats; everything is good. Everything is fine. See?" I lock the door behind me then place the keys behind the wall hanging, hidden away but very close by.

I ascend the stairs then unlock and open the door from the finished basement to the upstairs. My body tenses, but I know I am fine.

I push the door open and walk out, closing it, then locking it behind me. I walk through the house, ready to face the day.

After I warm up breakfast, I go about putting laundry in the washer and decide to dust and vacuum. I know it's a good day when I want to vacuum. The noise from the machine forces the cats to hide in a different room. The vacuum's roar fills the silent home, a home in which you could normally hear a pin drop.

On a good day, I can get through the entire downstairs without fear that something or someone will come from behind and grab me.

When the vacuum is put away and I feel as though I have accomplished something, I decide to open the curtains and let the light in. The cats love lying in the window seats in my parents' room and the living room, allowing the sun to warm them and revitalize them. I used to as well.

Chapter Six

Brock pulls up, thanks to my quick text to him. The step up into his Ford F250 truck is hard, but I breathe through the pain. I need to keep pushing no matter how bad it gets.

My head spins and my vision blurs, making me wonder how bad my injuries are. Then again, I can't go back inside, so it doesn't really matter. Mentally, I have to stay aware of what is going on, and if I get worse, I can always look on the Internet for home remedies. Either way, staying in the hospital is not an option. No one can know it was Jason Stanley lying in that hospital bed. No one can know about the fights, especially the one last night.

We pull out of the hospital parking lot, and I can't help smiling when I see we are behind the angel Lorraine's car. I have to know more about her, like why she seemed so jumpy when I approached. What is her story?

"Follow that car. I wanna see where she goes."

Brock smirks. "Damn, Cobra, don't you think you should get rid of Missy first? She's liable to claw your eyes out if she finds out you're on the scout."

I close my eyes. He is right about that. Only, I don't think she would claw my eyes out as much as she would put my balls in a vise, yet still try to ride my dick while I slowly lose circulation in my favorite man parts.

"I ended it," I say on a sigh.

"You ended it, and she didn't stab you or cut your balls off? When did that happen?"

"Today," I mutter, taking in Lorraine's Ford Focus.

It's not what I would expect for someone in their early twenties like me, and there is no way she is much older than I am. Of course, she has to be obviously college educated in order to be a nurse. She must make a solid income since she drives a newer car.

Brock is rambling on about Missy and what a mess the two of us are. I watch her pull into a decent neighborhood. It's not a gated community, but it certainly isn't the ghetto. The houses are cookie-cutter, American dream homes. She pulls into a two-story colonial's driveway.

Brock starts to follow.

"No," I say, clipped. "Keep driving."

Mentally, I take down her address: 415 Hollow Terrace.

"You wanna tell me what's going on?" Brock asks as he drives loops around the cul-de-sac.

I don't want to tell him, because I really don't know. Regardless, he isn't going to let me off the hook that easily; it's just not how we are.

"Ever meet someone and feel like you need to know more about them instantly?"

"That's some of that movie bullshit women believe in." He laughs at me, which only agitates me further. He looks over at me then; his eyes meet mine and he sees I'm serious. "You got the shit beat out of you. It's fucking with your head." He tries to excuse my mindset.

"Yeah, speaking of, you wanna tell me what the hell happened to me?"

He sighs. "Man, I'm sorry. They held me back. I couldn't get to you." I see the marks on his neck and the black eye I hadn't noticed in my haste to leave the hospital. "By the time I did, you were knocked out, swelling and shit. I got you to the hospital, but given what happened, I couldn't stay and answer questions."

I understand. If the shoe had been on the other foot, I would have done the same thing. With the league we are in, no way could he explain my injuries. The best thing he could do for me was drop me off and run.

We pull up to my place, and Brock comes up to help me pack a bag.

"You know she's gonna go bat-shit crazy," he says, confirming what I already know without a single doubt in my mind.

"If you have such strong feelings about Missy and the safety of my balls, why didn't you say something before?"

He doesn't miss a beat, doesn't hesitate, and he doesn't avoid my eyes. Brock lays it out straight like he always does. "You two have this twisted way that you seem to get off on." He shrugs. "I figured you liked fighting with her."

The truth hurts. I find it sad that even outsiders think we get off on the pain.

"Is that the kind of man you take me for?"

My longtime friend looks me straight on. "Yeah. Where the hell have you been? You do get off on it. She does, too. It's just the way you guys work. I don't know if it's the shit with Tatiana and Hitmaker or the blow you took to your head, but I'm glad you're ending this before she fucking cuts your ass . . . or worse."

Before we can make our exit, the shit storm that is my ex-girlfriend blows in.

"Jason, you are not leaving me!" she screams as Brock takes a bag of clothes and necessities out to the truck.

I only needed to get a few things and the keys to my car and bike so I can get set up somewhere else. If she doesn't pour bleach on the rest of my shit or light it on fire, I will get it once I have a new place to call home.

She slaps at my chest. My body is already in pain, and she only brings the blood rushing to the skin, making it sting with every hit.

"You. Are. Not. Leaving. Me."

"It's done, Missy. Get your hands off me."

When she slaps me hard across my swollen and battered face, I step back. My cheek throbs and my head pounds, but I will not give her what she wants.

"Come on, Jason, give it back to me. Give me something. Don't you leave!"

I step to the side, and she steps with me.

I just want to get away from her. I want out.

"This isn't healthy." I want to give in to the monster inside me. However, I know if I do, I will hate myself for it and then feel the need to comfort her. The cycle will begin again when this has to stop now.

She swings her purse at my head. The chain catches on my cheek and cuts me open. I feel the blood run down, but I don't advance on her, even as my every instinct screams at me to teach her a lesson.

If you want to hit someone like a man, be ready to take it back like a man, whether you have a dick or not.

She is pushing me. I will not give in to my urges. I will not put my hands on her. She will not get me to that place.

She keeps swinging her purse at my face and head. I back up. I clench my fists open and closed.

I want to hit her. I want to give her the pain. I want to let the rage explode. I have to get out of here.

Brock comes back in and watches, wide-eyed.

"Missy, fucking stop it, bitch!" my longtime friend commands, but she only swings harder.

"Bitch! Yeah, I'm a bitch! Jason made me this way!" Tears stream down her face. "Look at what you've done to me! Look, Jay! Look at the mess you've made of me, of us. You can't leave. You can't leave me like this."

Reaching out, I grab each of her arms firmly, and she freezes, bracing for impact.

Picking her up, I move her out of my way, and then I walk off toward Brock with her chasing me. She jumps on my back while I keep walking, dragging her out with me. I am twice her size. I could easily knock her out. However, I'm fighting the darkness inside of me. I will not hurt her.

"Missy, stop this now. It's over. This isn't healthy," I say, choking as she wraps her arms around my neck, trying to hold on to me. At the doorway, I reach up and force her wrists apart. "Done, Missy. We're done."

Pushing back, she falls on her ass, crying out as I keep walking. I don't look back.

I drop my stuff in the room at the Extended Stay and quickly follow up with my boss so that my job won't be in jeopardy from my absence. I got lucky the fight was on a Friday night. Now I just need to get a few days off to heal so no one will question what my outside activities are. I can take this time to find a new place to live and get my shit from Missy's. I'll also take the cash for the next three months' payments to the branch manager at the bank so that is handled.

I need to make a clean break and not give her any reason to seek me out. Old habits die hard, and she is a habit I don't need to get tangled with again.

My phone blows up with call after call from Missy. I

ignore each one. Breaking up is hard to do, but as much as this hurts her now, in the end, it is what is best for us both.

"Thanks for the help, man," I say as Brock brings up my last bag.

"No problem. You really need to stay away from that one. She's a viper."

I smirk. "She's something."

"All that passion may be hot in bed, but, Jay, that shit is seriously dangerous in every other part of life."

I run my fingers through my short blond hair and sigh. "That's for damn sure."

"Catch up later," Brock says, laughing as he exits.

Laying down, I rest against the headboard. My mind doesn't go to Missy like I would expect it to. After three years together, I should miss the woman I claim to love. After three years of creating something and thinking of a future together, I should mourn the loss or some shit. That's not where my head is, though, not in the least. No, I can't shake the blond angel in hospital scrubs.

She lives in a family home within a well-developed family neighborhood. Does she have a family? I don't remember a ring. Then again, I should still be in the hospital. Maybe my mind isn't seeing things clearly. Does she have a husband? Kids?

I smile, thinking of little blond, cherub-cheeked babies in her arms. Then I shake my head. What the fuck is wrong with me?

I can't help wanting to know more about this woman. In time, I will visit her again: 415 Hollow Terrace. It stays with me, as if her house contains all the answers to every question I have about the stranger who saved me.

My body is healing, and the pain has settled after the adrenaline rush of fighting and leaving Missy. I close my eyes and find myself drifting to sleep with Lorraine on my mind.

I blink in rhythm with the beeping of the machine beside me. The light gleams around her as she leans over me.

"Beautiful," I whisper, and she smiles.

Her fingers rest on my wrist's pulse point. The simple touch has me building a tent out of the thin hospital sheet. There is shyness in her eyes, but there is also a hidden boldness wanting to come out.

With my free hand, I reach down and stroke myself.

She gasps, but then I see the fire in her eyes.

"I see you're coming around," she says softly.

"When you're here, I'm definitely ready to come"—I wink—"around."

"Is that so?"

I continue stroking. "I think I could use a sponge bath, Nurse Lorraine."

She steps away and gets a basin with warm water and a sponge. I can't help laughing. She's really up for playing my game. Well, baby, so am I.

When she pulls back the sheet, I have no shame over the cobra I keep in my pants. With practiced ease, she removes the hospital gown and starts wiping me down, beginning at my neck. Her finger grazes my neck tattoo, and the beast inside me is ready to strike.

Squeezing the sponge, she drips water over my chest, causing my muscles to tighten. She licks her lips in appraisal, and I envision those same lips over my cock. With the sponge in hand, she slowly washes me, teases me.

At my hips, she traces the seam of my V, leading to the place I ache for her to touch.

"Baby," I groan, needing relief.

I close my eyes, feeling her small hand wrap around my

throbbing cock. She slides up, and I fight back the urge to thrust into her grip.

Up and down, she moves her hand. Then I feel the tightening of my balls.

Wrapping my hand around hers, I move her faster. Up and down, we slide over and over. I move to sit up as I release while she keeps stroking, working out every drop from me.

The wetness of the sponge hits me, and my body aches.

The pain wakes me from my dream. I am a sticky mess, and the open cuts on my hands burn from the contact.

Damn, I haven't had a wet dream since I was a fucking teenager.

This chick has me all twisted inside. I have never been this caught up in a woman.

The pain is intense, but my need to have her still tops everything I physically feel. I pop an over-the-counter pain pill from my nightstand then go into the bathroom to shower.

When I lie back down, anger hits at the thought of my situation. I can't believe I'm in a damn hotel without the luxuries of home while I'm laid up, broken and beaten. What a mess my life is, just like my fucking bed. Well, as the saying goes, I made it, now I have to lie in it.

Chapter Seven

Heidi

I don't normally venture out in the dark. You can't see everything as vividly. However, we sometimes have to do the things we don't like in order to find out the truths we seek.

The suspect list dwindles with each task I complete. Each time I give my attention to them, I can narrow down my focus. I have three people to watch now: Adrian, Charlotte, and Waters. I need to see what they do when the sun has set and no one is watching.

Target one this evening: Charlotte.

The house: 7930 Brown Avenue.

The time: six-forty-eight p.m.

The garage door opens as she pulls in her black BMW. Without shutting her garage door, she opens her car door, and her feet hang out in just her nylons. She tosses her heels from the car as she slides out with the grace of a ballerina.

She is certainly slow and smooth with her movements. Her day-to-day processes are thought out. Her dark hair is once again twisted up and away from her face. Even after a day of work, not a strand is out of place. If she were to slide back into her heels, she would be able to walk into a courtroom, boardroom, or any office as if it were nine a.m. That is how crisp and put together she is. Everything about her is clean-cut.

Opening the back door, she pulls out her blazer and briefcase, tossing the jacket over her arm as she walks into her home. At the door, she taps the button, and the motor slowly turns, closing off the garage from view.

I maintain my position in my car across the street. I can see into the main parts of the house as long as she doesn't adjust the blinds. She moves as a woman who has nothing to hide, but looks can be deceiving, and I can't be wrong about anything in this. There is too much at stake.

Staring at the kitchen window, I watch as she lays her briefcase and blazer on the table. With her standing at the sink, I pause, hoping she doesn't look out the window and find me staring in. She reaches up and lets down her dark hair before moving out of view.

I give it another few minutes before she moves into sight again, her profile in view, sipping a glass of wine. Her face is relaxed, her mind off in thought. Her day is done.

She's home for the night.

Moving on to the next target.

Suspect two this evening: Adrian.

The house: 732 East River Drive.

The time: nine-seventeen p.m.

His house is bright, the lights on and windows open. I watch as his wife brings him a drink. Baldy doesn't move. He sits in his recliner as the king of his castle. This irritates me. His demeanor is that of a tyrant.

Something is said, and he bolts up, slamming the

recliner shut and standing in his wife's face. His hands go up in the air.

They are having a domestic dispute. Noted.

She walks off, and then he settles back into his chair as the man in charge. All is well in his world. He is in control. The man is on his perch, and his subjects are back to their tasks. He is comfortable. His day is done.

He's not going anywhere tonight.

Moving on to the next target, I fight back a yawn.

Suspect three: Waters.

The house: 746 Wesley Drive.

I pull up as he pulls out. Okay, we are on the move.

I follow Waters's Lexus SUV outside of town until he turns and parks in an open lot. I pull over to the side of the road and wait, hoping to see him do something incriminating. Instead, I see a yellow taxicab pull up, and he gets out of his vehicle and jogs toward it.

What the hell? Why take a cab?

Questions play in my mind, but I don't have time to make notes except in my head.

His hair isn't slicked back tonight. He is dressed in jeans and a polo shirt. He looks younger, handsome, like he's going out for the night. Well, good. That means this isn't a waste after all.

I follow the taxicab about five blocks away until it pulls over in front of a club. He gets out and walks in quickly. The bouncer doesn't stop him, not even for an ID check.

I look at the neon sign over the entrance: The Lion's Den. I should get out more.

I park in the garage across the street then start to make a plan to follow him in.

Pausing, I look over my outfit of black leggings and a black fitted top with a whole lot of cleavage popping out.

Can I do this? Yes, I can do this.

Reaching into the backseat, I grab my boots: knee-high, five-inch heels, all black—hooker shoes at their finest. Digging in the glove box, I find a chain and lock from an old shed we haven't used in years.

"Thank you, Daddy," I mutter to the empty car.

Good thing he was driving this the last day he was in the shed and left me some great accessories.

Wrapping the chain around my waist, I hook it with the lock, letting it hang at a sexy angle that draws attention to my hips and ass.

Clubbing. I can do this!

I give myself the mental pep talk before I snag my ID and some cash to get me in. Stepping out of my car, I do a quick flip of my dark hair to give it volume before I reach back into the car and add some red lipstick.

My eyes pop without makeup needed, but I add mascara for the sultry appeal.

Well, here we go, boys. Time to follow Mr. Waters and see what he is up to tonight.

The bouncer moves the red velvet rope to close me off from entering. The man in front of me is a good six foot six, all broad shoulders and angry face.

"Invitation only," he clips out.

Cocking my hip out and pushing my breasts forward, I twirl my hair around my finger. With a pouty lip, I do the only thing I can think of. "I wanted to surprise Mr. Waters tonight."

I didn't want to use my mark's name, but he obviously got in without an ID. Once inside, I'm sure I can blend in with the thumping bass and moving bodies. If I get caught, they will just kick me out. Waters should be none the wiser.

With a wink, the velvet rope is unclipped, and the massive man steps to the side, letting me by.

"Your sir will most certainly be pleased, pet."

Sir? Pet? What the hell is he talking about?

The entryway is dark, and my eyes struggle to adjust. I see a dim glow ahead and follow it. When I enter the space, I am in no way prepared for what is in front of me.

Along a back wall are rooms, the bright white doors a stark contrast to the charcoal gray walls. Five doors, all numbered, and all have ribbons hanging on the handles as couples fill the spaces nearby.

There are women in nothing more than bras and thongs who are on their knees beside men with leashes hooked through collars. There are men in a variety of outfits—from simple boxer briefs to complicated leather pants with chains. They, too, are on their knees beside what I will assume to be their partners. Some sit with men, and surprisingly, others kneel before their women.

To the right are multiple couches and chairs, all of them full of couples in different stages of undress.

I watch as a woman rides a man, publicly fucking him, her cries warning of her building orgasm. Her partner nods to the woman beside them, and she leans in, pulling the woman's breasts from her bra and taking one into her mouth. The woman riding the man goes off with a loud wail as the man laughs under her, continuing to thrust upward with his hips as he reaches around the back of the woman sucking and begins to finger her. She rocks against him, losing her suction as the first woman reaches out and pulls her to her, returning the favor by sucking her breast.

I stumble as someone bumps into me from behind, pushing me into the open space. Desperately, I look for the flashing lights, music, or any sign of the nightclub life I'm used to. Instead, I'm deeper into The Lion's Den, and my body quivers in anticipation. This club was certainly named appropriately.

Mind back to the task; where is Waters?

Looking to the right, I see the soft glow of red neon lights following the length of the bar. I make my way to a stool. From here, I can scan the space inconspicuously until I find my mark.

The bartender, who is shirtless and in black leather pants with his Mohawk tipped in blue, smirks as he comes over. Mixing a quick cosmopolitan, he places the martini glass in front of me.

"On the house," he says, leaning onto the bar with a half-grin.

I push the cocktail back. "I don't drink." I try refusing his offer.

His half-grin moves into a full-out smile, revealing perfectly straight, white teeth. "It's your first time in The Den. You need to loosen up."

Reminding myself I need to blend in, I sip the drink and nod my appreciation.

"You look like a deer caught in the headlights. What's your kink?"

I nearly choke on my drink as I raise an eyebrow at him.

"Definite submissive. You'll make a nice pet for someone. Who gave you the invite?"

Shit, I have showed my cards too soon and to a stranger. I need to focus. Think, Hi, think! Kink, he wants my kink. Obviously, The Lion's Den is a private club. I needed a name drop to get in. Submissive, pet, my mind goes over the words used.

I blow out a breath, making my chest rise and fall dramatically. Leaning into him, I whisper, "Don't mess up the scene." I settle back onto my stool with a wink.

Mohawk man gives me a thumbs-up and moves away to serve someone else.

Okay, now back to my target. I scan the area yet still have no sight of him.

Casually, I sip my cosmo, hoping Mohawk man isn't watching for my partner to arrive.

A tall man in a snug, black V-neck T-shirt takes the stool beside me. His tailored, black dress pants are definitely accenting his ass and toned thighs as the shirt clings to his every muscle, making me wonder if the arms will bust at the seams from his size. The tattoo of a snake head striking stands out boldly on his tanned neck as the green eyes of the cobra seem to come to life, watching me from the side as he throws up a finger to the bartender for a beer.

Mohawk man serves him and winks at me. Shit, he thinks this is my scene. I move to slide off the barstool, accidentally bumping into snake man.

He turns. His spiky blond hair is devilishly styled, making his eyes pop. When the green hue meets my blue stare, he looks as if he is ready to strike, like the tattoo on his neck. His face shows signs of healing injuries, making me wonder what happened to him.

As he watches me, I can't help worrying he sees right through me, because that's how it feels. With every blink of his eyes, I feel like he is seeing deep into my soul.

"Angel," he whispers raising an eyebrow in question.

Breathlessly, I reply, "I'm no one's angel."

Chapter Eight

Tuesdays aren't my usual Lion's Den night. Swingers looking for an open fuck usually come on Sundays. Tuesdays are for scenes, training, and the occasional person looking for a new partner or a couple looking for assistance. Missy and I have come a few times and before her I frequented the club regularly.

I need release, though. I need a drink. I need to be in a place where names don't matter, jobs don't matter, nothing matters but getting off. I need to be here where no one cares who my father is. I need to be where no one cares about the secrets I hide from the world.

I settle on a barstool, and the bartender gives me a wink and a nod. I hope to hell he doesn't think I'm his type, because I'm fucking not.

"Shot of Jack and a draft chaser," I order, reaching in my pocket for some cash.

I pay the man and look left. Immediately, my eyes settle on the dark-haired beauty beside me. She's not dressed like the other kinky bitches in here, but I wouldn't mind tying her hands up in those chains around her hips.

She slides off her stool and bumps into me.

I know her type. She wants to play submissive tonight and then probably go home to her old man or maybe a vibrator. She wants to step outside of her comfort zone, but only by dipping her toe in. She's too timid to be excited, which means this isn't her scene.

I can see the steady tick of her rapid pulse in her neck. I can feel the fear along with the anticipation coming off her.

She looks up from behind that mess of dark hair. The blue of her eyes is soft and pops out at me. For a moment, I see familiarity . . . No, she can't be familiar. I focus. I see weakness, vulnerability. She is damn good at this game. I can't tell if it's an act. Maybe she is afraid to get caught, or maybe she didn't realize, once you walk into The Lion's Den, there is no turning back.

"Angel," I whisper wondering if her eyes are indeed one in the same of the angel I just met.

"I'm no one's angel."

She is fresh meat and could walk out any moment. The lions in this den seem to be very watchful of her. At her reply, I can't help but feel wound even tighter. I need release.

She glances around, noticing. Her eyes widening and shifting, she looks like a trapped gazelle. She could make an easy escape, but she doesn't. Her eyes train on me, almost begging me for something. I know what that something is. She is here for the same reason I am.

I turn on my stool and reach out, taking her hips and pulling her between my legs. "You're mine tonight."

Her eyes widen, mocking innocence. I know she wants to be here. If she didn't, she would have left. She came for something, and that something is going to be what I give her.

I tilt her chin up and lean in, rubbing my nose from her shoulder blade to her ear. I feel a gush of warm air escape her mouth and smell her sweet breath.

"There is something about the high of this place," I whisper against her neck. "The smell of arousal, the sound of a whip or flogger hitting bare, exposed, and willing flesh mixed with the cries of pleasure and sexual release . . . It can be addicting immediately. It can suck you in and make this addiction stronger than any drug on the street."

I lean back and look her in the eyes. She looks down, and I lift her chin up so her eyes are focused on me again.

"I'm nothing like these men, angel. I won't deny you a release just to build you up. I won't tell you not to look me in the eyes, because when my cock is in this mouth, between your legs, or buried in your ass, I want to see what it does to you. I want to see you on your knees, choking on me because you can't help trying to take me all in, because you're so hungry for my cock. I want to see you when I am hovering above you, feeding your little cunt male fucking perfection inch by inch. I want you looking over your shoulder as I start out slowly, rubbing the head of my dick around your rim before ramming it inside of your hot, little ass, making you scream because you're sure I have torn you in two. Then I'll rock in and out with ease as you dig deep inside of you, allowing yourself to feel the pleasure it will bring you."

Her mouth opens and closes a few times like she can't find words. When I place my finger on her lower lip and brush it back and forth, she glances sideways then back at me.

"You see something else you want? I'm not a fucking silver medalist, angel. I'm a gold. If you see something better, go for it." I push her hips so she steps back. "I'm no one's second choice."

She glances around again then steps into me.

"Change your mind?"

She nods.

I'm pissed. This little bitch isn't gonna play games with me. She can work for it. She may have the eyes of an angel, but she was right when she said she was nobody's. Well, for tonight, she's going to be mine.

"You're gonna have to prove it." I take her hand and place it on my erection. "Unbutton me."

She squeezes her eyes shut, but she doesn't pull her hand away. When she opens her eyes, she is feisty and full of fire, and I am no less turned on.

I reach up and yank her blouse so the buttons pop off, and she gasps. Then I unclasp her front closure bra so her tits are now exposed. Her eyes shift down, so I lift her chin again.

"Eyes on me."

She looks up.

"Get to work."

Her eyes narrow, and then she quickly unbuttons my pants.

"Now—"

I stop when she pulls my dick out and grips it firmly, her eyes still on mine.

"I'm in control here, angel." I give her the same look back. "Now, on your knees, looking up at me with your mouth full of cock. Show me who owns you tonight."

Her grip tightens as she glares at me.

I hiss because it feels fucking good, and her eyes flutter. Desire.

"That's a good girl. Now suck my cock."

She kneels down, and I slide to the end of the barstool, pushing my pants down as her hot little tongue flicks across my head.

"That's it, angel. Eyes."

Her other hand reaches up and cups my balls as she runs her tongue down my shaft.

"If I wanted to be teased, I'd be wearing leather, ass-less chaps. Suck my cock now."

She sucks hard. Her cheeks hollow out, but she doesn't choke like most women. There is a challenge in her stare. She wants to give in, but she desires to hold back. Push and pull, it's a dangerous game she plays.

While she works me with her mouth and hand, I close my eyes and let my mind turn off. That's what I came here for: escape, release. When shit with Missy got to be too much, I would come here to get away from it all.

The concussion really fucked with me, because the eyes staring up at me as she licks the head of my cock are the same blue eyes I woke up to in the hospital.

I almost dare myself to ask her name, but I don't. The Den isn't a place for names, only memories.

Just as my balls tingle and tighten, she pops off with a smile. Standing up, she shimmies over my rock-hard cock. The sensitive end pulses with need for her to finish the job.

"Games are not smart to play in a place like this, angel."

Her eyes never leaving mine, she challenges, "I'm no one's angel."

"So you continue to say." Leaning down, I pull up my pants before taking her by the hand and guiding her to a corner wall on the far side. "What are you here for?"

She looks all around me. Cupping her chin, I stop the movement. Her eyes meet mine in defiance.

"I'm not here to dominate. I'm here to control. I don't need to own you. I don't need you to give me power. I simply want to control our time together. Eyes on me at all times, angel."

Her chest rises and falls in rapid succession as she breathes deeply. I back her up to the wall, and her hands come up around my neck, her thumb rubbing against the cobra head tattoo.

I am ready to attack her when she rolls up on her toes, and her lips meet mine. Not one to give in, I open my mouth and invade. Roughly, I tangle my tongue with hers, not holding back. Trailing my hands down her back, I grip her ass and scoop her up. Her legs wrap around me, and her heels dig into the backs of my thighs.

Her nails dig into my scalp, and I get off on the pain. Public debauchery isn't my thing. From her shy demeanor, I don't think it's hers, either. However, we are both lost to the moment and the sensations.

She gives as much as I take, clawing at me for more. I rock my erection against her core, fucking her through her clothes. She throws her head back, hitting the wall as she slides over me.

Reaching down her pants from behind, I find her dripping wet. I slide my middle finger into her heat, and she bucks wildly, leaning forward and biting into my neck.

I need to be inside her.

With my hands still behind her, I slide her pants off her ass just enough to slide into her, since my pants are still undone from the suck-off at the bar. I tease her entrance and pull back just long enough to cover myself with a condom from my back pocket. As soon as I'm covered, I pull her up so that her legs are high on the sides of my waist and her pussy is lined up with my dick, and I slam into her.

She melts into me, giving me all of her weight and control as I slide in and out. Her pussy walls milk me as I look to her eyes then still.

"Eyes on me, angel. The orgasm I'm about to give you

is all mine," I growl into her ear as my frustration builds. I'm balls deep, and she gives in to me, but all the while, she is watching someone else?

Fuck no.

Her eyes meet mine, and I roll my hips to hit the sweet spot of her pussy and slam home, beating my dick into her. She shakes around me, holding my neck. Then I hear her whimper as I feel her body give in to the release.

"That one's mine. Cobra strikes and consumes."

She slips her legs down, my aching cock popping out of her. She watches someone behind us, no longer in the moment with me. She pulls her pants up, shyly avoiding my gaze.

My whole body is in pain from my injuries and my need to release. With a fierce need, I take off the condom and stroke myself. Closing my eyes, I envision her blue depths as I finish off. In my mind, her dark hair becomes the blond of Lorraine's. It's been too long since I've seen her because I swear these two could easily be one in the same. Clearly they are not, Lorraine was too skittish in the parking lot to find herself in a place like this. I open my eyes as I squeeze the last drop from my cock. Back in the moment with the raven-haired beauty before me.

With my come on my fingers, I dip them into her distracted mouth. "I don't know how you do a one-eighty so fast, but that's my come in your mouth, my cock that stretched your body, and my orgasm you're still feeling." Cockily, I tip her chin up to make her eyes meet mine again. "Next time, angel, it will be inside that pussy of yours. Next time, you won't have any distractions. Your only thought will be whether or not you can handle another round." I lean down and kiss her, tasting myself in her mouth. "And you will handle round after mother-fucking round, baby."

I marked her. Distraction or not, she is still going to feel me for days to come, and I will stay on her mind. Her eyes, those eyes will haunt me for nights to come. I consider this fair play.

I came here tonight for a release and found a whole new challenge. Tonight is just the beginning. I hope she is ready.

There is a twitch to her eyebrow, and then she brings her hands around my neck, pulling me to her. My mind races, unable to keep up with the whiplash in her behavior.

When she makes a mewling sound in my ear, I'm hard again and don't give a fuck about the game she is playing. My body craves being inside her more than my next fight.

She moves to push my pants down again, and I still as she cradles herself into me. Something is off with her. The feel of her near me, the smell of her perfume, and the fact that I didn't finish the way I wanted have me ready to be balls deep inside her heat once again. The hot and cold just to get hot again game is one many newbies find themselves unintentionally playing. She needs to calm down. I'll give her what she craves without pushing her beyond her limits.

"I know this isn't your thing," I whisper, thinking she needs encouragement. "You're a good girl who made me lose control. I have to have you right here, right now, in front of everyone." It's the truth. She's got some sort of black magic that has me out of my zone.

She looks around me nervously. "It is my thing. I can do better." She rolls up on her toes to kiss me.

I growl against her lips, "No, it's not. Don't lie to me. I don't judge you. I don't look down on you. This thing, even if it's just tonight, is open and honest. You and I don't lie to each other—not fucking ever—you understand?"

She nods her head with her eyes still scanning the area around us.

Anger fills me that she is thinking of someone else right now.

I press my body to hers, keeping her hidden in our corner. "You think any of these fuckers could make you come like I did?" I reach up, running my hand down her long, slender throat. Squeezing without cutting off her air, I lean in and whisper, "Do you think any of them could read you like me? Do you think any of them would be able to tell that you're not into the hardcore shit and not push you beyond your limits?"

I can feel her pulse pounding as her heart rate goes up. She blinks rapidly as I loosen my grip before rubbing my calloused fingers over the sensitive skin behind her ears then all the way down to her shoulders.

"I can promise you this, pet." I lace the word with the implied threat of violence. "My hands may be rough, but they will never be harsh. I can damn sure guarantee that any one of these motherfuckers would prefer to tie you up and flog your sweet, little ass until your skin is on the verge of splitting." I caress her neck. "I don't want to make you bleed, angel. I just want to make sure I leave you bruised and maybe a little battered inside so that tomorrow you remember it was my cock inside you. I want you to remember never to walk into a place like this without the man who not only owns your pussy, but will protect the lines you aren't ready to cross. You don't belong in a place like—"

"Yes, I do," she says, trying to sound strong.

"The fuck you do," I say, gripping her throat a little more tightly. "The only place you belong is under a man like me."

Confliction and confusion dance in her crystal-blue eyes. "Like you?" she asks as her pulse quickens.

"Only me," I say, loosening my grip before bending down and taking her mouth as I lift her up.

She easily submits to me this time. Fear and trepidation are gone, replaced by lust and need.

I slide her pants down enough to get in there again and release myself. It's a dangerous game, but I can't help sliding into her tight pussy without taking the time for a condom.

Skin on skin, I watch her eyes roll back in her head as I slide in and out. When she contains herself from the sensations, she once again looks over my shoulder, out into the crowd behind us.

Angry, I pin her to the wall, sliding all the way out to the very tip of my cock then slamming back into her. She cries out as her pain mixes with pleasure. Before she can decide whether she loves it or hates it, though, I do it again.

And again.

Over and over, I pound into her until she can't keep her eyes open or support her own weight around me. When I feel the buildup, I slide out and release my come onto the floor.

She drops her legs to the ground and holds herself steady against the wall as she fights to calm her breathing. Then, sliding her pants back up, she moves past me.

I tuck my dick back into my pants and zip up quickly in order to follow her as she walks toward the women's bathroom.

I want to know her fucking name. Any other time, I wouldn't give a shit. Those eyes, though . . . There is something in her eyes.

Patience has never been a character trait ascribed to me. Now is no different.

When I feel like a fool for standing outside the women's restroom like a fucking puppy dog, I grab a submissive by the arm. She looks up at me and licks her lips in desire.

"The dark-haired girl in all black and thigh-high boots —she okay in there?" I bark out.

The bottle redhead in front of me pouts, and my stomach churns. "She freaked and climbed out the damn window." She traces her manicured nails over my neck. "Whatever she can't handle, I'll willingly do, master."

Master, ugh. I don't aim to be a master. I aim to be a leader. I'm a dominant man, but I don't need a pet under my control.

Thinking of my woman tonight, I like the challenge.

"If I wanted a pet, I'd get a dog." I release the redhead then take off out of The Lion's Den and head down the block to where everyone parks.

I catch a glimpse of her as she gets into a black car. Hurrying, I climb in mine and take off behind her. It's not long before she turns into a paid parking garage. I try to follow her, yet once she gets out of the vehicle, I lose her while trying to find my own spot. Therefore, I move back to her location.

When I can't get a feel on her, I go back to my car. As I pull out of the garage, I realize I'm not far from Lorraine's house.

Her eyes come back to mind, and I hit the steering wheel, thinking of the mess I have made.

Tonight, I fucked a stranger raw while, in my mind, I gave her Lorraine's eyes and face. Sure, the hair was wrong, but the eyes, those blue eyes, were my angel's.

How hard did I get hit in the head? I should take my ass back to the hotel and call it a night.

I don't.

Instead, I make the turn onto her road and find myself silently sitting across the street from her house. This can't be healthy, but I can't seem to pull away.

I watch from outside as the lights seem to come on in a sequence. I make out the form of a dark-haired woman carrying a bat.

I get out of my car and make my way closer to the house. When I see the blond ponytail of Lorraine fall to the floor, panic fills me, thinking she is hurt.

Someone is in the house and has hurt her.

I rush in through the front door after easily picking the lock. Then I disarm the alarm by slicing a few wires with my pocket knife, without even thinking about how I have no explanation for why I am here. Instincts take over. I have a drive I have never felt before to get my ass inside to save her.

Chapter Nine

When his hand covers my mouth, I immediately scream. My body trembles, my muscles tighten, and I know I'm going to die. I am going to die just like they did, inside what was once a sanctuary to my family. A house, a haven, a home to a middle-class working family with two daughters, two cats, two cars, and too much love and happiness, just to be silenced with a blade.

It became a tomb, a hell, a house haunted by the gruesome and savage slaughter of a family. A house I couldn't bear to sell or leave because of the good memories still here.

Now, I am going to die just like they did.

The fight response comes on immediately. I claw, kick, and try with every ounce of strength I have to get free. I don't know how strong I am or that I even have it in me to fight, but I do.

I fight for three, and I fight for me.

My attacker's hand is covering my mouth, so I know

the screams aren't alerting anyone, but I refuse to die like this.

He is saying something, but I can't hear anything except my screams and the sound of my own heartbeat thrashing in my ears.

I see them. I see them in my sister's room. The blood, the mess, the death. I see Daddy tied to a chair with his throat slit, his white, button-down shirt covered in blood. I see Mom lying on the bed, her clothes sliced apart. She has cuts on her thighs, across her exposed pelvic area, and on her breasts. I see how her eyes are wide open, and she isn't breathing. I see my sister's dead, half-naked body bent over the end of the bed, blood staining down her inner thighs, her body and her throat sliced, too.

I see death.

I hear my own heart still beating. I scream. I fight. I thrash. Then my attacker drops to the floor, still gripping me firmly.

I hear his voice, but it's muted. My ears are filled with heartbeats and screaming and thoughts of how to survive.

I can't move my arms. The arm of my reaper surrounds me, trapping me. The leg of my soul's harvester wraps around me from behind, holding my legs down so I can no longer kick.

I can't get free. I can't move. I find it hard to breathe. I feel a wave of nausea, then heat, then cold, and then my body aches from fighting.

I close my eyes more tightly, and I see them. I see them surrounded by light, their hands outstretched toward me.

I miss them terribly. I miss them so much my heart aches.

It hurts. The pain inside hurts almost unbearably. Then . . . I feel . . . nothing.

I smell that familiar sterile smell and hear the beeping

and hushed bustle that make me feel safe. I am warm. I am—

I gasp and try to sit up, but Dr. Sam Bennett holds me still.

"Easy, Lorraine," Dr. Bennett says quietly.

I look around, confused. My eyes immediately feel heavy. I smell the ammonia again, now knowing this is not a dream.

"You're okay, Lorraine." Dr. Bennett's smooth, soft voice confirms what I now know.

I passed out, blacked out. It hasn't happened in a while.

"Do you know where you are?"

"Henry Ford." Embarrassment washes over me as I sit up again.

"Slow down, okay?"

"I'm fine," I say as I shake my head.

"Nurses definitely make the worst patients," he kids.

I look up at him and force a smile. "I apologize, Dr. Bennett."

"Do you know how you got here?" he asks, looking down at his clipboard.

Oh, God, I think. I was attacked is on the tip of my tongue when I hear a familiar, gruff voice from the other side of the bed.

"Of course she knows."

I look over at him, and his eyes narrow.

"Meet a new friend?" Dr. Bennett briefly looks up at me, and I can see he is not impressed.

"We've actually met twice, haven't we, Lo?"

Jason walks around and stands next to me. I'm confused, not understanding. His eyes narrow, warning me.

"Here at the hospital, and again tonight when we were out"—he pauses, and I am terrified—"together."

I swallow back fear, confusion, and embarrassment.

I look up at Dr. Bennett's suspicious eyes. "Will you give me just a minute?"

Dr. Bennett looks at Jason then back at me. "I'll be back."

"With release papers," Jason states.

Dr. Bennett straightens up to his full five-foot-eleven stature and looks at Jason. "We'll see." Then he walks out.

Jason walks over and closes the door behind him before he turns and stares at me, crossing his arms over his chest and looking me up and down slowly. Then he sighs, grabs the stool, and pulls it over so it is sitting inches from me. He sits down and looks up, running his hands through his hair.

"What the fuck?" he mutters.

"Was it you? Were you the one who broke into my house?" I gasp out, interrupting him. "The one who—"

"I came to save your ass." He looks at me, shakes his head, and then looks up at the ceiling.

I'm afraid of what he will say next.

"Thank you. I mean, I guess—"

He holds his hand up and stops me. "You passed out."

"Yeah, it used to happen a lot." I am horribly uncomfortable. I shake my head. "Thank you for bringing me—"

He leans in. "Shut it down." Then he stands up and leans over me like he is going to say something, but he groans, balls his fists, and turns his back on me.

"Jason, I—"

He whips around. "Not another word. Not one . . . unless you want to do this here . . . where you work."

It's a threat. He's threatening me.

I nod. "Okay. I—"

"Shut the fuck up, Lo."

Lo, the name freezes me. It's what she used to call me. I

feel tears building down deep inside. I have no clue what to do next.

The door opens and Sam Bennett walks back in. He stands toe-to-toe with Jason, eyeball to eyeball.

I watch as Jason's fists clench more firmly as he looks down at him.

"Now I get a minute."

"She's fine."

"And your medical degree comes from where?" Dr. Bennett walks around him and sits down.

I glance up and see Jason glaring at him.

"Medically, you are fine." Sam looks back at Jason. "I would like you to come to the house and stay with me."

Jason hisses, and Dr. Bennett looks back at him.

"A minute."

Jason looks at me. He's angry.

"We need a minute," I tell him.

"You've got two." He holds his fingers up. "Then we're out of here." He walks out the door, but the sound of his shoes stop, and I know he is right outside the door.

"How many times has this happened?" Dr. Bennett whispers.

"It's the first time since college."

"Are you sure?" he asks, concerned.

I nod. "Yes."

"I'd love to have you back. We miss you. Rochelle and Ryan miss you. They're both home for a week, and I know—"

"I'm really fine," I say quickly. He looks upset. "I am stronger now. I am—"

"Sweetheart, I know how strong you are." He places his hand on my wrist. "But I know, once in a while, all of us need someone. You have the four of us, Lorraine. Anytime." The Bennetts have always been my safe haven.

After talking to the police, I couldn't think of anyone to call but Dr. Bennett's son, Ryan, since they were . . . together. I went home with him and stayed until I could sort out my life.

"I know, and I hope you know how much I appreciate it," I whisper, hoping Jason doesn't hear. I don't want him to know anymore than he already does.

"Have you thought anymore about putting the house up for sale?" Dr. Bennett asks, and I shake my head. "I think you should."

"I feel close to them," I whisper.

"It's been five years." His tone is sad.

"I know."

"Have you let anyone inside? Have you had company?"

I start to answer, but Jason walks in. "I've been to her house."

Dr. Bennett looks shocked then confused. He looks at me. "Okay, then." He stands up. "We miss you, sweetheart."

I'm not sure if I am imagining it, but I think Jason growls. I look at Sam, but he apparently didn't hear anything.

"I promise I'll visit. I miss you all, too." What I tell him is a lie. I see him all the time, even Sarah, his wife. But his children, I avoid them. I have to.

"Use the back exit. Then the entire ER staff won't bombard you."

"Thank you." I nod. "Thank you so much."

Jason opens the door to his car, and I slide in. I have no choice. Something tells me he knows my secrets. Of course he does. He has been in my house.

He gets in without saying a word and starts up the car before quickly pulling out of the parking lot.

"A left at the light," I say, trying to sound strong.

"I know," he grumbles.

The rest of the ride is silent. I watch out the window as we pass the streetlights, counting them as we go by, trying desperately to take my mind off the awkwardness of the situation.

As soon as we pull onto my street, I grab the passenger-side handle, fear gripping me like a hand around my throat.

He pulls into the driveway and immediately gets out. Before I can pry my hand off the door handle, he is opening it, but I can't move.

"Let's go," he sneers.

I feel the tremble start in my hands. Then my body shakes.

"We need to pull into the garage," I manage to say before I feel dizzy. I know I'm going to pass out again, but then he dips down and scoops me up. "I can't!"

"The fuck you can't," he says with a fieriness I wish I could borrow. I desperately wish I could borrow it right now.

He marches to the front door and opens it.

"It wasn't locked!" I gasp.

He doesn't answer as he walks in and kicks the door shut behind him. He tries to sit me down, but my arms automatically wrap around his neck.

"Jesus Christ," he whispers, holding me more securely. "You've gotta stop shaking."

"I think I'm going to pass out," I whisper to myself, but apparently, it's out loud.

"I'm not taking you back to that hospital, so you better fucking not," he says softly as he leans against the closed door then slides down until he sits on the floor with me in his lap. Then he clears his throat and adds in a much harsher tone, "You've got some explaining to do, Lorraine Bosch."

I look up at him when he says my full name.

His eyebrows slowly creep up. "When I walked in here tonight to save your ass," he says snidely, "I saw the blocked-off stairway, the empty rooms. I mean, fucking empty. How the fuck do you live here? It's like the fucking Bates Motel. As a matter of fact, a shit-bag motel is more comfortable than this place." He shakes his head, and I start to look away, but he stops me by lifting my chin. "Where do your eyes belong?"

Shock overtakes me, and I gasp.

"I'm so fucking confused by you right now." He leans down and kisses me harshly on the mouth. I try to pull away, but he grips the back of my neck, stopping me. "You fucking kiss me now."

"I'm not. I'm—"

"Is it the doctor?"

I start to respond, but he shakes his head.

"He's fucking old enough to be your father." He stops and looks at me, almost like he fears he has offended me . . . almost. "He's too fucking old for you."

He starts to stand, nodding for me to move. I look around, then back at him. He clenches his jaw, and then I kiss him.

"Fuck," he whispers against my lips before cupping my face and positioning me to his liking.

His tongue is possessive, his touch rough, and as I get lost in the kiss, I feel my back hit the floor.

His hand runs up my side as he pushes my shirt up farther and farther.

"Don't ask me to stop," he says before bending his head down and taking my breast in his mouth.

"Oh, God," I whimper. "I can't. I can't."

He looks up, his mouth still around my nipple, sucking so hard it's a pleasure and pain mix. If I could let go, I would, but I can't.

"I just can't," I cry out.

He allows my breast to drop from his mouth. Then he pushes himself up with such swiftness it's almost animalistic.

He turns and grabs the door handle. "Take care—"

"Wait!" I panic as I sit up before crawling to him and gripping his leg.

"Jesus Christ, angel," he says, grabbing me under the arms and pulling me up. "I'm not doing this shit. I'm not gonna fuck around with some crazy-ass chick." He stops and looks around then back at me. "This is fucking insane, you know that!"

I nod quickly because I do know. "I know what it looks like. I know what it feels like. I know. I really do. But I can't . . ." I stop when tears begin to fall, and I wipe my eyes. "I am so tired."

I see him shift and think he is going to leave. I don't want him to, but I don't want him to stay, either. I don't know what I want.

The tears begin falling faster while both Boots and Socks emerge from the kitchen.

"Oh, I'm so sorry," I say, squatting down. "I am so sorry." They are not in their regular places.

I look up at him. "Can you just lock the door on your way out?"

His eyes squint together, and he slowly shakes his head. "The lock's busted. Alarm system is tripped. You'll need someone to take a look at it."

I close my eyes and shake my head, trying to get my thoughts together.

He squats down next to me. "I thought you were

getting fucking jumped. I followed a brunette woman here." He cups my chin and turns my head toward him. "You get what I'm saying, angel eyes?"

I look down. "I'm not crazy. I just. I just sometimes—"

"Pretend to be your dead sister and go to kink clubs to get fucked? Totally sane." He shakes his head and looks at me oddly.

"There are reasons."

"Care to fucking share?"

I shake my head.

"All right, then." He starts to stand. "You need to sell this place, because you are a little fucked up in the head, and this shit ain't helping."

He walks over to the stairway and knocks on the plywood. "Ghosts don't need doors, angel, and they aren't real. So what the hell is up with this?"

I clear my throat, stand, and whisper, "The cats. They go up there, but I can't."

He nods. "Because that's where your family was found murdered." I can't hide my shock. "Google 'Lorraine Bosch,' and you see pictures of a scared teenage girl. Google this address, and you know exactly why."

I feel my bottom lip quiver. "I was late. I was with a boy, and I was late coming home. If I had been here—"

"You'd have been dead, too," he interrupts, shaking his head. Looking around, his eyes search the place. The concern shows but there is an underlying emotion I can't quite figure out. "Where do you sleep?"

Dear God, I don't want to answer, but I do. "In the basement."

He doesn't even look at me like he did, like I'm nuts. "Got tools down there?"

I nod.

"Good, show me what you've got, and I'm gonna screw that door shut until I can fix it."

"Are you sure?"

He nods. "I said it, didn't I?"

I nod.

"While I'm doing that . . ." He looks around as if he's trying to find a task for me, something to busy me, like my father used to. "Do you have something to make a sandwich?"

I can't help smiling. "Yes. Yes, I do."

Chapter Ten

Insanity, chaos, post-traumatic, or any other thing that will take me to a padded room and throw away the key, I need to walk away from. The evil inside me is not what this chick needs. Some serious therapy, possibly some medication, and someone much better than me are what she deserves.

Grabbing a drill and some screws, I go to tackle the door I messed up. I can hear her humming in the kitchen as she makes my sandwich. What a fucking night.

I finish getting the door secured just as she comes over with a ham and cheese sandwich piled high. I raise an eyebrow at her.

"You're a big guy. I thought you'd be hungry," she says shyly.

I can't help wondering where the vixen from the club is. I also can't help wondering if we are both in over our heads here.

Biting into the sandwich, I smile. When was the last time someone did something simple for me like make a sandwich? My mind goes back. There isn't a time outside of when Tatiana stayed with me. Not my mom, not Missy, and sure as fuck not my dad.

I realize how late it is, so I take my plate back to the kitchen.

Lorraine seems on edge as she checks every window and door. Needing to connect with her, I take her by the hand.

"Breathe, angel. Let's get you to bed, and I'll make sure everything is secure before I leave."

Her eyes grow wide in fear, but she stomps it down.

Hand in hand, I guide her to the basement room. The two fur balls she has for pets follow us down like they are more than ready to settle in for the night.

Her eyes give too much away as she looks at me. The fear shows. The years of pushing her body beyond its limit show. The fatigue of too many unknowns shows.

I run my hands through my hair as I look around the space. There's not much here, but I can make it work.

"Get to bed, angel. I'll be here to watch over you while you sleep."

Her eyes grow wide.

"I'll be in the chair, not your bed."

She isn't ready for that, and I have too many questions that need answers before I can let myself go there again. I'm in over my head; she's been in over her head for more time than I'm sure she cares to think about. I need to walk away, but every time I look in her angel eyes, I'm drawn to stay. Those eyes keep me wanting more than I've ever wanted in my entire life.

Timidly, she climbs into the bed. It's after two in the morning, so she should be as exhausted as I am or more so.

The two cats climb in beside her as if they can finally rest, too, and I make my way to the recliner in the corner and sit. I don't close my eyes. I don't settle my mind. I allow my body to find its rest. I calm my heart rate and slow my breathing. What I don't do is sleep.

It's not long before she starts tossing and turning. Her words are incomprehensible until she wails, "I'm sorry, so sorry. Heidi, I'm sorry. Mom, Dad, don't be dead." She is screaming and all twisted in the sheets.

Getting up, I move to the bed. I don't touch her. I have had enough of my own nightmares to know not to touch her.

"You're okay, angel. It's okay." I try to bring her out of it.

She sits up with a jolt, and I move back to avoid her hitting me with her head. Her breathing is too fast, and she is covered in a sheen of sweat.

"Calm down, angel. It was a bad dream."

Her wild eyes shine in the darkness. "If only that were true . . ."

If only it were true . . . Regardless, I can't take that kind of pain away.

"You need to rest."

"You should go." She looks to the door instead of at me.

I slide my shoes off and climb into bed beside her. She looks at me with her hair a mess and surprise in her eyes, but she doesn't tell me to stop. I wrap my arms around her and pull her close. She doesn't relax. She doesn't fall asleep. If anything, she seems wound more tightly.

We lie together in the dark with both our minds in thought. Hers is most likely on her loss, and my mind runs wild with what to do next.

"Angel," I say, and she sits up to look at me. "You can't sleep. I can't sleep."

She gasps. "I'm not having sex with you. I barely know you."

I laugh even though I know she's the woman from the club. If this is what she needs right now, so be it. "That is a better idea than the one I have."

"Oh," she says shyly.

"Let's work out."

"Huh?"

"Look, we don't know each other well. I know more about you from the fucking Internet instead of from your lips, but it's okay. I have a hell of my own to live, and when I can't turn my mind off, I run."

"You want me to run with you? You don't want to have sex?"

"Oh, angel, I want to fuck you. I am a man." As much as I shouldn't want to fuck her, I do. As much as I should walk away, I don't. Instead, I tell her exactly what I think in the moment. "I will fuck you, but not right now. Your head's not there."

I sit up, taking her with me. Then she surprises me when she follows me out of the bed. I grab my shoes and head to the door.

At the top of the basement stairs, she hesitates. I take her by the hand and guide her out into the space of her kitchen.

"I-I," she stammers as she fights to get her breathing under control. "I don't go out at night."

I want to call bullshit, but now is not the time. My body is already amped up to feel the burn through my muscles.

"Angel, you're not alone." I kiss the top of her head and pull her into me. "You feel me? You feel me here with you? No more fighting the darkness alone. I'm here. Right. Here. With. You."

She nods against me.

Giving her a moment to get her breathing under

control, I simply hold her. When she is steady, I separate us, and then we head to the back door.

Sliding on my shoes, I realize I'm still in my club clothes. Not only do I desperately need a shower, but this is not ideal for a workout. Well, it will slow me down so that maybe she can keep up.

Silently, we pound the pavement together. The steady thumping of our feet is in sync with each step of our jog, becoming its own lullaby of sorts. It's not long before she is breathing heavily but steadily and seems to have worked out some of what is going on in that beautiful head of hers. My feet ache from the tight confines of my shoes, and I swear my pants are ready to bust at the strain of my over-sized thighs stretching as my muscles move.

When we slow, I look to see the sun rising. I can't stop the laugh that erupts from me.

Lorraine looks at me as if I'm as crazy as she is.

"What?" I hold my hand to my chest in mock offense. "I've never seen the sunrise with a woman before."

I haven't, not like this. Sure, I have taken women to bed and woken up with them, but never have I spent the morning on a run and watched the sun come up on a new day and a new beginning with a woman before.

"It's not my thing."

"You're a good man, Jason."

I tip her chin to make her eyes meet mine. "Angel, the only good thing about me is right in front of my face. I'm a monster inside, and you should know that."

Something I have seen too many times before flashes in her eyes—challenge.

Frustration grows inside me. Like a parasite, it latches on, and I feel the tightening in my chest.

"I don't see a monster."

My tone is sharp as I hold myself back. "Men like me don't change. Evil is in my veins."

"Then why bust through my door to save me? Why take me to the hospital? Why get me out of my self-made prison to see the dawn of a new day? If you're so bad, why be so . . . good?"

I trace my finger over her jawline. There is trepidation in her eyes, but the challenge remains firm. "There is no good inside of me. There is in you. I'm here for you, though not because I'm some knight in shining armor. Angel, you've gotta know, don't ever try to fix a man, especially one like me. You can't tame the beast inside me."

She thinks for a moment, her eyes glistening with a pain from long ago. "I may not be able to tame the beast inside of you. I may not be able to beat back the darkness in your depths, Jason. I may not be able to fix myself, and I know I can't fix anyone else, but maybe I can help you fight back, kind of like you are with me right now."

Never have I thought about someone fighting for me. The frustration I was feeling, the anger that was building from her challenge, changes. New thoughts invade my mind.

Could I fight back, put the evil inside of me at bay?

I would like to hope so, but I know reality is nowhere near as nice as fiction.

I pull my hand from her chin and notice how large my fingers look against her pale skin. These hands have brought pain. These hands have brought death. These hands are tainted with more darkness than anyone could ever understand.

"There's no help for me. I'm not sure I want it." I turn away from her and start the jog back to her home. I need to breathe, and I need the exertion. I need to push myself to the limit. I need to get away from her before she really starts to think she can save me.

She falls in step beside me, and then we head back to her house. She stops when I do and doesn't go any farther. She steps closer to me like I am some kind of armor for her. Then she looks up at me with lost eyes, and I know damn well I have to get her inside at the very least.

I walk in, and she follows behind me. I watch her do some sort of surveillance walk around the house, checking all the windows and doors. She looks over her shoulder at me, seeming to make sure I am there with her.

My stomach twists from knowing how terrified she is and that I am allowing her to think of me as some sort of hero. I'm no one's hero.

She turns around and looks me in the eye then back down. Her bottom lip is between her teeth, and fuck if I don't want it between mine. But I can't.

Missy was crazy, and her fucking issues and mine didn't mix. This girl is beautiful and fucked up at the same time, and I would just ruin her further. I would destroy the ounce of sanity she still holds, which is dangling from a very thin, invisible string. A string that would be sure to snap if I let anything more happen to her.

I want to fuck her again. I want her eyes on me, watching me, only me.

"I'll be back later to get your alarm reset. Until then, get some rest."

The challenge I saw in her eyes earlier is gone. She simply nods her head and lets me leave.

"She's got you fucking twisted," Brock says from the other side of the pad he is holding to protect him as I beat the hell out of it.

"I've got me twisted." I kick, and even with the

padding, he stumbles back two steps. "I'm everything I never wanted to be, but fuck if it's gonna change."

My entire body hurts. I shouldn't be here, not after the head injury I sustained, but I have to fight. I have to feed the need inside of me to fuck shit up. I have to release the aggression that builds day in and day out. It's fucked up. The Ping-Pong ball in my mind knows it's all wrong. Everything about me is wrong, but I can't control it.

I also can't get those angel blue eyes out of my mind.

I can help you fight back.

If she only knew what really lies inside me, she wouldn't help me fight it back. She would fight to be free from me. It would be the smartest thing she could ever do for herself.

She needs to get as far away from me as possible. I damn sure am not strong enough to walk away from her.

Funny, I can beat the shit out of men twice my size, but I can't resist the blond haired, blue-eyed pussycat on Hollow Terrace.

I told her I would fix her alarm, and I will. She is also going to get the fuck out of that house. It can't be healthy to stay there. Then again, it won't be healthy to stay with me, either.

I have to fight inside to keep myself away from her. She's a mess and I'm trouble with a capital T. She has no idea the monster she had in her bed.

Chapter Eleven

LO

I watch him walk away. His muscles flex in his clothes. He is strong, so strong, and I can't help wanting to absorb that energy. I need it for what we—I mean, I have planned. I know I'm a mess, but in order to clean up a mess, sometimes you have to become one.

He gets in the car and sits in his seat, running his hands through his blond hair. He looks up at me and nods, then twists his finger as if to say turn around before he points to the door. He mouths Go, and it's as if I can hear his rough, deep voice saying the words to me.

His voice, even imagined in my head, wraps around me like a shield of strength and protection. There is no hesitation or thought. I look around the house that built me then crushed me, that terrorizes and consumes me with the borrowed strength of a man who calls himself a monster. I know I can finish what we—I mean, I have started.

I lock all three dead bolts and the doorknob and then lean against the wall and slide down it, coming to a rest on the floor.

He is gone, and I am here . . . alone. I take comfort in the sun being up and in Jason, the man with a pain of his own, the man whose stature and stare could leave anyone trembling, the man I allowed to keep me safe from her—myself—last night.

Boots and Socks are sunning themselves in the window while I sit here, watching them in their relaxed state, envious of them. My eyes grow heavy, and I allow them to rest, but just for a moment. I know the house is locked and secure, because he made it so.

I jump when I hear a loud knock on the door. I rub the back of my neck as I stretch. It aches from the way I was positioned. I must have fallen asleep.

Socks and Boots jump off my lap.

"I'm sorry I scared you," I say to them as I crawl to the window next to the door and peek out.

Green eyes meet mine, and I instantly feel ease wash over me.

I unlock and open the door for Jason, who walks in with a toolbox and a bag. He is dressed in gray sweatpants and a black, sleeveless shirt, and he has a black baseball cap on backward. He looks every bit as strong as he did when he left, maybe even more so.

"I'm gonna fix this quickly. It shouldn't take long, and then I'll be out of your hair." I know by the look in his eyes he sees the fear inside of me. "I can't stay again."

I nod rapidly. "I know."

"You are off for a couple days. It was in your discharge papers from the doctor. Get this fucking place on the market. You need to move on," he says as he walks by, setting the bag by the door where the alarm wires were cut.

I watch as he works quickly, as if he has done this a hundred times before, and maybe he has. He is a mystery to me, a beautiful, strong conundrum of anger, attitude, and angst. I want to know more about him, but I know he doesn't want me to. I can't blame him. I am tainted and tormented by one horrible day. April 20, the day hell erupted from the depths and was no longer just a frightening story to scare a child into behaving. It became a reality, one I face every day.

I start to feel my body on the verge of shaking and trembling. I can't let this happen. Not in front of him. Not when I want him to stay.

Anxiety drowns rationality, and I scurry into the kitchen where I feed the cats first then quickly start to make two sandwiches, just to keep him here for a little while longer.

"I'm all set," he says from behind me.

I turn around and hold up the plate. "It's a thank-you."

He closes his eyes, and I immediately feel let down, rejected.

"Can I get it to go?" he asks with a forced, airless tone.

"Of course." I turn around and open the cupboard with parchment paper and cling film. I lay it out and wrap it in the paper, folding it into an envelope like I did when I was younger and worked at the sandwich shop on weekends.

I liked having my own money. Heidi had Ryan, and they spent all of their free time together. He showered her with gifts and affection. I didn't have time for boys. I wanted to work to buy the things I wanted, the things Ryan gave her that my parents thought were extravagant indulgences. Things a middle-class family couldn't afford.

At work, I met friends. I loved talking with the customers and got to know the regulars and what they would order. I also met a boy. The first night I agreed to meet Stephen after work was the night I was late.

Emotions creep up in my throat, but I force them back

as I wrap the cling film around the turkey and provolone sandwich on rye bread.

When I turn around, I force a smile, and he looks back and forth between my eyes and forces his own smile. I'm pretty sure it's the first time he has smiled at me. His teeth are perfect, straight and white. They don't match the rest of his rough exterior.

"You got a bag?" he asks.

"Of course." I know there is too much excitement in the response, because his shoulders automatically slouch in some sort of defeat.

I open the cupboard and push up on my toes to reach the brown paper bags I haven't ever used but know are in here.

I feel his body heat behind me as he leans close and reaches up to grab them.

"Thank you," I whisper.

He takes in a deep breath, and I look over my shoulder at his eyes looking down at me.

His voice is thick and gruff when he replies, "No problem."

He doesn't move. I am sure that him staring at my lips means he is going to kiss me. I close my eyes, waiting, wanting, expecting . . .

I feel his hot breath come closer and closer, and my body becomes tingly as heat rises from my toes up to my belly, intensifying the sensation.

A knock at the door causes me to jump. In doing so, my head hits his jaw. He groans.

"I'm so sorry." I turn quickly. He doesn't move, and I feel his erection against my stomach.

I quickly look up at him, and he takes a step back, rubbing his hand back and forth over his hat, before he walks to the door.

"Wait, don't open it!" I panic as I peek around the doorway to see if he listens.

He doesn't stop. He unlocks the door and opens it without even looking.

"What's up?' he asks in a somewhat cocky tone as he shoves his hands down the front of his waistband and adjusts himself.

"Good afternoon." I hear the familiar voice of Ryan Bennett and freeze on the spot. "I'd like to speak to Lorraine."

"About what?" Jason asks, not moving.

"A personal matter," Ryan clips back.

"She's busy," Jason hisses.

"If that's true, I'd like to hear it from her." I see Ryan push past him, and Jason grabs the back of his collar.

"Did I invite you in?" he snarls.

"Jason," I gasp as I walk toward them.

"You know this dickhead?" he asks as Ryan pulls away from him and stomps toward me.

I nod and swallow hard. "He was my sister's boyfriend."

"Christ, Lorraine." Ryan looks around and points to the stairway. "What the hell is this? Where is all your furniture, your photos, a sign of life?"

"Why don't you back the hell off, son?" Jason asks, walking toward me.

"Who the hell is this joker?" Ryan points at Jason.

"This is my . . . friend Jason," I answer.

"Friend?" Ryan asks, seeming unconvinced.

I look at Jason, hoping I haven't offended him. He seems to be questioning my answer as well.

"I certainly hope so," I whisper.

Jason's eyes widen just a bit before looking away from me to Ryan. "What can we do for you?"

"I heard through the grapevine she allowed someone to enter into her home," Ryan says, looking around, "if that's what the hell this is." He looks back at me. "This needs to stop, Lorraine. You need to move on, have a life. If you can't do it here, you can come back home. You smiled there, lived." He walks around, waving his hand about, and then stops and looks at me. "We miss you. Come home."

"This the doctor's kid?" Jason asks.

I nod and look down.

"Well, Ryan," Jason starts, "Lo has decided she's gonna put this house of hell on the market and get herself a new place. She is working things out."

"For two years, she's been working things out. If she's telling you that, she's lying to you and herself." I can tell by his tone that Ryan is angry at me.

I shake my head. "I'm not lying to anyone."

"You should probably hit the road, Ryan," Jason says firmly.

"Lorraine, you and I need to chat . . . alone. Please tell this . . . gentleman that you are fine with me here."

I nod. "You were leaving anyway. I'm fine, Jason. I truly appreciate everything." I look up at him, and he appears angry, but he finally nods.

"Take care, Lo."

I walk him to the door, and when he opens it, I grab his arm. His body tenses, and then he pulls away.

"See ya, Lo."

I feel an immediate sickness, a sadness, as he leaves without even a glance at me.

"Lock the door," Ryan says in a quiet calm that is all him.

I shut the door and lock it then turn to him.

He looks at me with hunger and sadness in his eyes. "I have missed you so damn much."

I don't know what to say to him, but I don't have time to say anything before he is in front of me, his arms wrapped around me. I hear a sigh as he kisses my head over and over again.

"Ryan," I say softly. "Please don't."

"I can't help it. I'm home now for good. I'm starting my residency at Henry Ford next week." He pulls back and looks at me. "Dad told me about yesterday. He worries about you and wants you to come home. We can handle it. We can. I know it. I just want you to feel safe again." He pauses, as if he is gathering his thoughts. "Lorraine?"

"Congratulations," I say, stepping back and away from him.

He nods. "Thank you." Then he turns and looks around the house. "I'm going to really help you this time. Let's call the Realtor and start making this place presentable."

"I can't live with your family again," I say quietly.

"That's fine. We'll get you a place." He walks toward my parents' room. "Somewhere in a building with security. Where the hell do you sleep?" He looks back at me.

"The basement," I answer.

"Jesus Christ, I can't have that. I can't allow you to do that. It's over. You need to move forward." He walks toward me and stops. "I've changed. I am ready to move forward and really live again. It's time for you to do the same."

Chapter Twelve

Jason

The getup frustrates me. The wig, the makeup, all the black clothing—it all eats at me. Watching her fluff her hair and smack her lipstick-covered lips irritates me more. What the hell is she doing? She climbs into her Impala, and even the car pisses me off. How do the levelheaded eyes of an angel nurse go from one extreme to another?

I need to walk away. I don't.

No, I keep coming back to her eyes. Every time I close mine, I see hers.

I came here because I'm a fucking glutton for punishment after she sent me away to have a talk with him. I should have left it at that. She made her choice. I would have sent him away. Instead, she had me leave. I shouldn't care what happened after I left. The dismissal she gave me earlier still stings, but what the hell can I do about it? I should let it all go and let her go. I damn sure shouldn't be here watching, seeking, and waiting for whatever the hell comes next.

I can't. For some messed-up reason, I can't walk away.

Knowing I left her with him, I had to come back and see for myself if he got to stay. What kind of crazy game is she playing? Why does he have this pull over her? Why does his family have such a connection to her? He asked her to come home. His whole family wants her to come home. It's just nuts.

Home. I mean, really? The girl lived with them for some time obviously, but where did she end up? Back home. She brought herself back to the same nightmare that haunts her to this day. I have heard of people trying to overcome their fears by facing them, but this is so much more fucked up than holding a damn snake to get over your phobia.

This shit . . . This shit she's doing—living in the basement of the house her family was murdered in—is the stuff that is made for TV or something. It blows my mind. There is no way I could live in a place like that, and I had a far from ideal childhood.

My father deserves to die brutally, and still I wouldn't want to sleep in the same house it happened in, no matter how much I know he earned it. She had a loving family, and to live in the place it all came to an end . . . I just can't wrap my head around it.

She backs out of her driveway, bringing my attention back to the urge to follow her. She's in that car, in the outfit. The outfit that tells me Lorraine isn't out tonight. No, my angel has tucked herself away. Why? I can't help questioning.

I shouldn't care. I should turn around and sort my own life out. Missy keeps calling, I keep ignoring. Missy is no longer my problem. I am my problem.

But every time I close my eyes, I picture her blue ones

staring back at me. I picture Lorraine, leaning over my hospital bed like a vision of an angel.

I should take my ass back to the hotel and find a new place to live. I have enough problems of my own. Do I do the responsible, smart, and normal thing, though? Do I leave the woman I barely know to her own troubles?

No. I follow her instead of my instincts. I sit back and try to sort out what she's doing.

She drives without checking her rearview, and like the sick fuck I am, I follow her.

Our first stop is on Brown Avenue. She parks her car in front of house number 7929 and sits. She doesn't get out. She doesn't move. She simply parks, turns the car off, slides down into the driver's seat, and waits.

What the hell is she waiting for?

When I see the garage door open to the house across the street and the black BMW pull in, there is no doubt in my mind who is driving. Charlotte Whittaker, the most put-together woman in the district. She is a fierce negotiator and will stand toe-to-toe with any man in her perfectly tailored suits and high fucking heels. She's one of only a few people my father actually respects.

Charlotte enters her home, and still, we wait. I look around, trying to figure out why we are here since there is no other activity in the area. After thirty minutes or so, the taillights flash on Lorraine's car before she pulls away.

Keeping my distance, I pull out, following her to the next location. We stop on East River Drive. She repeats the same process of sitting still and watching. I can't figure out what she's watching. The upscale neighborhood is quiet.

My mind goes over why she would be here. I come up empty.

We aren't here nearly as long before she pulls off again.

We stop next at Wesley Drive. I immediately know who lives across the street from where she has parked.

Gavin Waters is a shrewd businessman with an appetite for the finer things in life. He also goes so far back with my dad he's my damn godfather.

It's not long before the man I have known my entire life comes out in jeans and a polo shirt with his hair styled in this shaggy way that is the polar opposite of his usual slicked-back business look. His Lexus backs out, and I am shocked when Lorraine—or I guess I should call her Heidi since she's in the getup—pulls out, following him.

Five blocks later, he parks his car and moves into a waiting cab. I know the routine well. This is how you make sure you aren't tied to The Lion's Den when you are a married man.

I shake my head, trying to shake off the thoughts of a man who is like a second father to me spending time in a kink club. The times I have been in the club my mind was never focused on the male patrons. He could have walked right by me and I wouldn't have given it a second thought.

Without missing a beat, she follows the cab. We seem to have come full circle as I follow her into the parking garage for The Den. Now it makes sense. She was watching him that night. That's why she was distracted. Lucky for me, he didn't spot me.

Disgust hits me like a punch in the gut. No way is this beautiful woman going to this club for a slimy bastard like Waters. He is as much a monster as my father.

I slam my hand down on my steering wheel. Shit, I fucked her like a damn whore when I knew it wasn't her kind of kink. It showed.

I fucking knew it.

Why did she go inside? Why did she let me fuck her?

She got off, so I know she enjoyed it, but why go through with it?

More than anything, I can't stop thinking, Why come back?

My anger boils over when she climbs out of her car in black, peep-toed hooker heels, fluffing her hair and adding more makeup. She starts to make her way over to the club as I park and jump out of my car, following her.

My phone rings. Seeing it's Missy, I ignore the call, not having time for her bullshit right now.

Anger runs through my veins. Is there one woman in my life who won't fucking play games?

Lo knows what this place is. She knows what people come here for. If that's what she wants, then I will be the one to give it to her. Me, my inner asshole screams. It will be me who gives it to her, not some bastard playing games his wife won't play because he doesn't have the balls or the talent to give his woman what she needs first. She came here tonight dressed to play. Well, then game fucking on.

"Lo," I start but stop myself. "Heidi," I call out, and she stops.

My Internet search said the Boschs were parents to twin girls: Heidi and Lorraine. Hi and Lo. If only they knew just how different their two girls would turn out when they named them in such a way.

Reaching her, I guide her by the arm to the alley beside the club. Her eyes grow wide in fear, and I am conflicted.

The dark hair, the red lips, the tight clothes—they make my dick hard. At the same time, they make me angry.

"You come here to be fucked like a whore?" I growl, angry at myself, angry at her, angry at the fucking world.

She licks her lips, and I crash my mouth to hers. What was meant to diffuse the situation and keep her from going inside after that bastard turns into something so much more. Somehow, the tables turn, and she takes as much as I give her, moaning for more.

She bites my bottom lip when I try to pull away. With my body against hers, pinned to the brick wall, I rock my erection into her belly. I fight not to tear her clothes off and take her like a wild animal. She makes me crazy.

"Feel me, Hi," I whisper, and she moans again. "Is this what you came here for?" I swear she purrs. "You want cock? You want my dick so deep inside you it's almost as if you can feel me in your throat?"

She doesn't answer verbally. She nods, biting her bottom lip.

Not good enough. I want the words.

She pulls at my neck, but I hold back. Then she traces the snake.

"You want Cobra?" I ask. If she's going to play this twisted game, I will give her the monster inside me. In the moment it's not about Hi or Lo or anything in between, it's us and I'll take her as she is right here, right now.

"I want you." She looks up at me with lust in her blue eyes.

I crash my mouth onto hers and grab the back of her thighs as she wraps her legs around me. Thank fuck she's in a skirt.

Hoisting her up, I rub her pussy with my hand as I unbutton my jeans, releasing my cock. I love the feel of her soaking wet silk panties against the roughness of my skin.

I don't think, and I don't stop as she rocks on my hand, soaking it with her juices as she looks for release. I don't wait. I push her panties to the side and slam into her.

She arches, hitting the back of her head on the unforgiving wall as I pound into her. In and out, in and out, I slide as she claws at me for more.

Leaning down, I bite her neck, making her cry out as she goes still, tightening against me.

"Cooobra." She trembles as her orgasm starts.

Her body shakes around me while I keep going. In and out, I slide as she rides through the aftershocks, her inner pussy muscles contracting around me.

After a few more thrusts, I go off inside her. I don't even give a fuck about the risks.

"Hear me now, Hi, and let's be clear. It's my come inside you. It's me who's marked you. You're not walking into that club." I run my nose along her jaw and down her neck, inhaling and exhaling deeply. I feel the goosebumps erupt on her skin, and it turns me on again. "I don't give a shit what Waters is up to. While my jizz drips out of your hot cunt, you're going to be with me. After I get you cleaned up, it's me you'll still be with. While we figure out whatever fucking game you're playing with me and with yourself, it's me you're going to be with."

Lost in her post-orgasm emotions, she nods her head as I slowly set her legs down. She's unsteady, so I guide her back to my car. She doesn't fight me, doesn't argue. She moves with me like she wants this as much as I do, and I thank fuck for that.

I will get Brock to pick her ride up later. For now, we have shit to sort out, and it needs to be sorted immediately. I'm not a methodical man. I take life as it comes at me. But this Hi/Lo insanity needs resolution. If she can't fight for it, I will.

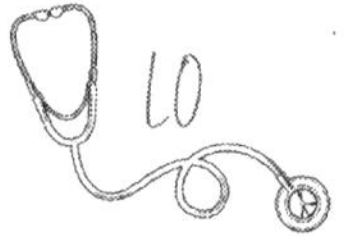

Chapter Thirteen

The wild abandon with which he took me outside the club rocks me to the depths of my soul. I knew when Waters switched to the cab, I shouldn't follow. I know what the club is about. Yet, I came anyway. It's a sickness the way finding their killer has consumed me. The lengths I have gone to in order to survive this mess both mentally and physically are beyond any definition of insane. The only way to do this is to become someone else. Heidi deserves retribution and becoming her gives her that.

Somehow, Jason sees through it all. He sees me. Somehow, this man who calls himself Cobra can read me like a book. Somehow, I have allowed myself to get into his truck and ride with him—home. Only he doesn't take us to my home like I expect. Silently, I allow him to take me and the craziest parts of me say I would follow him anywhere. I don't even know why.

As soon as we walk into his room, he turns and pulls the wig off me then drags me into the bathroom.

"Sit," he says. He is so angry, so very angry, so I do as he asks.

He turns his back to me and grabs a washcloth then turns on the water. "Why the fuck do you do that?" he grumbles. "Why fucking go there?" He wrings out the washcloth and squats down to wash my face. "You hide your face, hide behind a wig, behind too much fucking makeup, and go there looking to get fucked! Wasn't the doctor's son enough for you? Don't answer that. I know it wasn't. You need to be fucked like a whore by a real man."

He is angrier than I have ever seen anyone.

"Don't even try to deny it. I saw it with my own eyes," he continues. "The way he looked at you, and you looked at him. He's fucked that tight little cunt of yours. He fucking thinks he owns it. You and I both know better. He doesn't satisfy your craving. He can't fuck you hard enough, can he?"

"It's not what you think," I whisper as tears start to fall.

"Oh, no? You gonna lie to me now?"

I shake my head, and he stands up, crossing his arms in front of himself and looking down at me.

"Then fucking tell me how it is!"

"He loved her!" I yell at him. "He loved her and missed her, and so did I. I would never—" I stop, because it's not true. I did. I did! "Yes! Yes, I slept with him, but it wasn't me. It wasn't truly me!"

"Oh, fuck!" he roars, throwing his hands in the air, acting as if the entire world has just exploded. "Just how fucked up are you? Tell me, are you bipolar, schizophrenic, or just so fucked up you don't even know the truth!"

"He was fucking her! He was fucking me, all the while pretending it was her." I stand and point at him. "I don't expect you to understand it. It's wrong. It was so very wrong, but it happened, okay? It happened, and there isn't anything I can do to change it!"

I feel my body shake and my stomach twists in a knot. I have never talked about it, never told anyone. Now that I have, it's even more real and upsetting.

"Did you fuck him tonight?" he snaps, balling his fists at his sides.

"I'm gonna be sick," I say, turning around and dropping to my knees in front of the toilet.

I throw up over and over. Nothing but liquid comes out. Nothing has been in my stomach all day.

When I finish, I lean back on my heels and see a washcloth in front of my face.

"When's the last time you showered?" he snaps.

"Yesterday morning," I answer, wiping the refreshing, cool cloth over my face.

I hear the water in the tub start.

"Get in."

"I just want to sleep," I say, holding my stomach.

"Get. In." He is already lifting me, his hands under my arms.

"Let go!" I yell as I try to fight my way out of his arms. "Dammit!"

I throw up again.

"You've got to be fucking kidding me."

"I warned you!" I cry, pulling my knees to my chest as he still holds me up.

I feel him pull the waistband of my skirt and underwear down, and then they are off. He sets me in the tub none too gently then pulls my shirt over my head and yanks my bra off.

"You're such an ass," I grumble, pulling my knees to my chest and covering my body.

"And you stink," he sneers as he grabs a towel and

wipes up the floor. Then I hear him stomp out of the bathroom, and the door shuts to the outside.

I quickly dunk my head under the water and grab the two-in-one shampoo then wash my hair, scrubbing vigorously. I then lie back and rinse my hair, submerging my head completely, wishing I didn't have to come back up, wishing I could just stay here in the weightless state. I think of the past five years and what I have become: nothing.

He pulls me up by my arm. "What the hell are you doing?"

I yank my arm away and wait for him to yell at me. I want him to yell at me. I want him to run from my insanity, but I don't want to lose him. I want him to fight me and then for me. Instead, he steps back.

"You need to calm the fuck down," he says in a low grumble.

"You need to walk out of here and let me finish," I say just as quietly.

He nods once then walks out.

I wash my body in privacy, taking my time doing so. It has been years since I soaked in a bath. I can't honestly remember the last time I felt safe enough to do so. While away at college, I lived in the safety of numbers and the chaos that is college. I showered during busy times so that I knew the bathrooms would be full, and I wouldn't be alone and afraid.

I look up when I sense he is watching me.

"You're taking a long damn time in here. Just making sure you're okay."

I lean against the side of the tub, covering myself as much as I can. "I'm fine. I just . . ." I pause and gather my thoughts. "I forgot how much I enjoy baths."

He looks at me and nods. "You need clothes." He holds

up a T-shirt and a pair of shorts then sets them on the counter.

"Thank you, Jason."

He nods again. "It's late."

"I'll get dressed, and then I guess I could walk—"

"Did you fuck him today?" he interrupts.

I shake my head.

He runs his hand through his hair. "You sure?"

"I'm sure," I answer, setting my forehead on the cold porcelain tub.

"My cock was the only one inside of you today?" he asks in a rumble.

I peer up at him. "Yes."

He pulls his shirt over his head swiftly and pushes his pants down before stepping out of them. He then steps toward me. "I need a shower. You need to get out and get dressed. Then get your ass to bed. I'm done tonight. Tomorrow, this shit gets sorted."

I dress quickly, deciding to leave while he showers. Facing the night is less scary than facing him right now. I have a task to complete, a job to do. I can't have him involved or in the way. I know how this ends, and then, and only then, will I feel safe again. Then, and only then, will I forgive myself for being late.

After quickly dressing, I reach out and slowly open the door to leave. A large hand reaches from behind me and slams it shut.

"Bed," he sneers.

"You don't want me here. I'm no good for you," I say without turning around.

"I'm not letting you leave tonight. I need sleep; you need sleep. I want to know what the hell the angel from the ER with the blue eyes who helped me needs in order to stop being the bad girl sneaking around at night and letting bad men fuck her—fuck you.

"You like it hard, don't you? Are you a whore, Lo? Are you a slut? How many men have been inside that tight, little pussy of yours?" His hand wraps around me and pulls me against his rock-hard body. "I'm a bad man. None of that shit matters to a bad man."

His lips push against mine as his hand flattens and runs down my belly inside the shorts he gave me. "Tell me, do you like to be tied up, spanked, fucked until you can't walk, fucked in the ass?"

I shake my head as his hand cups my flesh, and he presses his palm against me.

"No? I find that hard to believe." He pulls his hand out of the shorts and spins me around. "Tell me how you like it."

I shrug and look down. "I don't know."

He lifts my chin up and searches my face. "You aren't hiding behind that fucking makeup and wig, Lo. Tell me how you like to be fucked. Tell me how the doctor's son made you come and how all those boys from high school and college chasing you around fucked you."

I close my eyes and swallow as I shake my head again.

"Open those blue eyes, look at me, and tell me the truth."

Slowly, I open my eyes, but I can't speak when his intense, heat-filled green eyes are searching mine.

"Tell. Me."

I shrug and pull my face away. "Ryan was the first."

"So twins really do share everything, huh?" he growls.

I don't like what he implies.

"It wasn't like that."

"Then tell me how it was."

"It was after her . . . after she . . ." I can't say it. "He needed her, and so did I." I push past him when he looks confused. "I already told you that."

He grips my hips and spins me around again. I glance up into intense, angry eyes.

"No one before him?"

I shake my head.

"I keep telling myself to walk away. Thoughts of you suck me right back in. I don't know what to do with you," Jason growls and I remain speechless. I don't know what to do with me, either.

He pulls the shirt over my head then bends down, taking my breast in his mouth as he slides his hands down the back of the shorts, pushing them off. He then cups my ass and lifts me. I grip his muscular shoulders, holding on for fear I will fall, as he walks us to the bed and leans down, lowering me until I am lying under him and staring up into his eyes.

"No one before him?" he asks, and I shake my head again. "I am sorry, Lo. I'm sorry for what you have gone through, and I should be sorry for what I am about to do to you, but I'm not. Not one bit."

His lips touch mine less harshly than before, but his groan is no less harsh, maybe even more so.

Without moving away, he says, "Open." And I do.

His mouth surrounds mine, and he sucks before pushing his tongue inside, stroking mine slowly up and down. He cups my face, his calloused thumb stroking my cheek sweetly, yet its roughness is still there. His chest rises and falls against mine before he slowly pulls away from our kiss, his kiss. He kisses my lips and moves down my jaw, my neck, and then he is hovering over me, surrounding my nipple with his mouth. My back arches against him, and I cry out from the pleasure that soars through me.

He reaches between us and pushes my legs apart before

he cups me, his fingers running up and down the outside of my sex, teasing, tormenting. I raise my hips up to meet his hand while he sucks hard, tugging on my breast then letting it fall out of my mouth with a pop.

"You smell so damn good." He groans before taking my other breast in his mouth as he pushes a finger inside of me.

"Jason," I cry out.

"Mmm," he moans, sucking harder and harder on my nipple as he moves his finger very slowly in and out of me. "I can't wait to taste you." That said, he starts kissing down my body. The sensations of his soft lips and the scratch of his scruff contradict each other. It feels so very good.

He kisses down my belly as he shoves his hands under me, cupping my ass and spreading me wider. He then sits back on his knees, staring down at my naked flesh, before he loosens the towel wrapped around him, allowing it to fall on the bed. His cock springs free, and he grips it tightly, stroking it in sync with the finger he thrusts back inside of me.

I watch his strong grip on his vast erection as my hips thrust against his touch while he is looking at the most intimate part of me.

"Your pussy is stunning." He takes in a deep breath, and his eyes hood. "Smells delicious."

His mouth covers my crotch, and the sensation is overwhelming.

"No! Oh, God, no."

I try to pull back, but he grips my ass, and his licks turn harsher. He pushes his tongue deep inside me until I cry out again.

I fight the sensation while he holds me steady as he devours me until I can't fight the feeling anymore. The intense burn builds deep inside of me. I buck against his face and grab his hair.

"Yes, oh, yes," I cry out shamelessly.

He sucks and licks and feasts on me as wave after wave of pleasure rips through my core like it never has before.

"Stop," I whimper when I feel like I won't ever recover from what I know is the most intense orgasm I have ever experienced.

He doesn't listen. He pushes a finger deep inside of me and then another as he sucks and licks at my clit.

"Oh, no," I cry, gripping the pillow as the burn comes again. "I can't, Jason. I—"

"Come for me, Lo. Come for you," he growls.

"I don't think—"

"You have the prettiest pussy I have ever seen. You taste so good." He flattens his tongue against me, and I cry. He looks up at me. "Don't ask me to stop. I won't."

His mouth and fingers continue to pleasure me, and I hold nothing back. My legs are now like rubber, and I am out of breath from trying to hold back.

Finally, he pushes himself away with a look of regret.

He then bends back down and kisses me there again before he kisses his way up my body.

With one hand, he holds himself above me, and with the other, he strokes himself. It's beautiful. Everything about him is strong and controlling. I feel safe with him.

"I'm gonna fuck you now."

I nod.

"Look at me, angel."

I open my eyes wider. I would do anything to please him right now, anything.

"I'm gonna fuck you."

I spread my legs wider so his large body can fit between them.

He rubs his cock up and down my seam, coating it with my wetness.

"So wet, so hot, and so fucking greedy for my cock, aren't you, angel?"

"Yes."

"Tell me what you want," he says, continuing to rub against my highly sensitive pussy.

"I want you, Jason. I want you."

He slams into me then bends down to taste my nipples and then my mouth. He draws back from our kiss as he pulls out almost fully.

"See how you taste, Lo? How fucking good you taste?"

He rams into me again and kisses me harder this time. Then he pulls out.

"No. Please, no," I beg, wrapping my legs around him and pulling him toward me.

"Fuck!" he roars and slams into me over and over and over again. "Come, Lo. Fucking come," he pants.

"I can't . . . Oh, God," I cry out.

He pounds into me until I feel my orgasm rip through me again. Then he pulls out, grips himself, and falls back on his heels, still stroking himself.

"I'm gonna come so hard."

I sit up quickly. "I want it. I want your come."

"Aw, fuck, Lo," he hisses, looking at me adoringly. "Open up, angel. It's all yours."

I lean in and open my mouth. He grips the back of my head and pulls me closer until I feel my throat muscles contract. I gag as his hot, thick liquid gushes into my mouth while he cries out my name.

My name.

When he pulls back, holding himself, he rubs the head of his cock across my lips. "Thank you."

I lie back, unable to take my eyes off him, this man

who makes me feel so much more than fear, so much more than pain. He just makes me feel so very good.

I smile and close my eyes. "No, thank you. That was . . ." I stop, not wanting to feel shame or embarrassment.

"Tell me, angel."

"In a way, you were my first." I keep my eyes closed. "I've never been with anyone who didn't think or pretend they were doing it with her."

"Are you kidding me? High school? College?"

"No. Just him and you. But really, just you."

I feel the bed dip, and then he is beside me, pulling me against him. "But you were with him."

"Not without a wig," I whisper. "No one has ever said my name like you did, Jason." I yawn and scoot back against him. "No one."

He rubs his rough hand up and down my arm as a soft growl escapes him. "Sleep, angel. I've got you."

I whisper, "I don't want to go back there."

"You won't. Tomorrow is a new day, Lo. Tomorrow, your life begins."

I fall asleep in his arms. I feel safe, I feel loved, and for the first time in forever, I feel comfortable. I feel comfortable because of him.

I wake to hands squeezing my ass and a low chuckle. "Get up, Lo; it's noon."

"I'm starving," I say immediately.

"Go hop in the shower. I'm gonna take you on a breakfast date."

I roll over and look at him. "A date?"

"Yeah, angel. It's the least I can do after deflowering you last night." He winks. "Now go."

I can't help smiling. "Well, okay, then."

When I'm done with my shower, I am excited about

the idea of a date. Pretending he is my first is wrong, but for some reason, it makes me happy. Deliriously happy.

I have no clothes. I laugh at myself when I open the door to come out. Then I freeze when I hear Jason arguing with a man.

"I ended it with Missy days ago, Dad," Jason snaps.

"She threatened to go to the media about the son of the mayor's abusive behaviors if I didn't buy her a plane ticket and give her money to get back to her family in Massachusetts."

"Our relationship ended because she is crazy as fuck. She pushed me. I couldn't do it anymore," Jason growls. "It was toxic."

"I guess you know how to push everyone's fucking buttons, don't you, son?"

Jason's methodical laugh is low and angry. "If that's what you want to tell yourself, fine. But a seven-year-old boy who spilled some fucking milk certainly shouldn't be considered a button pusher, old man."

"You never listened," he spits at Jason.

"Tell yourself whatever the fuck you need to. Over the years, I took your beatings for doing fucking nothing. Make sure you know, if you ever raise a finger to me again, I will snap your fucking neck."

"Your threats don't scare me, son."

"Good, 'cause I'm not threatening. That's a fucking promise. Now get out."

"I paid for your whore's silence and to get home. I won't do it again. Whoever the whore in the bathroom is better never find out who you are, or so help me God—"

"Don't talk about her like that. Don't ever talk about her like that. She's no fucking whore."

"Someone from work, Jason?" he snaps. "Not smart."

"No, her name is Lorraine Bosch. Does that ring a bell? You know the name."

There is poignant silence. "Jason, what the hell are you thinking? The girl is messed up. Do you have any idea—"

"She's been through hell, but so have I, haven't I, Dad? Don't you worry about me or about her; both of us are more fucking normal than you."

I fall back against the wall and cover my mouth. Jason is the mayor's son. Oh my God, he is Jason Stanley.

Chapter Fourteen

Fuck! Missy and her bullshit brought my dad here.

His eyes told me all I need to know about his past with Lorraine's family. He knows something, which means her following the people she is following is dangerous. Her being involved in anything surrounding my father does not sit well with me. I have work to do.

First, I have to make sure Missy is on a plane and gone for good. Calling the front desk to my building, I am informed of her departure and the key left behind for me. She also asked to be removed from the complex owner association papers, and as long as I sign off on it, then it's a done deal. Well, as much as I want to bitch at her for blackmailing my father into a plane ticket, I am just happy to have her gone. She needs a fresh start, and I need to breathe without worrying about her showing up somewhere to shoot me or stab me.

After looking around at my meager belongings thrown around the hotel, I gather them up and into my bag. Once that's done, I look at the bathroom door and can't help wondering what is taking Lo so long.

I go to the door and listen.

Silence.

I knock. "Lo, you okay in there?"

"Yeah," she says, her voice sounding weak. "I, um . . ." She pauses. "I heard voices. I didn't know if your company left."

Shit, she heard my father here. Does she know who he is? Does she know something he's hiding? Was he involved in her family's murder? It wouldn't surprise me. The thought alone has me needing to break something, though.

I step back as she makes her way out of the bathroom and over to the bed. Every time I tell myself I am walking away, I get drawn back in. With everything between us, I can't stop myself from wanting her, from feeling things for her I've never felt before. She wrings her hands together nervously, wearing one of my T-shirts and boxers, all of it swallowing her completely. She avoids eye contact, which bothers me, too. One thing I have always done is face things head-on. This is no different.

"Do you know my father?" I ask, wondering if I really want to know the answer.

She bites her bottom lip and nods, looking at me with her blue eyes sparkling with emotions. "I know you."

I point to myself. "Me?"

"We were at your house. It was a campaign dinner or something. Anyway, just me and my dad made it. My sister was sick, so my mom stayed home with her. My dad worked for your dad. You were eight, maybe nine. I knocked over a plate of food. I was afraid I would get in trouble, so I didn't tell anyone. I cleaned it up, but your father saw the white carpet stained with salsa from my chips and dip." She doesn't move her eyes from mine. "Your father saw you with a plate of salsa and grabbed you harshly. I followed when he took you into a side office on the first floor of your house."

I wish I could remember which event specifically she was referring to. I don't. This same scenario played out on more than one occasion. Anytime things didn't go perfectly or not enough money was raised or my father was simply mad at the world, I paid the price. In the end, one event blurred into the next, and as much as I tried to hide out to avoid them, I wasn't successful. What she saw happened so many times.

She swallows then brings her hand up to stroke my cheek. "He . . ." She pauses, and I see the pity in her eyes.

I tense and step away. Everything in me goes tight. My heart seems to stop beating. I never want to see that look in those heavenly blue eyes. I never want her to have any sadness or negative emotions associated with thoughts of me. If there is one thing I never want to see in her eyes, it's pity.

Pity for me.

"Don't finish the fucking sentence. I know what happened and whatever you remember is probably mild compared to what I endured. It was a long fucking time ago. It's done. He's not a part of my life except when it's expected or situations like today where he couldn't reach me and had to relay information." I pause, watching her rapidly blink, processing what I just said. I don't let up and give her time to think on my childhood. It's over. I have moved on, and she needs to let it go, too. "Look, my place is free. I'll take you there until we can sort out yours," I say roughly, needing to breathe.

I don't need anyone to feel sorry for me, least of all her. She has no idea what growing up like that has done to me. She witnessed one time. She saw a little boy who had no choice other than to take on the problems of a grown man's inability to control himself. She doesn't know that it started when I was so young I don't remember a time he didn't hit me.

She doesn't know how many times my mother begged me to be a better boy so I wouldn't keep upsetting him. Never once did my mother fight for me. No, all the fight had to stay inside of me, never to be let out.

The thing is, as much as I hate my father, as much as I never want to be anything like him, it happened despite my best intentions. The same little boy grew into a man much like the one who just left here.

No, Lorraine Bosch need not pity me.

She should fear me.

There is a moment of hesitation before she moves to put her shoes on so we can leave. After I grab the rest of my stuff and toss it haphazardly in the bag, we head out. My father's unexpected arrival killed any thoughts of breakfast. I can't stand that she pities me and I wonder, yet again, if I should walk away.

The ride to my condo is quiet. I need it to be that way. I don't know what to say to her, and I'm sure she has no clue what to say to me.

I'm not a little boy anymore, and she can't save me even if she thinks she somehow can.

Getting out, I walk toward the front door as she follows. There is no need to disillusion her to think I'm the kind of man to open doors or cover her with my jacket because she's cold. Sure, my instincts pull at me to do these things, but she doesn't need to find good in me. Knowing what I came from, she should know what I'm destined to become. I tried to fight inside to make the change; that didn't happen. In fact, with Missy, I sometimes think I was worse.

At the doorway, I stop her in front of the security man.

"Max, this is Lo." He extends his hand, and she takes it. "She's free to come and go in my place."

Seeing her hand in his, I fight back the rage inside me that another man is touching her. I shake my head, trying to brush off the thoughts of crushing the man who matches my size and skill set just for being polite. I have never been this jealous of a touch before. Even Tatiana and Caldwell didn't make my blood boil to this extreme.

Stepping away, I guide her to the elevator and to my condo.

"Security is top-notch. We didn't always have a doorman, but now there is someone here twenty-four hours. There are four men who do a rotation. As long as you are here, I promise, Lo, you are safe."

I shouldn't tell her this. I shouldn't give her this false sense of security. She is safe here—from everyone but me.

Entering the front door, I check the alarm. No surprise there; Missy didn't set it.

I look at Lo. "Give me a four-digit number you won't forget."

Her response is immediate. "Zero, four, twenty." It makes me angry.

"No," I say, clipped. "I know that is the day all was lost for you, but you cannot carry those ghosts here."

"Zero one, two, eight."

I arch an eyebrow at her. "Meaning?"

"The day I met you," she whispers.

"Okay," I say, resetting the code for the alarm. I then walk her through the steps to arming and disarming the alarm before I take her to my bedroom.

I walk in and can only shake my head at the mess Missy has left behind. My bed is slashed, the sheets have paint poured on them, and my lamps are busted. I guide Lorraine back out.

"I'll get a new bed delivered today. My ex and I had this place together. She didn't take the breakup too well."

"I don't have to stay here. I have a house."

"No, this is a fresh start. You're letting go of all that. You can stay here as long as you want, and I can stay at the hotel if you don't want me here." I look at her, knowing as much as I stand here and say the words, I can't make myself stay away.

I feel like we need some space, and she needs to know she's safe. There is a part deep inside me that doesn't want to give her an inch of space. There is this need in me to be all over her, in her, and never let her go. I fight inside not to consume her. She needs to work out her past and I need to find a way to overcome mine. One part of me screams we are no good for each other. We are destined for disaster. The other part of me screams she's a heaven-sent angel. We are destined to save each other. The more I try to tell myself to walk away, the more her eyes pull me right back in.

"I'll go handle getting a new bed, and then I need to hit up the gym just to check in. Make yourself at home."

"I'll just call a cab to get my car."

I can't let her go.

"Lo, I'll get your car. You better be here when I get back. If not, I'll find you, and when I do, I'll pink that ass for my effort."

Her mouth drops open. "You wouldn't!"

I smirk. "Oh, baby, I would, so get comfortable. You have the alarm. Let me get you a new bed, and I'll pick up a few things at your place for you." I pause, not believing I'm going to do this. "I'll also pick up the cats, their food, and their litter boxes."

At the thought of her pets, she smiles softly and seems to settle. "Don't forget the cat condo. Boots loves to nap in it, and Socks uses it for a scratching post." She pauses as if to think, "If I'm going to be here for a while then I'll need scrubs for work."

Mentally, I try to make a list of everything I need as I grab my gym stuff and give the place a once-over for more damage from Missy. In the kitchen, I find everything is gone. Every plate, every utensil, every pot and pan. Looks like my ex wanted to hold on to the non-fine china. I don't give a shit. The woman needs to stay away and if cleaning out the kitchen does that for her then so be it. Looks like I need to stop at a store for some new dinnerware.

Part of me doesn't want to let Lo out of my sight. I'm afraid she will run from me. The other part of me knows we both need time. I need her to know she's free to come and go as she wishes. She needs to know she isn't leaving one prison to enter another. I need to think on my own. Having space between us, I can think over her reactions.

When I climb into the ring or octagon for a fight, I study my opponent. Overcoming whatever shit Lorraine is doing as Heidi is my new opponent.

Heidi is hot as fuck, but she doesn't hold a candle to Lorraine and the connection we share.

I don't want another woman who is going to drive me mad. I want someone to cherish who can see beyond all the bad.

Everything in her world changed the day her family was murdered. All the people she is following are tied to districts and high-priority positions. Her reaction to my name is even more telling. I can't help but wonder if her father stumbled upon something at work he shouldn't have.

Sitting down on a bench in the gym's locker room, I pull out my laptop. I start researching her father. Then it hits me. He once worked for my father. Hell, they came to a party my parents hosted once, years ago.

My stomach churns and my mind dances with more questions than answers. My father is a ruthless man in business and in life. There is no doubt in my mind he would kill anyone who went against him.

The question is, what did Mr. Bosch do that wronged my father?

The more I dig, the less I seem to figure out.

Needing to take my aggression out on someone, I call Brock to meet me at the gym. It doesn't take long before he arrives, and we get to work.

"You need a fight with Caldwell," Brock goads me as we warm up.

That's for sure. The bastard could meet me hit for hit.

"He's done."

"Shit, do you blame him? If you had a hot piece like mouse at home, you'd consider your risks a little more carefully, too."

I smirk. "Damn straight I would."

"Wanna tell me what's up with the black Impala I had to drop off for you?"

"Nothing to tell." I try to avoid the conversation.

"Bullshit, fucker." He knows me too well.

"I don't have enough answers right now." Which is the truth.

I don't have enough information to explain what is going on with me and Lo. I will, though. Mark my words, I will figure her out and figure us out. This is far from over. In fact, it's just beginning.

Chapter Fifteen

When he leaves, I take a deep breath and look around the condo. It's large and very wide open. I take comfort in being able to overlook nearly every area from where I stand in the foyer. There are no curtains covering the wall of windows overlooking the city, so I don't have the fear that someone is hiding behind them.

Curtains. Who in their right mind has to make the decision whether curtains could be a life or death choice when considering the décor of a home?

Someone like me.

Jason thinks he is dangerous and damaged.

I am, too. I am damaged and I am determined to be dangerous to those who killed my family.

I walk to the window and place my hand on the cool glass, still not heated from the afternoon sun. I look at the balcony where two plastic chairs and a large barbecue grill sit. I wonder why it's so scarcely decorated. After all, there was a woman who lived here.

I would love to sit outside and read or sunbathe or listen to music. Heidi and I used to do those things. We were carefree, not a worry in the world. We were two lives, conceived together, born minutes apart, and nearly inseparable. We had a language of our own as children. No one but she and I knew what we were saying, not even our parents, for the most part.

It was always Hi and Lo, never Lo and Hi. She was the courageous one, the sassy one. Heidi was the one who could stand alone socially, the one who looked anyone she came in contact with in the eye and smiled.

I remember when she dyed her hair black so that maybe we could have more independence from one another. Shortly after that, she started dating Ryan and hanging out with some of his friends. I loved to watch her shine, and honestly, as upsetting as it was at first, I started to enjoy not being called Heidi.

I remember the night she and Ryan had their first lovers' quarrel. She begged me to dye my hair with her. She even brought home the box of color. She said she'd hoped I would try like she was to stand out, and then she finally realized how silly it was. She said she missed us being just alike, and in the state she was in, I agreed to become the same.

For a week, it was Hi and Lo again. For a week, she avoided Ryan's calls. She never would tell me exactly what happened between them. Then, out of the blue, they were back together again, and she was happy.

I got a job and ended up loving the independence. Having work friends, people outside of the tight little circle Hi and I kept, wasn't as frightening as I had thought it would be.

And then, within weeks, she was gone forever.

Heidi, oh, how I miss her.

I press my face against the glass to soothe the burn preempted by tears. I will not let anything stop me from finding out who tore us apart, who killed the other half of my soul and the two people whose love made us.

I feel a strength burn from inside when I think of her. I borrow it to help me through difficult times and rely fully on it while I try to do the unthinkable. Lo would never try to find the killer. She would be too afraid to do it on her own.

The police found nothing that would connect my family's murder to anyone: no enemies, no coworkers with a grudge, no clue as to who might do something so hideous, so heinous. None of our neighbors saw or heard anything suspicious. There were no fingerprints at the scene of the crime, but my mother's jewelry box and purse were emptied. The case was deemed unsolved, and the only conclusion they came up with was that it was a home invasion.

I wrap my arms around myself and step back from the window. I close my eyes and shudder as the vivid memory of their deaths pops into my head like a glossy photo.

The thought of selling the house has always been terrifying. It was as Jason said. It's like the Bates Motel, but lightning doesn't strike in the same place twice. I take comfort in that thought.

In the time since Jason came into my life, I see hope in the freedom from my past. He says he's a monster, but I have dark thoughts myself. I have a plan, and for my family I will follow through, consequences be damned. He has turned everything upside down. Even though our first sexual encounter was as Hi, he takes me as I am completely. He fights to keep Lo going, not letting me fall into my old habits. Rather than take me home and leave me, he brought me here.

I want to ask him about his past. I want to ask him about his ex, especially after seeing the damage to his room. She took everything from the kitchen as well. I hate to tell him that. I don't know his financial situation. For as much as I don't know about him, he still is a soothing balm to all of the open wounds to my heart and soul.

I see a chair in the corner of the room, liking the fact that there are two walls with nothing behind them. I walk past the wooden coffee table and stop when I see a Men's Fitness magazine and a copy of Cosmo. I take the Cosmo and grab the black fur blanket off the back of the sectional leather sofa in the middle of the room and make my way to the chair. It doesn't match the rest of the place's white and black décor. It's a dark blue.

I sit down in its oversized comfort. I pull my legs up under me and drape the soft blanket over myself. Then I rest my head on the side of the chair and open the magazine in hopes of getting outside of my head and living in this moment. It has been years since I have felt this restful.

I am a guest to a man I consider my true first; I am not worried what is hiding behind curtains or what I am allowing the curtains to hide me from; and I am wrapped in warmth high above the streets of Detroit in a tower that has guards and security. Although the tattooed, gorgeous man who has seen devastation and caused it himself is not here, I can smell him, and I feel the safety he promises surrounding me.

I feel fur against my face and hear soft purrs. His scent is stronger now, and so is the scent of . . . barbeque?

I open my eyes and see Boots's big eyes looking into mine as Socks seems to be trying to hide under the blanket with me.

"Hello, my beauties," I whisper, giving them my attention while looking around for Jason.

As I stand up and walk toward the window, I hear a song playing from the balcony. Its beat is hard and fast. Angry.

He is sitting in one of the chairs, shirtless. His tattoos are works of art and no doubt hold emotional connections. The cobra is what I assume he feels he needs to be: quick, fast, strong, and deadly.

It doesn't scare me anymore than him being the son of that monster my innocent eyes saw beat him. I remember running to my father—my protector and the strongest man I ever knew—to get him to help the little boy who was kind enough to help me clean up my mess. My father followed me into the room where Jason was curled in a ball in the corner. His father looked up at us, his eyes filled with venom, and my father pulled me behind him, shielding me.

I don't remember what was said that day, but I remember Jason looking at me emotionlessly. I remember smiling, or trying to smile, and then I remember him looking away. He stood up and walked quickly out the door, past us, and I didn't see him for the rest of the night.

My heart bleeds for the little boy whose father didn't protect him like my father did. I'm sure Jason's father never looked in closets and under beds when Jason had a bad dream, because he would only come face-to-face with himself. He is a monster.

Jason leans back and runs his hands over his hair then throws his long, strong, and muscular legs up so his feet come to rest on the concrete wall that surrounds the balcony. He grabs a brown, long-neck bottle off the floor next to him and takes a drink. Then he wipes his lips with the back of his hand. He sets it down and clasps his hands behind his head and rubs them up and down his neck, rubbing into it as if he is working out the stress he carries there.

I slide the door open, and the low rumble of music I heard is now loud. He is still rubbing his neck when I walk up behind him. My fingers itch to rub away his worry. I reach out to do just that and immediately realize it's a bad idea.

In one swift move, his hands grip my wrists, and I am effortlessly pulled over his shoulder and land on his lap.

I open my eyes wide as I stare into his, which are just as shocked. Then I can't help laughing. He looks at me like I'm insane, and maybe I am. Then he smirks, giving me a glimpse of the dimple that is rarely visible.

I put my finger on it. "That's a treat."

His eyebrows shoot up. "Is that so?" He quickly moves his head and catches my finger between his teeth, winks, and then releases it.

"It is." I smile, getting more comfortable on his lap.

"You better stop doing that. You're technically poking the snake, angel."

I wiggle my bottom again, and he immediately stands with one arm wrapped around me. His lips crash down on mine, and he moans. His tongue thrusts inside my wanton mouth and takes possession of it. His feast is short-lived, though. He abruptly pulls away and steps back, leaving me wanting more.

He looks me up and down, his eyes hooded and dark. Then he turns around and walks to the grill. "Sit down and relax."

"I think I've done a lot of that today."

He looks over his shoulder and nods. "You needed it."

"So do you," I say quietly as he flips two of the biggest steaks I have ever seen in my life.

He walks back toward me, grips my hips, moves me to

the side, and grabs the beer before walking back to the grill and dousing the meat with it.

"I'm good," he finally answers.

Yes, he is, whether he believes it or not.

Basketball shorts, muscles, and tattoos combine to make up the most beautiful sight. I tear my eyes off the vision and turn around, facing the city's skyline. It's beautiful, but not so stunning that I can get lost in it like I can him.

"You slept," he states.

I turn back toward him and lean against the wall, nodding. "Total indulgence."

I see him smirk as he closes the barbeque and turns around. "Fifteen minutes more to feast. Another indulgence."

"You're spoiling me, Jason."

"Feeding you and letting you crash here is spoiling you?"

I shrug and turn back around to look over the city.

I hear him walk toward me. I feel the heat of his nearness, and a chill runs up my spine.

"It feels good to be free, doesn't it?"

I turn around and am eye level to his chest. I want to tell him I feel far from free. I feel consumed, protected, bonded, and owned.

I lick my lips and lean in. I want to be closer to him. I want to feel his skin touching mine. I want to taste his skin.

He cups my face and lifts it so I am looking in his eyes. "I need a shower. You need to eat something." Then he steps away, and I feel insecure, stupid . . . "Then I'm gonna fuck you, angel."

. . . desired, impatient . . . dirty.

I wait until I see him disappear into the bathroom. Then I walk inside and close the door behind me quietly. I sneak up to the bathroom door and wait until I hear the water running. I look down when I feel Boots tangle between my feet.

"Not now, buddy," I whisper and step around him.

My heart is pounding. I need to be brave. I think of Heidi and consider pretending just for a moment that I am her. However, I don't want her to linger between us, to be in my head. I don't want to feel like I did at The Lion's Den. I want him. I want me. I want the feeling of his strong body next to me, his skin touching mine, his mouth against mine, his hands on me.

Me.

Just me.

I walk into the bathroom and take a deep breath before pulling his T-shirt off my body and shoving his shorts off. I step toward the shower, but then stop, remembering what happened on the balcony.

I stare at his shoulders and take in the strength in them. Then I allow my eyes to travel down his strong back and watch his muscles work as he rubs his hands through his hair. His waist tapers in a—dear God, his muscular ass is beautiful.

I want him.

I take a deep breath and knock on the tile. He looks over his shoulder.

I open my mouth, planning to say something incredibly sexy, but nothing comes out.

His eyes narrow, his jaw flexes, and he runs his hand down his face, ridding it of the excess water. His eyes run from my toes slowly up my body, leaving goosebumps in their wake. When his eyes meet mine, he takes in a deep breath and licks his lips.

"You need my cock?"

"I need you," I say with a tremble in my voice as I watch him grip his cock and stroke slowly up and down.

"You need my cock." He groans.

I nod, watching him.

"Get in here."

I do.

"Foot on the stone bench." His voice is thick with desire and demanding.

I obey.

"Show me how you touch yourself."

I look at him, not moving.

"Now."

I slide my hand between my legs and rub my fingers between my sensitive lips.

"That's it, angel," he hisses, and I continue. "I want your finger in your pussy. Spread your legs wider."

I do.

"How does it feel, angel?" His hand pumps his cock.

"I want you," I whisper.

"Say it louder."

"I want you," I repeat more loudly.

He releases his cock, grips my hips, lifts me up, lines his wide head up against my pussy, pushing me against the tiled wall, and without warning, he slams into me fully.

"You can't come in here like that," he hisses. "I can't control myself." He pulls out and slams back in. He groans against my neck as he swivels his hips, stretching me.

"Then don't," I pant.

He slams in and then out. "I can't go easy." He pulls out then slams in again. "I won't go easy." He does it again. "Get there." Out and in. "Now, dammit."

"Oh, God," I cry as his pace increases and his thrusts become more powerful. My body explodes in a surge of pleasurable waves as he pulls out and comes on my inner thigh.

When I walk out of his bedroom, he is putting broccoli on a plate.

He glances up. "Didn't you see the bag?" he asks, referring to the bag of my clothes he brought over.

"Yes," I say, walking toward him wearing a different pair of his boxers and another of his T-shirts.

"Nothing you like?"

"I wanted to wear yours."

He stops cutting up the steak, looks over at me, and nods.

A few minutes later, we sit across from each other, our eyes connected as we eat. He devours his steak while I pick at mine. I'm not hungry for food. I'm hungry for him.

"Not good?" he asks before taking another bite of his steak.

"It is."

"Not hungry?" he asks after wiping his mouth.

"Starving," I answer, looking away. "I've been starving for years."

"Then eat, angel."

I look up at him. "Not for food."

His jaw clenches, his eyes narrow, and his nostrils flare. "Two more bites . . . please, Lo."

He eats fast, and I do as he asks. He then gets up quickly, walks behind me, and pulls out my chair. I stand up, and he turns me toward him and lifts me.

"I'm gonna feed you my cock all night long."

He walks quickly toward the couch, but as soon as my ass hits the leather, someone knocks on the door.

He grabs the blanket and hands it to me. "Cover up."

I watch him open the door without looking through the

peephole. “Perfect timing.” He holds the door open wide, and two men walk in carrying a mattress. “Right in there.”

Twenty minutes later, the two men leave with the mattress his ex destroyed.

I get up, lock the door behind them, and turn to see Jason leaning against the doorjamb.

“Get in here.”

I do.

Chapter Sixteen

Sleeping with her next to me is something unlike what I shared with Missy. The way she fits beside me, the way she relaxes and rests, calms the beast inside me. Today, I have to work and so does she.

My alarm goes off, and I get up quietly, sliding out from under her as I silence the damn thing. Socks and Boots look up at me lazily from their cozy corner at the end of the bed, and I look back at them, thinking, When the hell did I become a cat man?

I have lots of love for pussy. I love a variety of pussy: dark pussy, light pussy, even multicolored, tattooed pussy. I have had smooth pussy and fuzzy pussy, but never did I think I would get up in the morning and worry about feeding pussy rather than feasting on pussy.

Making my way to the kitchen, I open a pouch of the fish-smelling, tuna-flavored cat food and split it between the two bowls. The cats wind around my legs, their fur soft against me as they purr and prowl, waiting for me to step back so they can dive into what they find delicious.

Moving to the bathroom, I empty their litter boxes first

before beginning my routine. I brush my teeth and rinse with my mouthwash. The tingling on my tongue and all the thoughts of pussy have me in need. I can spare twenty minutes to wake Lorraine up properly, I think with a sly smile as I make my way back into the bedroom.

Before me lies an angel. Her blond hair is spread out over the black of my sheets. Her face is soft and features delicate as she continues the steady rise and fall of her chest. Climbing in beside her, I slide back the sheet. She stirs yet doesn't wake. I part her legs, and she whimpers.

"Sleep," she whines as I let my hot breath hit her inner thighs.

Naturally, her legs fall open, and I slide her panties over and blow on her lips. The curls of her pubes move, and I see the glistening on her lips. I swipe my tongue between them, parting her. Up and down, I lick and lap her up before I put my nose under her hood, making circles as I thrust my tongue in and out, curling it at her clit with a flick.

I gaze up to see her wide eyes looking down at me as she props herself up on her elbows. Using my bottom teeth, I graze the sensitive skin under her pussy. I suck her clit, and her legs instantly wrap around my head, holding me in place as I devour her through her orgasm. She throws her head back in ecstasy as her stomach trembles in bliss.

I lick her through the aftershocks and give one last minty blow against her sensitive mound. Then I pull away and stand.

"What a way to wake up," she whispers.

I laugh. "It's better than Folgers in your cup."

I don't say another word. I leave her to her post-orgasmic moments while I head to the bathroom to finish preparing for my day.

I'm not in there long before she comes in behind me.

"Um," she starts shyly.

I lean down and press my lips to hers. Then, as I turn to move to the shower, she grabs my arm.

"What about you?" she asks, pointing to the tent in my boxers.

"We don't have enough time for me to do all the things I want to do with you before we both have to be at work."

"But, you um . . . you gave me—"

"I wanted pussy for breakfast." Her eyes grow wide at my bluntness. "I wanted your pussy for breakfast. I had it. Now tonight, you can have cock for dessert. Baby, I gotta get ready for work, and if you stand here much longer, looking as fucking delicious as you do, neither of us are going to make it in today."

"Oh," she says, biting her bottom lip.

"Yeah, you get me that worked up. You do that, Lorraine, not anyone or anything else. You have that power over me. Now let me take a shower before I take you in the shower, and like I said, if I let myself get started, neither of us are going to make it to work on time or at all."

She smiles almost proudly before she rolls up on her toes and places her lips against mine. "That was definitely the best way to wake up."

"It started my morning off right," I say with a wink before stepping out of my boxers and into the shower, blasting it on cold.

Once I have my cobra under control and my body and hair washed, I step out. Wrapping a towel around my waist, I move to the bedroom where she is waiting to take her own shower. Instantly, my cock starts to harden, and I try to think of my grandmother to keep my erection down.

I dress for the day and give a quick knock on the bathroom door when I hear the shower turn off.

"I'm off to work, Lo. See you tonight after the gym, baby."

"Okay," she says with hesitation in her voice.

"You need me to stay till you're ready?" I ask, thinking about her fears of the world. When her answer isn't immediate, I go over all the security in the place. "I'll set the alarm. I'll have the doorman on the lookout for you. If you aren't comfortable with that, I can wait." Thinking, I realize the one thing I forgot to show her. I'm a hands-on man who is used to fighting, but I also keep a weapon in my home. "There is a handgun in the nightstand," I inform her. "It's loaded. Just flip off the safety, and it's ready to go, baby."

She creeps out of the bathroom in just a towel with her hair dripping wet and water beading on her body. I swear today is a battle of wills, and I'm going to fucking lose.

"Show me," she whispers.

I move to the nightstand and pull out the Glock, placing it in her small hand with my large hand covering hers. Taking her other hand, I guide her to hold the gun properly and stand with her legs shoulder-width apart for optimum direction in her shot. I show her how to slide off the safety, how to aim, and then I explain how to pull the trigger.

"Don't waste time. If you are in a position you need to use this for any reason, disable your guy and get the fuck out. Don't hesitate."

Tears fill her eyes as she nods. I let go, and she holds the weapon firmly in her hands.

"Why do you have a gun living here?" she asks and I can see the fear start to creep up.

"Do not be afraid here, angel. I have it because I fight,"

I answer her honestly. "The night in the hospital, it's an underground thing. No one can know where, who, and the how, so don't ask me." Her eyes grow wide. I wish I had more time to explain. "Look, I have aggression and it's a safe way to get it out."

Still holding the gun firmly, she looks to me. "I wouldn't call it safe with the way you came in," she whispers, and I revel in her concern for me.

"Sometimes it's not. I need it, Lo. I don't have time to explain it. There is a time for Jason to be Jason and sometimes I have to release the cobra to get the snakes out of my system. It will not ever touch you. I give you my word, the life I lead as a fighter will not ever touch you."

She studies me and the gun before looking at me firmly. "You can go now. I'll get ready and be on my way."

I watch as she slides the safety back on and secures the gun into its place. With a quick kiss to her forehead, I step away before I can't stop myself and end up taking her on the bed, leaving us both needing another shower.

Work is a pain in my ass, but it's a means to an end. I get paid, and I get paid fucking well to be a paper-pushing motherfucker. The more I try to work, though, the more my mind goes over the people Lorraine follows as Heidi.

I tried to do an Internet search for disorders of people assuming someone else's persona. However, I couldn't figure out the psychobabble and realized I should have paid better attention in Psych 101. I don't know what to do for her. I feel helpless, and if I'm feeling that way, I can only imagine how she feels.

She was there and witnessed my father's way of dealing with me firsthand. She knows my past without me telling her—well, most of it. I have warned her I'm a monster. She can't seem to stay away as much as I can't seem to hold back, though. Can two totally fucked-up people find a way to make something good out of some seriously bad pasts?

I don't have an answer. After Missy, I am afraid that one experience doesn't bode well for my angel eyes and me.

I also don't have any more clues to the murder of her family than she does. The police called it an invasion. In their findings, they felt it was a random thing, yet Lo goes out at night as Hi and follows these city officials . . . for what?

My mind goes over and over following her. The one thing all of those people have in common is my father. Would he be capable of putting a hit on the Boschs? There isn't a single doubt in my mind that he could and would without hesitation if he felt threatened.

I just don't see what her family has to do with him. I don't see where her father could have had enough blackmail on my family to even pose such a threat. The pieces to the puzzle don't fit. The only thing that replays solidly in my mind is, if I find out my father had something to do with it, I will kill him.

He can beat on me all he wants. He can tear me limb from limb. He can tell me I'm not good enough, that I will never be anything—I'm used to all of his shit anyway. But I won't let him get away with destroying a good family like Lo had. I won't stand for it, and he will pay.

My phone rings, bringing me out of my thoughts. I see who it is, and rather than avoid her any longer, I slide to answer.

"I'm gone for good!" she screeches.

I move to step outside of the office.

"Thank fuck for that. What do you want, Missy?"

"I just wanted you to know I'm out of the condo."

"Yeah, I got a visit from my father. You're a dumb

bitch. Don't come back. Don't ever come back. You got involved with the wrong Stanley man now."

I don't listen to what she says next; I simply disconnect the call.

I gave her time to get her closure. If she called thinking I would beg her to come back, she was wrong. After involving my father in our business, she is dead to me. That's the one button she knew never to push, and her running to him makes me realize she wasn't the one, because through all of our fucked-up relationship that was an understood, accepted, and never-to-cross line.

Her call only drives me harder to keep the distance between us. I'm not usually the kind of guy to give up on anything. We had three years to get it right, and with every passing day, it seemed to get worse. My mind moves from the struggles and fights of trying to make something work that was doomed long ago to the ease of having Lorraine in my space.

Closing my eyes, I lean back in my office chair and picture her hair spread out over my pillow like it was this morning. I think back to the fear she has in her home. I think about her taking on her sister's identity to follow people, people I know. I just don't know why she is following them specifically.

I also wonder if she's had help, psychiatric sort of help—shit, good ol' Dr. Sam would've noticed the need, right? I keep coming up with more questions; the why's are bombarding me.

I'm glad she has a good job she loves, and it suits her. Only, her life in every other aspect stopped that night in April and I feel compelled to help her figure out why.

Chapter Seventeen

Today is a seven-to-seven shift. Three on, three off, but I always pick up extra shifts. Normally, I want to run to the comfort of the hospital. Today, I don't want to leave the comfort of this place. His place.

I sit down, and Boots jumps on my lap. He is already accustomed to Jason's condo. Socks shows trepidation, though. I feel a twinge of guilt for having given him anxiety—my anxiety.

My first week home after graduating college, he ran outside in the dark. I was terrified, but I couldn't leave him outside. I ran around the backyard, calling for him. Panicking, my heart raced so hard I thought it would come out of my chest. When I found him, I was so angry. I held him to me and cried. This was after boarding up the damn stairs so he wouldn't go up there. It was not my finest hour. It was the first night I slept in the basement room—my father's old home office—and it was the last day the stairway to hell was opened.

My hysterics and the sounds of me using my father's tools probably caused him to seek comfort in the same place I did—the basement. From then on, I fed him there and tried to protect him from my demons, ones I gave him.

I pet Boots, holding him as I stand and walk to the bedroom where Socks is hidden under the covers. I sit down and pet them both until they purr almost in sync before standing up.

"You're safe. Go soak up the sun." I pet them again and look at Boots. "Take care of him."

As I ride the elevator down to the ground floor, I watch as the numbers light up. With each passing floor, the fear of the box I am in eases, yet the thought of someone coming in becomes no less terrifying.

Reaching the ground floor, I let out a deep breath as the door opens. I walk out, looking both left and right.

"Good morning, Miss Bosch," a dark man says with a nod. "Mr. Stanley asked that I let you know your car is parked in front and that he was the last in it."

"Thank you," I tell him, looking away.

I pull my sunglasses over my eyes and walk outside to my car sitting right up front as promised.

I don't understand why he insists he isn't good, why he says he is bad. Everything he does shows me the total opposite. He is considerate of my feelings, and he doesn't judge or run from the knowledge of who I am or the piece of craziness that lives inside of me.

The way he touches me isn't monstrous—not to me, anyway. The way he wants me as much as I want him is not wrong, even though it sometimes feels a bit possessive. It's also protective, and to a girl like me, that protective and possessive manner coming from a man who wants me is the best type of feeling I have ever felt.

I need him; I want him; and I will have him until I can't.

I turn the key in the ignition, and the car starts up. I

put it in gear and press on the gas pedal. Then I look in the rearview mirror as I pull away from his building and smile, thinking about returning to him tonight. Until then, I will push through today, get lost in the need to save lives, and help those I have been trained and educated to help.

This morning . . . definitely better than Folgers.

I sit down in the break room and sigh. From the moment I walked through the door, it has been nonstop. Normally, I love a day like this. When we are busy, time flies by. Add three MVAs (motor vehicle accidents) to an average day, and I am already exhausted.

I pull my phone from my scrubs pocket and re-read the text message Jason sent me this morning. It was simply, Have a great day, angel.

Angel, I love it when he calls me that. I love it when he calls me Lo, too. I love how safe he makes me feel. I love that he wants me.

I know I will never be normal, but I also know the chances of feeling somewhat normal are far better outside of that house.

He was right; I need to get the house on the market. I need to do it now. Therefore, I Google realtors, and Rock City Real Estate is the first to pop up. When they answer, I tell them I would like to sell my house and give them the information. I explain the fair market value is fine as the house will be "as is." I don't tell them it's because I don't want to spend anymore time there. I don't tell them about the triple slaughter of a family. I don't tell them any of that. I can't.

An appointment is set for them to come out and take pictures. I make it for the evening of my day off, hoping Jason will be there with me.

I don't want to do it alone.

I don't want to be alone.

Not anymore.

I sit and stare at the phone and read his message again.

Have a great day, angel.

Five words, just five, that make me feel like I matter.

Have a great day, angel.

God, how am I going to do this without him knowing? How will I be able to look at him and lie if he asks any more questions?

Have a great day, angel.

How am I going to leave him when it's time? Things have to be made right and I can't stop Hi, and really . . . . I don't want to, revenge is a necessity.

Have a great day, angel.

Now that he knows what I am doing, it has become real, I no longer can hide behind Hi. Hi is no angel, and now neither am I.

"Code Blue," squeaks over the intercom, and I welcome the chaos outside my own.

Sitting at the desk, entering patient information, I look up when I see Dr. Bennett walking toward me. He isn't relaxed and all smiles; he looks pensive, concerned, very much unlike himself.

"How are you, Lorraine?" he asks, setting his tablet down and sitting next to me.

"Busy." I smile. "It's been a crazy day. How are you?"

"Concerned about you."

"Don't be. I am actually doing very well." I lean in and whisper, "I put the house on the market today."

"Good, then you'll come home?"

I look down. I don't want to see the disappointment in his eyes. I can't go back to his home, their home. I can't go back to living the twisted life I lived while I was there. I also can't explain it to him, because he doesn't know what Ryan and Hi were doing. Sam's a good man and would never understand. He took me in in good faith not realizing Heidi was along for the ride, but at the time, I didn't know that either.

"I understand that you are asserting your independence, and no one appreciates that more than I do. I appreciate and respect that."

I can't look at him and see the sadness. He and his wife have been nothing but good to me. I can't imagine how disappointed he would be if he ever knew. I suspect Rochelle, Ryan's stepsister, knows.

Rochelle was kind to me at first whenever she was home from college. She was kind to me for a long time. Then . . . she wasn't.

I remember the night I was in his bed, and she walked in Ryan's room. I didn't see her, only heard her.

"I knew it! I—"

She stops when Ryan flies off me and out of the bed. I cover myself with the blanket, terrified that we have been discovered. I don't know what to do.

Several minutes later, I hear the door open then shut and lock.

Ryan slides back into bed, and I start to get up.

"Don't go. We weren't finished, Heidi."

"She saw us," I gasp.

"She saw a brunette in my bed. She didn't see you," he says, pushing his hand between my legs and inserting two fingers. "The wig is actually perfect. You can be Heidi for me and you."

"This has to stop," I tell him.

"You're so wet, though, love. Let's not deny us. This can be the last time." He lowers the blanket and hovers over me. "Don't hold back. Do it like her. For you, for me, for all of us."

After that night, I never felt comfortable in the house

again, even though he assured me Rochelle knew nothing. Every time we were together, him always Ryan, me always Heidi, I worried.

The late morning is filled with sick children. I hate to see kids in pain and ill. It used to bother me more when the babies came in. They can't tell you what is wrong with them, and they don't understand why you aren't helping them. If that's not enough, they look at you like you are evil. At least with older children, they can tell you where the pain is.

I walk into a room with a mother and child. The child's teeth are chattering, and she is whining. The mother holds her close, trying to comfort her.

As soon as I close the door behind me, the mother looks up.

"She has a hundred and four temperature. She's been vomiting for two days. This is our second trip to the ER. Why can't you help her?" I hear panic in her voice.

My instinct is to ask her to stay calm. Her child needs her to stay calm.

"I'm sorry. Let me look at the chart." I click on the tablet and see that she was at an urgent care center two days prior. "Kelsey was diagnosed with a virus?"

"Yes, but nothing has helped. Alternating pain relievers is a joke. I'm sure she is vomiting them up."

"Kelsey, can you tell me if there is pain specific to a spot?"

"My tummy," she cries. "Everywhere."

"When the pain started, where did it start? Can you remember?" I ask.

"My stomach," she whimpers.

I look at her mother. "Did they run labs or do any scans?"

"No. They said it was a virus and to wait it out. There was nothing they could do about it."

"Okay, let me grab the doctor."

I walk out in the hall and see Dr. Bennett. "Room 18 has a little girl. She can't eat; she has a fever; and she has been vomiting. They went to urgent care and were told it was viral and sent home. No lab work or scans. Her pain started in her stomach."

"You disagree?" he asks, tapping on his tablet.

"I think they should have done something to rule out appendicitis," I answer.

He smiles and nods as he walks toward the room. "That's my girl. Thank you." Dr. Bennett is unlike many of the doctors I have worked with. He actually believes in his nurses' abilities and judgment. Most of the others think they know everything. The God complex.

He opens the door. "I'm Dr. Bennett, Kelsey. I want to get some pictures of your tummy, okay?"

When he walks out of the room a few minutes later, he looks for me and nods. I walk over to him.

"I ordered scans for her, and I agree with you. My guess is appendicitis. Good job, Lorraine."

"Thank you."

"Get her hooked up to an IV, recheck her vitals, and if radiology isn't already here waiting for you to finish, then you and I will take her there."

Less than half an hour later, Kelsey is being wheeled to the surgical floor. Accompanying the surgeon is the other Dr. Bennett, Dr. Ryan Bennett, son to Dr. Sam and Sarah Bennett. He smiles at me then turns his back and puts his hand on Kelsey's mom's shoulder. I assume he's comforting her before her daughter is put under the scalpel.

It is calm enough now in the ER that I am able to think about catching up on paperwork.

Walking toward the desk, I see the older Dr. Bennett motion me over.

"Come to dinner this week. Promise at least that."

"I'll give it some thought. I need to sort everything out with the house being on the market," I tell him in hopes to appease him.

Completely out of character for him, Dr. Bennett reaches out and hugs me. "You belong with us. Come home, and we can help you with the house and deciding what comes next."

After a moment, I back away. "I know."

Chapter Eighteen

"Watch yourself," Brock says, leaving me at the café. "Don't mix up one obsession with another."

"It's not like that."

"Sure," he remarks.

I shrug my shoulders and make my way to my car. I have a chef salad for Lo that I need to get to the hospital before my hour is over. She seems more relaxed at my place, but Brock's words hit me in the stomach.

I don't want Lo to be a replacement for anything in anyone's eyes.

Missy and I were long done; I just didn't want to face it. We were so bad for each other. Love shouldn't be pain. Tatiana told me that. I can see it now. If you love someone, you should swallow your pride at times and walk away, not push until the evil spews out.

Once upon a time, we had a chance for something, but it wasn't meant to be. She's a crazy bitch, yet I do hope she finds someone to balance her instead of push her.

I know that's what I need. I don't need someone who

gets off on my anger. I need someone who knows when to pull my head out of my ass and also when to back off and let me come around on my own. I see that potential in Lo. I see the good we could be for each other.

Brock's wrong. It's not replacing one obsession with another; it's holding on to hope. It's holding on to the idea that, as dark as I am inside, there is a light and a chance I can break the cycle.

Rushing inside, I don't pay attention when I hit the check-in station to get buzzed back to the emergency department for Lo. When a dark-haired woman steps from behind a desk to grab my arm before I head to the door, I am shaken into the moment. Her eyes meet mine and I need her to let me go. With a wink and a dreamy kind of smile, the lady clicks the button, opening the door.

At the station, I see Lo talking to none other than Dr. Bennett. Fury fills me as I walk up to him talking about her coming home again.

"I'll give it some thought. I need to sort everything out with the house being on the market," she softly replies with her back to me.

His eyes meet mine as he pulls her to him for a hug. "You belong with us. Come home and we can help you with the house and deciding what comes next."

She backs away. "I know."

Two words and I feel like everything is for nothing.

Why did I ever think I could hold on to something good even if it's tangled up in a mess? She knows? What does she know? She knows she belongs with them? She's wrong; she belongs with me.

Setting the Styrofoam container on the counter beside them, I don't speak as she looks over her shoulder at me. I won't push her. I have done that before, and it ended up killing a piece of me and Missy. Pushing each other only destroyed what once had the potential to be something beautiful.

"Jason," she says with a smile, not knowing I heard their little chat. Dr. Bennett knows, though. He stands there smugly without giving me time with her in private.

I take her by the waist and pull her to me, kissing her temple, and she moves into me with a soft sigh.

"Brought you lunch. I've gotta get back to work."

She blinks up at me, her angel eyes calming the monster inside me. "Okay, thank you. I'll see you at home." She slips out of my embrace, and I stare at her.

"Is it home?" I whisper then turn away to leave.

"Jason," she calls out, and I turn to look over my shoulder. "With you, it is."

"Remember that, then," I say before I stroll away. I feel her eyes on me, but I refuse to look back again.

Going back to work, I'm amped up. What is the Bennett family's deal? Why the obsession with Lorraine? Heidi was Ryan's woman, and she is dead. I get the connection, but these people are taking it too far.

The more I'm around Lo, the more I want to protect her, the more I need to provide for her, and the more I simply need her.

Taking off mid-afternoon, I head to the gym. I'm in the locker room, wrapping my hands, when I see movement out of the corner of my eye. The tattoo taunts me. In seconds, I'm up and slamming him into a locker before he can react.

"You and your fucking crew knocked me out and left me." I press my forearm into his throat as he tries to pull me off.

"Hey, man, I didn't know they would do that. You had me; they handled it." His knee comes up and connects with my balls.

I back up and fight to catch my breath. He's not quick enough, and I recover, slamming him back into the lockers, making the metal clang again.

"Cheap shot, cheating ass, bitch boy. Watch yourself, Chainz. There won't be a next time for you to get me down."

Brock comes in and pulls me off him. "Not here, man. You know they won't tolerate damages and insurance shit." He looks at Chainz. "Not so tough when you don't have your boys at your back. Watch yourself."

Chainz spits at Brock. "You should watch yourselves, Brock. That spitfire redhead who warms your bed sure would be fun to break." He taunts my friend and sparring partner with his fight name.

He looks at me as Brock reaches up, latching his hand around his throat. "Heard you wrapped yourself up in a crazy one, Cobra."

"If you come near either of them, I'll make sure you never enter a gym or fight again. I'll fuck you up so badly you won't make it out of the hospital on your own two legs," Brock warns, releasing him with marks on his neck just as the door opens and a trainer walks in.

"Problems?" he asks, raising an eyebrow at Chainz.

"Nah, just having a chat," he answers smartly.

With a shoulder bump, he pushes past us. I see the flare of Brock's nostrils. As wound up as he is, this should be a damn good session. Chainz crossed a line with me and my man that he shouldn't have. Brock will make sure he gets the message, too.

Two hours later, I'm sweating, my heart is pounding, my muscles burn, and my face, ribs, and legs all hurt. Brock stood toe-to-toe with me and maintained power on the ground. We were evenly matched in every round.

Cooling down, we walk the gym, trying to get our breathing regulated and hearts to slow out of cardio rate.

"How's it feel?" he asks, and I raise an eyebrow at him. "Going home to someone who isn't ready to start a fight every two seconds."

I sigh. I have been so in the moment I didn't stop to let myself think of how it feels. I don't dread going home anymore.

Home.

I have never given a thought to being at home until now. My entire life has been spent wanting to avoid being at home. First, it was because of my father and then because Missy would spend her days deciding what I did wrong for our nights.

I knew I wouldn't be able to fight for a while. The quiet and inability to release my stresses physically was going to kill me.

Having never had a normal family life, I guess I never knew what a real relationship should be. Maybe this is the feeling I should have had all along. Though Lo is still far from normal, but we'll fix that.

"Damn good," I answer with a smile.

"She's got some magic in those angel eyes." He laughs. "You've never smiled this much."

"Fuck off," I give back to shut him up.

He's right, though. I have never been this relaxed or happy, which means I better find a way to hold on to it. I also need her to find herself and move beyond what happened to her family. All of this brings me back to needing to know if my father set them up.

She told me she was late that night. If she had been there on time, she wouldn't be here to be my angel now. There is no doubt in my mind she couldn't have saved them. She would be just as dead as her family.

Brock and I hit the showers then leave the gym. I feel both exhausted and energized. I'm not already halfway angry going home, something I haven't felt in so long the feeling is odd to me.

I make my way inside and find Lo cooking in the kitchen.

Going up behind her at the stove, I turn off the burners. She looks at me, but before she can speak, my lips crash down on hers.

"You give me good, Lo. I'm gonna give you the only good I have," I growl into her ear as I push her pants down.

She steps out of them, holding on to my shoulders for balance. "You okay, Jason?"

I back her to the countertop. "I need you, need to feel you, need to be one with you. I realized some shit today. You've gotta know, Lo, that you and me . . . This is it."

I release my cock from my pants, not bothering with my shirt or hers as I slide into her, holding her up by her ass. I take all her weight easily and rock my hips, rolling to her sweet spot.

"This is home." I slide back out, then in. "Home," I growl, and she moans. "Say it," I command as I drag my cock almost all the way out, teasing her entrance. "Tell me this is home for you."

She moves her hands from around my neck to cup my face. "This is home," she whispers with her angel blue eyes locking on to mine as she drops her hips, taking my cock deep inside her. "Home," she mewls.

I can't hold back. I pick up my pace, my body breaking out in a new sweat. This may be the biggest mistake of my life, but I can't be without her.

I slide in and out as she trembles around me, her orgasm building.

"Home," I grind out as I thrust two more times toward my own climax as she reaches hers and slumps against me in satisfaction.

"Home," she whispers, kissing me softly before separating from me.

Damn right we are home.

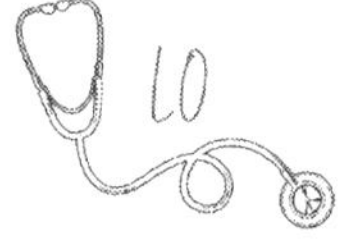

Chapter Nineteen

I watch him sleep beside me, unable to do the same. I upset him today. I upset him, and he ravaged me.

Me, not Heidi.

Me.

I still have to remind myself that Jason wants me, Lo, not Hi.

"You give me good, Lo."

I wrap my arms around myself, knowing I'm not all that good.

"I need you, need to feel you, need to be one with you. I realized some shit today. You've gotta know, Lo, that you and me . . . This is it."

I hold myself more tightly, trying to keep myself together, knowing what I am going to do can and will make that impossible.

"This is home."

I press my eyes shut, unable to look at him when I know that's what I want. I want to give that to him and take it for myself, yet I know I have something to finish first.

"Home." He growled it as if he was taking without permission, promising without reserve, and giving regardless of the fact that I can't give him back what he is promising.

"Home," I responded, knowing if I could, I would make it so . . . for as long as he would have me, while my crossed fingers stayed hidden from him.

I open my eyes and look at him again. The tattoos forever stain his skin, and the faint pink scars across his back are something he will carry forever. I know in some way, shape, or form, I am going to scar him, too.

I turn my body to get out of bed, but he grips my thigh. "Lo, you need something?"

"You," I answer honestly. "I need you."

He opens his eyes then cocks his head to the side as he raises his arm up above the pillow. "Then get over here."

I rest my head on his strong, hard chest. His arms surround me, and his lips touch the top of my head.

"Sleep, angel."

I do.

On Wednesday, Jason holds my hand as he pulls me out of the vehicle.

"Don't let him see you sweat, angel. He'll think he can walk all over you." He looks at the Realtor, his eyes narrowed, before looking back at me and kissing me hard, possessively. I borrow strength from him that this place depletes me of.

The Realtor is waiting. He is almost six feet tall, in his thirties, and average-looking. He wears a suit, tie, and a big smile.

"James Rock." He holds out his hand. "I've already gotten the outside photos. Now let's see the inside."

"It's—"

Jason squeezes my hand. "It's all ready." He looks down at me and winks. Then he nods to the door.

When I walk in, I hold my breath and keep my eyes on the ground.

"Beautiful entry," James comments. "And look at that stairway."

I tense up, waiting for him to yell, What the fuck is wrong with you? Instead, I get, "Beautiful wood. Absolutely stunning, the center of the home. Perfect shot."

Slowly, I look up and see the stairway to hell looking like it did when the house was a happy place. I lean into Jason's protective embrace and look up.

He doesn't have a look on his face begging for praise. He gives a small shrug, squeezes my hip lightly, and looks back at the Realtor.

"You get whatever pictures you need. We're gonna grab the last of the boxes out of the garage."

He holds me snugly against him as we walk into the kitchen where all the cabinets are open and empty. He opens the door to the garage where four totes sit.

"This was all in her room. I didn't want to throw any of it away."

I nod then shake my head, turning into him and hugging him tightly. He drops his arms low around my waist and leans back.

"Eyes."

I look up. "I have no idea how to"—I pause—"how to thank you."

"It's really nothing. The place was clean, Lo. I just needed to get rid of some things." He shrugs.

"You only knew two days ago. How . . . ?" I stop when he sighs.

"My angel works twelve-hour shifts. I work eight. I

have some extra time. No big thing." He shrugs again. "Let's get these boxes in the car."

He calls me angel, but I know better. I know he is mine.

Over the next couple days, I push aside revenge and vengeance and surround myself in him as often as I can. When I return back to work, he brings me lunch every day. Every day for three now.

The way my coworkers look at him should make me jealous. The way he looks at me and only me, though, tells me jealousy is unnecessary.

Like every day since the first, he is home before me, waiting by the elevator door when it opens, leaning against the wall so the first thing I see is him. The look in his eyes is fierce, his chest tightens, his jaw squares, and the muscles in it flex. Then his tongue swipes quickly across his lips as his nostrils flare. His feet are bare and so is his chest. He wears low-slung shorts or sweatpants.

He looks at me the same, regardless if I am in scrubs or naked. His green eyes bore into me with hunger. His kiss is possessive. His touch is protective. His thrusts scream that he is claiming me, marking me, ensuring that I will never forget him.

I never will.

We eat dinner, staring at each other. I look down when I feel like I may crawl over the table and demand to feel him.

"How was work?" I ask.

"I hate my fucking job," he answers point-blank.

"Then why do it?" I ask before taking a drink of water.

"Paycheck," he answers then takes another bite.

"I wish you loved your job," I say quietly.

He smirks and shakes his head then points his fork at me. "How was your day?"

I shrug. "Nobody died."

He smiles and nods. "That's a good day."

I smile back because his is spectacular and the dimple is even more so.

His smile straightens. "Bennett?"

Oh, hell, how could I forget?

"I agreed to go to dinner."

I watch as his eyes narrow.

"When?"

"Tomorrow, five o'clock."

He stands up and grabs his plate then mine and stalks to the sink, dropping the plates in. "I'm gonna step out for a bit."

I jump up and walk to him. "Where?"

He holds his hand up, stopping me. "Don't."

"Let me go with you," I begin, feeling anxiety build.

He shakes his head and starts to step around me, and I move in front of him.

"I'm telling you I need a fucking minute, Lo," he snaps.

"Angel." I use his endearment to me and remain unmoving.

He lets out a deep breath, crosses his arms, and leans back against the wall. "You don't cage a man like me." I smile, refusing to believe him, and he gasps. "I told you I'm a bad man, Lo."

I step toward him, shaking my head from side to side. "You're not bad to me."

He looks up with hunger in his eyes as I walk closer.

"I'm not afraid of you." I take his face in my hands. "Eyes on me."

He looks down, his eyebrow cocked.

"I agreed to go to dinner." He growls at that, and it sparks desire inside me. "I told him you would be coming, too."

His eyebrow rises higher.

"I need to do this," I tell him. "They were good to me."

He sighs, still not saying anything.

"You need to be there, because . . ." I shrug and look down, feeling vulnerable. His fingers touch my chin and lift it, and our eyes meet. "I need you."

His body tenses, but he doesn't move. He stands as strong and tall as a statue.

"I need you, too, you know. I need to feel you, to be one with you. I realized some things the day you broke into my house and saved me from"—I shrug—"myself. You have to know, Jason, that you and me . . . This is it." I close my eyes after using the words he used with me, the words that play over and over in my head almost hourly. When he doesn't reply, I say it out loud, like a prayer begging to be answered. "Home."

"Eyes," he snarls.

I give him what he asks for, opening my eyes and searching his as they search mine.

"This is home. Decisions get made together. And listen to this really well, Lo." He grabs my hips, lifting me, before he stalks to the kitchen island where he sits me on it, gruffly putting his hands on either side of me and leaning in so his nose almost touches mine. "Never ask me to sit across from the man who fucked your sweet, innocent, mourning pussy. A sick fuck who touched your body, making you pretend to be less than the angel you are. You don't know the monster inside of me. You don't know that I want nothing more than to rip him apart, limb by motherfucking limb."

My pulse quickens; my chest rises and falls rapidly; my body is near combusting from how badly I want him.

"Fuck me," I beg.

He growls then laughs a haunting laugh before

reaching behind me, and with one swipe of his arm, he sends everything on the counter tumbling to the ground. Excitement grows hotter and hotter inside me.

He pushes my back so I am lying on the hard granite countertop, then grabs my scrub bottoms and rips them from my body. I start to sit up.

"Stay. Fucking. Down." He covers my entrance with his mouth, and then his tongue circles my clit.

"Yes!" I cry out.

I have been on edge since he met me at the elevator, half-naked and wanting me, so I knew I wouldn't last long.

His tongue thrusts inside of my pussy, and I contract around it. My hips thrust upward, and he grips my thighs and spreads me wider. His tongue slows, and I try to thrust into his face again, needing more, but he digs his fingers into my thighs, stopping me.

"Please," I beg, knowing I'm there.

He removes his mouth, steps back, shoves his pants down, and then wraps his hand around himself tightly, groaning as he pumps his thick cock.

I push myself up and slide off the counter, dropping to my knees before him. He rubs the tip of his cock across my lips, and I lick him, tasting the salty pre-come.

Then he steps back and pushes his erection into his shorts.

I shake my head, and he nods.

"Why?"

"You pissed me off!" he snarls.

"Let me finish." I grab his leg and pull myself across the smooth wooden floor.

"Dammit, no." He steps back.

"I don't understand?" I nearly cry.

"I don't understand, either, but I'm making this decision for us, just like you made one for us."

"That's cruel," I snap.

"Damn straight it is." And he walks away.

After my shower, I walk out completely naked and crawl into bed. He lifts his arm for me to curl up next to him, and I do. I look up at him, and he looks down.

"Kiss me."

He does.

My hand runs down his chest, his stomach, and I grip him.

He pulls away from my kiss. "No."

I close my eyes. Inside, I weep. He doesn't need to push me away physically and emotionally to teach me some sort of lesson. I know I am new to having a relationship, but this can't be how we handle things.

I wake up to Jason pushing my knees apart with his thighs. His cock is in his hand, pumping himself hard and fast. It's beautiful. His neck muscles are strained, and every vein is visible in his strong forearm as he strokes faster and faster.

"Oh, God," I say as the fire inside me blazes from just the sight of him.

"Fuck!" he snaps. "Fuck. Fuck. Fuck!" He releases his cock and pulls me close. Then he lines up, thrusting harshly inside me. He comes hard, groaning sexy obscenities as his cock pulses inside of me. He leans forward and grazes his teeth across me from hip to hip. Then, in the blink of an eye, he pushes himself off the bed.

"Jason?"

"My come better be inside you when I get home." He walks toward the bathroom then turns back. "That decision was mine alone. I came hard inside the pussy I fucking own. You made a decision yesterday and didn't consider me one damn bit."

I gasp as I am both angry and elated that he marked me in his own way. "You're serious?"

"You're damn right I am."

After his shower, he comes out completely naked and dresses quickly.

"You're an ass." I pout.

"I'm the only ass that has ever owned that pussy and made it a priority."

"Well, that changed," I say, rolling so I am looking away from him. I have learned to make myself my own priority . . . because of Jason and our time together, but I'm not telling him that right now.

"Today, as you fight to keep my come inside of you, wishing you could get off, I'll be trying to figure out how the fuck I'm gonna keep from killing his ass tonight." He grabs my shoulders and rolls me over, kissing me harshly then growling as he stands up. "This is fucked up, Lo."

"I trust you can handle it. I need you there with me!" I yell at his back in desperation. We have never had this type of moment together. I can feel the heat coming off of his body as he fights inside with his own emotions.

"You give me too damn much credit, angel," he barks as he walks out of the bedroom.

I wait until I hear him leave then get up. I don't know what to think. Actions speak louder than words and Jason's actions with me have always been good. After my shower, I dress, determined to find out who killed my family. More than ever, I need closure.

I need to be smarter now. I need to get this done. I need to either live—truly live—or smile when I see the bright white light at the end of the tunnel, knowing that I have done my family proud. I have been in a relationship that I could never walk away from, because as angry as I am at him now, he is my home.

At four-thirty, he walks in the door, and I feel my body heat up. I'm pissed about this morning, but seeing him lessens the anger drastically.

He drops his bag and storms toward me, pulling me up from the barstool and kissing me hard, taking my breath away. He then shoves his hand down the front of my leggings and pushes his finger possessively inside of me. He sighs against my mouth and pulls away.

He then takes my hand and drags me behind him to the bedroom. "Bend."

One word is filled with so much promise.

I do.

He pulls my pants down and thrusts his thick cock inside me. Lazily, he moves in and out. Each time I try to push against him, he holds me still.

I feel him pulse and whimper, "I'm close."

He spurts off inside of me then pulls out.

Kissing the back of my head, he says, "Tonight, when you sit at dinner across from that piece of shit, know that my come is filling your pussy. I own it."

"I am so pissed at you."

"Uh-huh," he says. "But when you're in that house, whose cock will you be thinking about wanting? Don't answer. It's mine, Lo. Mine."

"All I want is you." I almost can't fight back the tears. I need him. I want him, and he is punishing me.

"You're damn right you do," he snaps.

Chapter Twenty

I'm an asshole. Time and time again, I have told her there is a monster inside me. She wants to find the good when there is none. I'm punishing her, and I'm punishing myself. I don't want to fuck her angry, but I need her to know she claimed me as much as I claimed her. This is us.

This is different. I don't want to hurt her. The thought of my hands on her in anger makes me sick. I just want her to see that we need to do things together. Punishing her, I am punishing me. The push and the pull runs through my veins. Every breath I take is a fight inside not to repeat the same mistakes. Everything between us pushes me not to push her too far. I find the ways to hold back; even when I don't think I can, I do.

I am quiet as we make the drive to the Bennett family home. Tonight will be our make it or break it. I will be here where she needs me. Before I put my mark on that pussy anymore, though, she needs to know exactly who she crawled into bed with. To do that, she needs to know my past. She needs to know I have the power to hurt her, and I don't just mean break her heart.

There is a poster at the gym: a real man owns his mistakes. a real man uses the fight inside to face them and never make them again.

We are not going to be another mistake in the long line of mistakes I make in life. Tonight, I will lay it all out for her. If she chooses to walk away, I will use the fight inside to let her go. What I won't do is make the same mistakes again.

Reaching over, I squeeze her hand as I park the car. Hand in hand, we make our way inside the overdone home.

As we enter, I can't help tensing up. It reminds me of the lavish place I grew up in. Behind such beautiful doors were many secrets. Is this house the same?

Dr. Bennett comes around the corner to greet us. He quickly hugs Lo tightly, not hiding his look of distaste for me.

"Lorraine, we're so glad to have you home," Mrs. Bennett says, following not far behind her husband.

She gasps as she looks at me. I want to laugh because I see the lust in her eyes as she licks her lips, looking me up and down. She keeps watching me as she hugs Lo.

The collar of my shirt hides my neck tattoo. I'm not the pretty boy in dress pants and a button-down she thinks I am. I want to tell her I'm not the pool boy or her tennis coach, so she need not ogle me further, but then Ryan Bennett comes down the stairs, and my eyes meet his narrowed ones as rage automatically runs through my veins.

Hugging Lo, he sneers over at me. Then I hear him whisper, "What did you bring him for? This is a family dinner."

"She asked me to come." I step up with her back now against my front, my hands on her shoulders.

His hand grazes my abs as he pulls away from her.

Dr. and Mrs. Bennett smile politely while giving their son a stern look before escorting us to their dining room.

Pulling out her chair, I make sure Lo is situated before I sit beside her. Then I reach over and give her thigh a squeeze just as a raven-haired woman walks in with a surprised look on her face.

"Jason, this is Rochelle," Lo introduces. "She's Ryan's stepsister."

"Oh, has the good daughter come home?" Rochelle asks, plopping down rudely across from me.

Ryan sits directly across from Lo as his parents sit at the ends of the table.

Ryan jerks his eyes to her with fury. "Rochelle, Lorraine is more than welcome to come home anytime she wishes."

Mrs. Bennett smiles at Lo. "I would love to have you back. Sam tells me you are selling your parents' house." She blinks as if she's fighting to contain her emotions. "Letting go is hard, but it is healthy, you know."

Ryan drops his head at her words before his father chimes in. "When Ryan first started dating Heidi, we all became close. We just knew they would be together forever. We knew we would all be a family together." He sighs and looks at Lorraine with sadness. "Ryan hasn't moved on since your sister, either. Like my wife said, we know letting go is hard, but it is healthy."

I try to push back the thoughts in my mind. I try to take these people at face value. Lo trusts them and has a deep bond with them, no matter how fucked up I think it is. I wish I didn't have this feeling that there is so much more to the Bennetts and their love for Lorraine.

Dinner is awkward at best, as time and time again, all

of the Bennetts except Rochelle push for Lorraine to come home to them. They have no regard for what Lo wants or the fact that I am sitting right there among them. Meanwhile, the more Ryan looks at her, the more I want to break his face.

"I think it's time to go home, Lo. I'm sure the cats are ready for bed," I finally say, getting up from the sitting room after our meal. My clothing is the normal business attire I would wear with a sports coat at work, so I want nothing more than to get out of it.

Lorraine looks at me for a second too long, making me question whether she is ready to leave or not.

Mentally, I prepare for a fight. My gut twists as my past haunts me. Please don't fight me, Lo, I silently beg with my eyes. My adrenaline kicks in as I tell myself it's time to go and she's with me, so she goes, too. Only, Lorraine doesn't argue. Other than the pause, she nods, smiles, and says her goodbyes.

"Thank you for taking care of Lo when she needed you. Dinner was delicious," I tell Dr. Bennett, shaking his hand. I don't bother with the others before I guide Lo to the car with my hand at the small of her back.

I don't speak on the car ride home. I am at war with myself. Part of me is battle ready. I feel like I'm walking on a ledge, and I could tip at any moment. My brain is running a mile a minute, waiting for her to fight with me.

She paused. I must have done something wrong. I retrace our night. What did I do for her to react in that way? What will she say when we get home? How hard will she push me?

She nods to the doorman as I guide her inside my building with my hand at the small of her back. The elevator ride is quiet and tense. I feel my blood pumping in preparation for war.

She makes her way inside, immediately stepping out of her heels. The cats come over, and she rubs their heads before making her way into the kitchen.

I move to pass by when she turns sharply to me.

Here it comes.

I steel myself for the verbal blows.

"Jason," she says softly, "I'm sorry if I upset you. I didn't—"

"Fuck you, Lo!" I roar, interrupting her. "I hated every minute of being in that house. I'm not that kind of man. I don't know what I did in there, but—" I stop my pacing back and forth. "Wait a minute."

I look at her wide eyes and see the fear in them. My mind automatically went into defense. There is no reason for it.

I back myself up against the wall. "You're sorry? Did you say you're sorry?" Why would she not attack me, push me, and take it farther?

She nods and takes a step toward me.

I raise my hand to stop her. "Don't. Please don't come near me." I'm too amped up. I need to work this out for myself before she can touch me.

I fight to calm my breathing. I fight to get myself under control. I was prepared to defend myself and us, and it wasn't necessary. I was ready to blow up and fuck her up, fuck this up, and it would have been wrong.

I move to the far side of the living room, and she follows me into the dark space yet keeps to a safe distance. I look out the window onto my balcony and see the city lights.

My voice is low and scratchy when I tell her, "I'm a bad man, Lo. You really need to stay away." I look over my shoulder and see her take a tentative step closer to me. "No." I stop her again. "You need to know." I sigh. "Before we make plans and I tell you all the ways you are not going back to the Bennetts', I have to face—no, we have to face who I am." I take a deep breath and tell her, "I am not Ryan Bennett."

I hear her mutter, "Thank God for that."

"Lo, I'm serious. I don't have a father who will care about your well-being. I don't have a mother who will sit at dinner and smile because she misses you."

"I don't care who your parents are," she says barely above a whisper with hesitation in her tone.

"You should care. You should care that the man you've been sleeping with is a monster. You should care that I am the fucked-up son of an even more fucked-up man."

"Jason, I know about your childhood. I saw."

I hold up a hand to stop her, refusing to look at her. "I know what you saw, and I don't want to talk about it. You have to know, Lo, that I've done bad things. I've hurt a lot of people."

"But you haven't hurt me, Jason."

I shake my head. "I will. I came home tonight, ready for the fight. My instincts were screaming that you were going to push me, and I can't stand here and tell you I'm so sure I wouldn't have pushed back. Lo, when I push back, I'm gonna hate myself, and you're going to hate me, too."

I feel her move up behind me, and then she wraps her arms around my waist. "I'm not going to push you to the dark. I'm going to hold you in the light."

"I hurt her, Lo," I say with a rasp to my tone. I don't want to go here. I don't want to continue to give power to Missy. She has it, though, with everything that happened. Missy still has the power. My anger still has the power. As much as it kills me and it may kill what I'm building with Lo, I have to take back the power within myself. I have to fight inside to admit my shortcomings so the anger and rage don't hold power over me anymore.

"Who?"

"My ex, Missy. I put my hands on her," I admit, looking down at my trained hands. "I fight in the league to get out the aggression. Somehow, it wasn't enough. She would start, and we ended up hurting each other. We built this thing together, and we destroyed it. I don't want to destroy what we're building. I don't want to destroy you."

She squeezes me. "You brought me out of the scariest of places. You don't let me face things alone. You accept me for me, not my dead sister. You, Jason Stanley, have given me something to want to live for. The only way you will destroy me is if you walk away before we can find out where we can go with this. The only way you will destroy what we're building is if you don't give me a chance to help you the way you give me the strength to move on."

"I'm a monster," I admit, pleading with her eyes that she will take off the rose-colored glasses and see the darkness that is completely me.

"I lived in a house that haunts me, because I was afraid of the world. You came and saved me. You aren't a monster, Jason. You just don't see the good you have inside."

I have no words. I have laid it all out in front of her, and she isn't running scared. She should be, but she's not. Somehow in her eyes, I'm not a monster. She sees the good inside me that I can't find. No one has ever seen anything good in me . . . other than Tatiana who wasn't mine to hold on to. Could this be my chance at something real? Can she really accept me for the damaged and dangerous man I am?

I turn around and press my lips to hers. I don't think. I

don't fight. I don't push her away. I take her as she is, just as she takes me.

Slowly and tenderly, I take her on my living room floor. I let the day wash away as I sink inside of her.

With her, I don't need to fight inside. I just need to fight alongside her for whatever lies ahead.

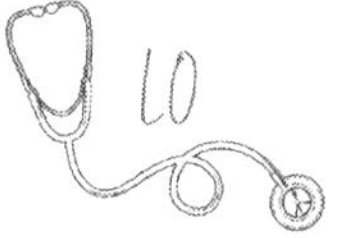

Chapter Twenty - One

After Jason has left for work, I lie in bed, staring at the ceiling, feeling satisfied. He made sure of it. On the floor, he apologized to my body sweetly, softly with his body. In the shower, he apologized with his kisses and the way his rough hands washed me gently, tenderly before I did the same in return. In bed, he gave me more. He gave me—Lo—what I now crave: the ability to lose myself in a moment of unrestrained, out-of-control sex.

I roll to my side, thinking about what he told me last night about the monster he thinks lives inside of him, the fear he will lose control with me. I know he won't. I know by his touch, his need, his protective nature, and his possessiveness. In the arms of the man who calls himself a monster, I feel safer, more protected, and more alive than I ever have in my life.

I hate to even think about the fact that I always lived in the shadow of my sister. I love her and would go back in time to stop what happened. It feels wrong to think about the fact that, for the first time, I feel like I am my own person, and a man, a beautiful man, wants me. Just Lo. It feels selfish to be content, happy, and unafraid.

I sit up and pull my knees to my chest, watching Boots and Socks lying side by side. My chest squeezes, and I close my eyes tightly. Brothers.

Boots reminds me of Heidi, always stronger, and Socks reminds me of me, the scaredy-cat.

I lean down and scratch under their chins. "We're getting stronger."

I don't want to deceive Jason. He told me his deepest, darkest secrets, the ones I didn't already know. However, I can't give him back the same. I can't let him know what I have planned. If I get away with it, I will be able to give a name to my feelings for him. I will be able to do that and not worry about the ramifications to him or to me if he can't tell me the same back. I will be strong enough to deal with the loss that may follow.

I am falling in love with a man who calls me an angel and himself a monster. He has no idea that the opposite is true. I hope he never will.

I look in the mirror and sigh. "Today, you are not Lo. Today, you become stronger. Today, you get answers so that, maybe tomorrow, this can end for you and for them."

I am Hi. I have to be. I need the strength I feel when I pretend to be her.

I sit in the car, feeling stronger. I have on my wig, dark glasses, and I am ready. I open my bag and see the gun and know why. Today, I am armed. If I am found or if one of them comes after me, I won't be vulnerable.

I look in the rearview mirror and nod at myself. I have on my armor. "Today, I am Hi."

Adrian, Charlotte, and Waters are my prime suspects.

Waters has become the one I believe most capable. He obviously has a dark side since I followed him into The Lion's Den. I don't trust Charlotte, either, but the crime scene was gruesome, and I have to ask: Is a woman capable of such things? Adrian is sketchy. His schedule didn't waver much. He didn't do anything out of the ordinary like Waters.

Today, I follow Adrian to a café on the waterfront. I sit and wait.

I should just say fuck it. I should just do what they did—they took away three lives. An eye for an eye.

I run my hand over my face and shake my head, trying to rid myself of the hate, the extreme hate I feel inside for these people I want to kill, the entire lot of them, when I don't know who actually did it.

God, it's so confusing now. Jason sees both, he shows me who I am, he chooses me, now this game has become more difficult. I use her strength, become her, take on her persona, in every situation that I want to hide from.

When the police questioned me—her, about who might have killed my family, I—she couldn't think of a single person. We were a normal family, a happy family. My father enjoyed his job, but he didn't live it. The same thing went for my mother. I—she felt helpless.

While away at college, Lo made a notebook and wrote down every possibility. My parents weren't close with their families, but when I looked into it via social media, the posts and tweets made it apparent that no one in our family was anywhere near Detroit on that day. They hadn't been in years.

The last time Dad's sister visited, she borrowed money. I overheard him tell Mom he knew she wouldn't pay him back or be back, and that was fine, because as he said, our family was more than enough for him.

Mom was an only child, and her parents had been traveling out of the country since they retired. My family's tragedy brought them home long enough to offer . . . Lo the opportunity to travel with them and to attend the funeral. It was very rough on them. They loved us. When they left, they called every week, then every month, now on birthdays and holidays. It's sad, but they should move on.

Everyone should.

Two years after their deaths, Lo remembered overhearing our parents talking about an argument with the city council about some error in accounting. Dad was angry they weren't looking into it. He said something about a three-hundred-thousand-dollar discrepancy. Mom told him he had done his job, and it was up to them to take action. She also told him she wanted him to try not to make waves since retirement was on the horizon, and she couldn't wait for them to retire and move east, closer to her parents.

I put on my gloves, pulling them down and flexing my fingers inside for the best fit. Then I pull the gun—the Glock—from my bag and hold it in my hand. I don't think about the repercussions to Jason. I only think of a solution to my past. The more time that passes the more I need to have closure. Desperation is a strong emotion. Its heavy steel looks large in my hand. It is large, but from the way he told me—her to hold it, I know I can handle it.

I am strong.

I see two cars pull in one behind the other. I immediately recognize them. Charlotte and Waters.

I knew it; I feel an emotion swell. Pride maybe. The fact that these three are meeting together outside of the office is highly suspicious.

"Good enough," I say out loud and look down at the gun. "It's time to end this."

The passenger side door swings open, and I hold the gun up, pointing it at whoever is coming for me.

When I see green, angry eyes, my hand shakes.

"Don't!" I scream.

He reaches out and snatches the gun from my trembling hands. "What the fuck are you doing?"

I turn away from his enraged eyes, unable to answer him.

"Lo, I asked you a goddamn question."

"Hi! Hi, not Lo."

"The fuck you are," he snaps before he gets out of the car, storms around it, opens my door, and leans in. "Move over."

I don't move.

"Now!"

I scramble over the console to the passenger seat, and he gets in the driver's side and adjusts the seat. Then he starts the car and throws it in drive.

As soon as the tires hit the road, his head whips around, and he yells at me, "You have some explaining to do!"

I don't say a word.

"I'm not fucking playing, Lo. I gave you everything last night. I gave you everything I had, and you can't even give me a word."

"Hi! Not Lo!" I scream, then raise my knees to my chest, burying my face in them.

"No!" He smashes his fist on the dashboard. "She's dead, dammit! She's fucking dead, Lo. You're here. You're here, and I need you to tell me what the fuck is going on so I can help you!"

When I don't say anything in response, he leaves me alone. I know I'm irrational but I can't tell him because I'm not sure.

"My fucking car is at the riverside at that little café. Grab it for me?" I assume he's talking into his phone, but I don't look. Then he says nothing.

When I was little and afraid, I kept my eyes closed, becoming invisible to the world. I did it when I was in trouble for something, too. It sucks to know I'm not invisible. It sucks to know I again have disappointed him, made him angry. As fucked up as this all is, though, I want him to believe I am Heidi. I wish he would believe it like I make myself believe it.

I look up when he slows down. We are at his apartment building.

Home, I think and my heart aches.

"You can't park here. You just can't."

"The fuck I can't," he hisses.

I start to open the door, but he grabs me. "I swear to God, you're pushing me, Lo. You're fucking pushing me on purpose."

"I can't let anyone see this car! I can't, or I won't be safe. You won't be safe!" I use this car when I am Hi.

"Jesus Christ," he hisses, putting the car back in drive and passing the building. "Where the fuck is your car, Lo, and what the hell are you doing?"

"The same place it was when you followed me the night you saved me," I whisper.

Now I cry for him and what I am doing to him.

He holds my purse in one hand and my hand in the other as we walk off the elevator, not exchanging words since we dropped off the car and got mine. He pulls me behind him and opens the door.

As soon as I'm inside, I look down and see both Boots and Socks walking toward me. I drop to my knees and pet them. Socks purrs the loudest. I scoop him up and hug him tight.

He is growing comfortable here. He is happy here, and I know I am not going to be welcome soon.

Jason opens the fridge and grabs a beer. I look at the time. It's nine in the morning.

"You're late for work," I whisper as I walk by the wall of windows and set Socks next to the scratch pole.

He laughs a low rumble. "I called in sick to work today. I wanted to spend time with you." I hear the bottle knock on the counter. "Apparently, you already had fucking plans."

"If you had told me, I would have stayed," I say honestly.

"Oh, no. I wanted to surprise you. I went to the gym and came home to an empty fucking place and no note. You didn't answer your fucking phone, so you know what I did, Lo?"

I shake my head.

"I went to the same goddamned places I followed you around to yesterday, trying to figure out what the hell you're doing. I was all set to come back here yesterday and fuck you right, but where were you?"

I hang my head.

"You were out stalking city council members!"

I look up quickly and scowl at him.

"I thought it was Waters. I thought my Lo"—he hits his chest hard—"my Lo might have a thing for that tool, because she followed his ass to The Lion's Den twice. But I buried that idea because, when I followed you to Adrian's, I knew no way in hell would you want that dick when you have my cock. Then Charlotte; I knew damn well you weren't the type to eat pussy when you like cock. More specifically, you like my cock!"

"I love it. Yes, I do." I take a step toward him, and he throws his hand up.

"No, Lo. No fucking way is this gonna end up in bed. You're going to tell me what the hell is going on in your head, or you don't get my dick, my tongue, my . . ." He snaps his jaw shut, closes his eyes, and shakes his head. After what feels like an eternity, he opens his eyes. All anger is gone, and I see pain. "I gave you everything last night, and you give me nothing."

"Jason, I can't," I whisper. "I don't want to be anywhere except here, but I can't tell you. You protect me against your demons. I am protecting you, too, okay?"

His eyes change, turn angry. "I don't need your fucking protection!" he roars. "I need your honesty. I need you to let me be the fucking man I want to be for you, or you, Lo, need to leave, because I can't let this get ugly. I won't let it get ugly, not with you. Not ever!

"You want to hide things from me, make me feel weak, when all I want you to feel is strong. As good as your pussy is, as much as I want it—want you, crave you—you want to hide. You need to leave."

Panic strikes, and I hold my hand over my face.

I can't hold back anymore. I can't walk away from the thing that makes me the happiest.

"She's going to kill them. She's going to kill them and make them pay for what they did. Heidi deserves retribution."

Tears fall and silent sobs build deep, making my body tremble.

In less than it takes to start, I feel his arms around me, lifting me, carrying me, and whispering, "Sh . . ." against my ear.

"I can't stay here," I cry loudly. "I won't let go, Jason. I won't back down until I finish what I started, and I don't want you involved."

"Lo, taking my gun involved me. If you had shot them,

it would have been me who got arrested." He sounds annoyed with me, assuming I didn't know the gun would tie him to it.

"You were at work. You had an alibi."

"No, I wasn't at work, and the guys at the gym don't care much for the cops. I would have been suspect number one," he says. "And you live here, have access to my piece, so you would have been as well."

I look up when he sits, holding me on his lap.

"I don't care if I go to jail. I would be proud that I avenged the death of my family."

"That wouldn't work for me, angel." He shrugs, and I see pain in his eyes again. "I don't want to be without you. I want us. I want you; and I want me; and I want a peaceful fucking existence."

"I want that, too. I do, but how can I find true peace when I know . . ." I stop and wipe tears from my left eye as he rubs his thumb under my right. "It wasn't just a random home invasion. There is more. I know there is, and I have proof."

"Why haven't you gone to the police?"

"Because Ryan didn't believe me, I let it go, then I knew I couldn't anymore. I tried going to the police. They said it was a closed case. I was weak and left it alone. No one believed me or my suspicions."

"I believe you."

Shocked, I throw my arms around him and hug him so tightly I fear I may hurt him, but then he lets out a noise telling me otherwise.

"Thank you."

His body trembles as he hugs me back just as tightly. Then he sighs and pulls away. I'm not ready to let go, so I hold on more tightly.

He reaches back behind his neck and pulls my hands apart then pushes me back. "I need you to sit down."

When our eyes meet, the emotion I felt in his embrace isn't shared through his eyes. He's angry again.

"I am," I say nervously.

He lifts me by the hips and sets me on the bed. Then he stands up and begins to pace. He does it long enough that I know . . . I know this is too much for him. I know what's going to happen next.

He stops pacing and turns toward me. "I believe you, Lo. I do. But I can't do this."

"Jason, please," I plead.

"I can't think of any way to do this other than demand you go to the police. You and I are not good together."

"We are," I sob out.

"You don't trust me enough to tell me what the hell is going on, and I don't trust you at all after this shit."

I cover my face and silently sob. "I didn't want you to get into trouble."

"That's not your fucking call!"

I look up at him. "Yes, it is! It's the only way I could protect you!"

"You have no clue what you're doing, who you're messing with."

"I've been watching them, online, in newspaper articles, and on the news for years. Now I have been following them for three months."

"And still, you don't have it narrowed down." He shakes his head. "You were just going to what, kill three people?"

"Yes." I nod furiously. "Yes, and then they could rest peacefully. Then I wouldn't feel like I should be dead, too. Then I would be free to embrace everything you make me feel. All the good things, Jason."

He sighs as he walks closer to me.

"I just want to be able to be with you and be happy without"—I strangle back a sob—"without disappointing them."

He kneels in front of me and looks up. "You are making this so difficult."

"You're gonna ask me to leave, aren't you?" I whisper.

"I'm gonna make you promise me, without hiding behind the bullshit of being her, that you will let your man do what your man is best at: taking care of you. I can fucking promise you no one can do it better. No one."

Him saying "your man," emphasizing it not once but twice, makes me smile through the tears.

"But if you can't promise me, Lo, then yes, I'm gonna have to ask you to leave because I can't ever be in the position to be so angry with you that I want to work it out with my fists. If I ever touched a hair on your head, I would not allow myself another breath."

I shrug and shake my head. "If I could let it go, I would."

"You made a promise to them; I get it. Justice. I understand, Lo. Your word is gold, right?"

I nod.

"Then give it to me or keep this up and walk out the door." He stands and steps back. "If you walk, understand you're killing two people's chances at a life neither one has known before and never will again."

"I promise," I say quietly.

"I can't hear you, angel," he says, allowing his emotion to flow into his words.

I stand up and walk toward him. My toes touching his, I look up into his eyes. "I. Promise."

"Thank God." He wraps his arms around me securely, protectively, and possessively. "Thank God."

We hold each other for a long time until we are interrupted by two meowing cats.

Jason steps back and lifts my chin. "I promise you, I will find out."

"How?"

"Angel, I have their work lives at my fingertips. I can look to see when they traveled, where they ate—hell, I can probably find out when they shit." He winks. "I hate my fucking job, but right now, I love it. Process of elimination, Lo. No need for me to kill three if only one did it."

My eyes widen. "You can't kill them."

"One person is slated for heaven, the other for hell. Nothing can change that. So yes, I can, and if that's what my angel needs in order to keep making me happy and allowing me to do the same, that's exactly what I will do."

"Jason," I whisper and look down.

"Don't you see, Lo? You mean a lot to me."

"Promise me you won't."

"I promise you that, if that's what needs to be done, I will make sure you know before I slink off behind your back and do it. If one of them needs to die, I'll make sure you know before I do it."

"And if I ask you not to? If I tell you I need to be the one to do it?"

"We'll cross that bridge when we get there. But, Lo, we're together on this and every other fucking thing we do except work. Feel me?"

"Then the same holds true for you." I look up at him. "If you're gonna take the day off that I have off and run to the gym—"

He laughs with his whole body, and it is the most beautiful sound my ears have ever heard. "You jealous of the gym, angel?"

"Maybe I am," I say, pretending to be annoyed.

"Good, you can start going with me."

"Yeah?" I ask, trying not to smile.

"Hell yes." He smiles back.

J A S O N

Chapter Twenty - Two

Taking Lo to the gym is one of the worst ideas I have ever had. My focus is shit. I watch her on the elliptical or the treadmill, and my dick twitches. I watch her hit the bag, and I want to bury myself in her from behind. I watch her jump rope, her tits bouncing up and down, and all I picture is her riding my cock. I need them in my hands.

I see her look up at me as I am staring while I spar with Brock. The fucker jabs me with a left, knocking me down, and I'm pissed.

"You need to focus, fool. Either that or you aren't going to be ready for the fight in ten days." He barks out a laugh as I get up off my ass and swiftly uppercut him.

He falls back into the ropes, and I laugh.

"You don't have to worry about me in a fight."

He shakes it off and pushes off the ropes. Then I am all focus and fury.

My fight-or-flight response has been in training for years. It took a long time to get used to immediately striking back, but it's like second nature now. I taught my father that lesson when I turned sixteen, and then I walked out the fucking door.

I lived and breathed the gym after that, and I cut off all ties with the bastard. But then he came to collect me, using my mother as an excuse to lure me back. She was sick, he lied. I bought it hook, line, and sinker.

Sick my ass. She was no different than before; only now my polished ass knew what a pill popper, alcoholic, drug addict looked like when they weren't bathed, pampered, and clothed in designer duds. One week on the street was all it took to open my eyes to her issues. Worthless excuse for a mother.

After I left her room, I walked down the stairs, and there stood my father, Waters, and a couple other businessmen. The two I didn't know held my arms back while Waters sat down, drinking scotch, and watched as my father proceeded to beat the shit out of me for taking off.

I learned a lesson that day. My father isn't the only piece of shit out there. The world is full of them. In order to beat them, you have to become them, and I did.

"Ease the fuck up, man!" Brock's voice booms, snapping me back to the moment.

"Shit." I step back, seeing blood running from his nose. "My bad."

He rolls his eyes. "I should have known better. Break."

I nod then look away. She's watching me. She saw me lose control. Fuck!

She sighs and walks toward me. The girl should be running the other way, yet she's walking toward me.

I hop out of the ring, and she hands me a towel.

"You okay?"

I shake my head, but say, "Yeah."

"What were you thinking about?" she asks softly.

I can't answer.

She takes my hand. "I understand it's hard to talk about everything, but remember our promise?"

"Of course I do." I sit down on the bench and bring her down on my lap. "He's been calling, leaving messages, pissing me off. Then Brock sucker punched me."

"Stupid man," she whispers, taking the towel and rubbing it over my sweat-drenched head.

"Brock is a good guy, angel. I lost control. It should scare the hell out of you." I close my eyes.

"I'd never hit you," she whispers, and I open my eyes. She smirks and leans in. "I may be a bit crazy, but I'm not stupid."

I stand up and set her feet on the floor. Then I take her hand and walk quickly into the locker room, locking the door behind me.

"What are you doing?"

"I need inside," I answer, turning her around so she faces me, then walking her back toward the row of lockers.

"There are people," she whispers as her back hits the dark wooden doors.

"There is you"—I hook the waistband of her shorts with my thumbs and pull them down—"and me."

I drop to my knees, and she looks down. "You can't."

"I thought you weren't a stupid girl," I reply, licking my lips.

"I've been sweating." She gasps as I lean in and lick the outside of her pussy. "Jason—"

"You smell so good: all female, all Lo, all mine." I lift her knee and pull one foot out of her shorts before getting the shorts off that leg and throwing it over my shoulder.

"Oh, God," she cries as I pull her hips toward me and push my face hard against her. "Jason."

I lick her hard, the way she likes it, parting those soft,

fuzzy lips. I rub my nose down her opening, and her hands fist in my damp hair as she cries out.

Egged on by her noises, I grip her hips and shove my tongue deep inside of her. I feel her soft, wet, velvet walls clench around my tongue, and I fuck her faster with it. Her body tenses. I need her closer.

I pull back and pant, "Hold the handles on the fucking lockers and don't let go."

As soon as she complies, I lift her other leg and push her back against the lockers as I fuck her hard with my tongue. She loses all control and drops her hands from their grip.

I can't get enough of her: her taste, her smell, her moans, her cries. I lick her harshly, driving my tongue in, curling it up, tasting and tormenting her, praising my angel's sweet, hot, slick pussy. My reward is when her hands fist in my hair, and she rides my face, grinding her hips, taking what I give her and begging with her body for more.

"Yes, yes. Oh, Jason, yes." She stiffens, her cunt strangling my tongue, and her juices soak my face.

I grip her to keep her in place and turn so I can lay her on the bench. I shove down my shorts and push her quaking body up so I can slide onto the bench. I then rub my cock up and down her slit. She is glistening, swollen. Her clit peeks out from its hood, and I can't help tapping it with my aching cock.

"Please," she begs softly.

"Please what, angel?" I ask, tapping it again.

"I want you," she moans.

"You want my cock inside of your pussy?"

"Yes," she whimpers.

"Tell me," I growl.

"I want your cock inside of me. I want you to fuck me. I want your come."

Restraint gone, I slam into her and hiss. "You want my come?"

"Yes. Of course, yes. I want everything."

"I'm gonna come so hard for you," I say as I grip her hips and slide her up and down the bench. Her pussy glides down easily on me. "So fucking wet."

"For you," she cries. "Always for you."

"Fuck," I hiss.

I need in deeper. I want to be buried inside her. I want to come so hard in her it makes her body tremble under me.

I stand, still connected, lifting her, and plunge in deep, hard, fast. Her pussy walls contract, and my balls are so tight they almost ache.

"I'm gonna come so hard for you."

"Yes. Oh, please, Jason, please."

My dick thrashes inside of her as hot liquid fires hard into her, unloading everything I have . . . for her.

She lies in our bed, exhausted from her workout and from the pounding I gave her at the gym and then again at home. I can't get enough.

I lie next to her, equally as drained, and push her hair off her face. "You wanna go again?"

I see her thighs clench and can't help chuckling.

"Did I wear you out?"

"I'll give you anything you want, but can you allow me ten minutes of rest?" Her smile is a sweet plea.

My phone rings, and I nod at her as I reach toward the nightstand and grab it.

Without looking, I answer, "Hello."

"You either stop avoiding me or I come over there and

question you and that little"—he pauses—"lunatic you're fucking."

"I have no fucking clue what you are talking about, Father, but you watch your fucking tone when you—"

"The letters!" he bellows.

"What the hell are you talking about? What fucking letters?" I look over at Lo. Her eyes are wide. She looks terrified, and my stomach is in knots.

"I warn you, Jason, if you try to get revenge on me using that little bitch's tragedy, you are going to find yourself in a situation that I will not be able to, nor would I, help you out of."

"What fucking letters?" I repeat, staring directly at her.

"Don't you lie to me!"

"I never have," I tell him honestly. "You are barking up the wrong fucking tree. Good night." I hang up the phone and look at her, asking the question I already know the answer to. "You know anything about letters?"

She cries herself to sleep on my lap after I calm her down. Now she is afraid again. She's afraid because she thinks they will come after both of us. I don't doubt they will, but they can't get to her here. I know it. I have explained it, and I think she believes it. Regardless, tomorrow, Brock will be outside this building while I'm at work, looking for answers.

I want to pull my hair out.

Apparently, a few prominent members of the city council all received the same fucked-up letter.

As I scour the Internet to find anything I can on the three people Lo thinks may have killed her family, I have an angel on my lap, a tablet in my hand, and two cats at my feet. Women are a pain in the ass.

Three of the six have already been ruled out. As for the last three, well, I have serious doubts it's Adrian. Charlotte could be it, but the woman never has a hair out of place; therefore, I don't see her leaving a crime scene like the one that was the Boschs' home.

Now Waters is a whole different story. I have known the man my whole life. He's as much of a son of a bitch as my own father. Is he capable of killing? Without a doubt.

Then again, so am I.

She is still asleep when I get up to leave for work. Work comes early. No gym today. I have to act quickly to get any information I can before they start covering their asses.

These letters obviously have them all on edge if they called my father. What do they all know? What are they all covering up?

My mind and body are wound tight. I can't seem to get to the bottom of this. Sure, there were funds missing, but I can't find the paper trail attaching anyone specific to the money yet.

I can rule out Adrian's and Charlotte's involvement. Both were out of town and that gives them a solid alibi. It's documented travel, receipts received, and if I look deep enough, I know I could probably find more. But I don't have time.

Waters, on the other hand, has nothing saying he was in town or out.

What I do manage to pull up gives me a partial insurance plan against retaliation as I dig more. I look into the finances from over five years ago, trying to find what Lo's dad may have stumbled upon. In the end, I can't prove murder, but I am able to download a year's worth of his work onto a thumb drive. Thanks to my time rooming with a hacker in college, I can do this without leaving a trace behind.

When I walk into the apartment later, she stands at the counter. She forces a smile, but then her lip quivers.

I hold up the thumb drive and give her a reassuring smile. "Things are going to be okay. Two of the three were out of town. I'm not saying they are not guilty of something, but their hands are clean of this."

She walks up and hugs me around the waist. "I'm so sorry."

"Angel, I'm sorry you went through what you did. I'm so sorry, but let me ask you something." I tip her chin up. "Did you feel safe today?"

"Yes, I did. But I was terrified for you. I put you in danger. I never meant—"

"You felt safe today in my home—our home." I pull away and look down at her. "I have insurance, angel. We're good. Nothing is going to happen. It's almost guaranteed."

With both of our minds on trying to figure out this unsolved case, neither of us say much or eat much for dinner. As bedtime comes, I hold her as she sleeps. I can't shake the feeling that my father and the rest are more worried about the damn paper trail than being brought up on murder charges. It should make me feel damn good, but it doesn't.

If they are not guilty of this, if I can prove they didn't have shit to do with it, my girl, my angel, will be looking over her shoulder forever. She will never be free or whole.

My chest tightens at the thought. I look down and kiss her head. She will have me, though. I will be her protection, and I will gladly take her as she is . . . more than gladly.

Chapter Twenty - Three

It's the weekend, and Jason is asleep next to me. I watch him. He has been going over and over my dad's work, and he knows now there is a discrepancy, but he doesn't know how it led to such a brutal massacre.

He has become obsessed. Between work and my problems, the only time he isn't inside his head is when he is inside me. I feel useless unless I am under him. The selfish girl in me loves it.

I go to work, knowing the black Chevy truck following me is his friend from the gym. I know it's his way of making sure he knows I get there, and that kind of protection means everything to me.

"What are you thinking?" he asks in a tired whisper.

Without thinking, I respond, "That I should walk away so you aren't so stressed."

He sits up, now wide awake and angry. "Do you really think that would help?"

Before I can respond, I am on my back, and he is kissing the life out of me. I can't breathe, but I don't want it to stop. I could die like this, and I would be happy.

He pulls away, panting, his green eyes ablaze. "Have I not proven to you every day that I want you here?"

"Yes, but—"

"Have I not shown you how much I want you, need you?"

"Yes, but—"

"But nothing." He whips the covers off me. Then I feel him push up my nightgown and yank down my panties. He grabs himself and thrusts almost viciously inside of me as he cries out my name then pulls back. He thrusts in, pulls back, thrusts in . . . "You leave, and I will find you."

My body trembles. He isn't just fucking me; he is fucking away my insecurities.

"I love you!" I cry out.

He stills. His eyes show emotion—pain, I think. He doesn't respond. He clamps his eyes shut and fucks me through orgasm after orgasm after beautiful orgasm. Then he comes with a roar, his heavy, thick cock twitching wildly inside me, but he doesn't stop. He continues fucking.

I watch through my half-closed eyes as he glares at me. His body—oh, God, his body—is glorious. His muscles flex as he works me and himself into another release.

He then falls on top of me, panting, his chest rising and falling against mine. He dips his head down and rubs his stubble across my tight nipples, and then I feel him growing inside me again.

He pushes up on his arms, and this time, he slowly pushes in farther. Then he bends his head and kisses my cheek, my ear.

"If that's true . . ." he pants. "If what you said is true" —he pulls out until his thick, broad head is the only part inside of my raw, sore pussy—"then you better never run from me, Lo. And you better never think that you are a burden." He drives into me. "Together?"

"Yes," I say as tears roll down my cheeks. "Yes!"

Slowly, lazily, he thrusts in and out.

I cup my breasts, and he groans, "Fuck."

His pace quickens, and then he falls apart. He kisses me, pulls out, and steps off the bed.

"Don't you move."

"I don't think I can," I whisper.

He smiles. It's a small yet very pride-filled smile. "Perfect."

I hear the water running in the shower, and as much as I enjoy our lazy morning showers together, I can't move. So I close my eyes and let exhaustion and the safety of knowing he wants me here as much as I want him lull me back to sleep.

I wake up to the smell of bacon and the feeling of stickiness between my legs. I force myself up and look at the clock. It's nearly noon. I never sleep this late, but I also never had sex like that first thing in the morning, either.

In the shower, I think about the fact that I admitted I love him. He didn't say the same, which should worry me, but it doesn't. He shows me as much every day. I just hope he never feels like I am taking more than I am giving or will someday be able to give.

I love him. I love him madly. Never in my life have I or would I be able to feel safer than I do with him.

I get out of the shower and grab the white, terry-cloth robe he brought home for me. In hot pink on the back, it says Cobra. It is the first thing a man has ever bought for me.

I smile as I dry my hair and then laugh as I walk out. I am met with cold eyes.

"Good morning."

He holds up my phone. "What's this?"

I shrug, having no idea what he is talking about.

"Messages from Ryan Bennett, asking why you blocked him."

"He was messaging a lot, asking when I'm coming home"—I shrug—"so I told him I was home. He sent a few more, and I blocked him."

He lets out a deep breath. "You decided not to tell me because . . . ?"

"Because we have enough between us, and we don't need him added on, Jason. I blocked him. I have no idea how he got back through."

"I will deal with him," he snaps.

I shake my head. "No."

"Excuse me?" His eyes bug out, and I can't help laughing. "Did I say something funny?"

"No, yes, maybe?" I sigh. "He would absolutely press charges if you did something, Jason." I look down. The next part, I whisper, partially because he didn't return my sentiments earlier. "I don't think I could handle life without you."

I glance up to see his chest visibly expand as he takes in a sharp breath. "Jesus. Come here."

In his arms, I agree to block his calls, but any messages Ryan sends, he wants to not only know about, but he wants to see them. I make him promise to do the same with Missy.

He looks down at me and tries not to smirk. "She's called twice. Does that make you jealous?"

I pout. "Very."

"Hmm . . ." He pulls my head to his chest, and I swear he is chuckling.

"It's not funny."

"Sorry, angel, but it actually feels really good." He pulls back and looks down. "I'm fucked up."

"Then we are perfect together."

"Damn right we are."

We eat brunch, and then I make my way into the bedroom to change the sheets. He smirks when he sees me carrying them out, and I giggle. He makes me feel that way—happy.

"Lo, these boxes have been stacked up in the living room for a while," he points out when I come back through.

"What's in them?"

"Stuff from your sister's room: a few photo albums, some jewelry, and a diary I found under her mattress. There's also stuff from your room in that basement. Not all the granny panties made it."

I feel my face turn beet red, and he laughs.

"I'm kidding. No woman ever looked hotter in briefs, Lo."

I don't say anything because I am seriously concerned with my wardrobe now.

"Lo?"

"I need to go shopping," I declare. "I ordered everything, and I know it's probably not what you're used to, and I—"

"Slow down, Lo. I was joking. To be honest, you in scrubs does it for me. You naked ensures you'll always do it for me."

"I want to go shopping," I repeat.

"Then we're going shopping." He nods. "But understand, I'm gonna be making you try on everything."

Jason places four bags in the backseat of the car then climbs in. He looks over at me, and I see that he is happy, so happy.

He leans over and grabs the back of my head, pulling me to him. "I can't believe you wouldn't let me watch you change." Then he kisses me.

"I can't believe I didn't, either," I grumble, narrowing my eyes at him.

"That's on you." He reaches over and grabs my seatbelt, snapping it in place before starting his car.

I remain quiet, thinking about how very jealous I am of the way the salesclerks and shoppers looked at him. He is hard to miss. Over six feet tall with spiky, blond hair; piercing green eyes; and a light shadow of a beard dusting his square, chiseled jaw. He has on black, worn jeans that hang low on his narrow hips and a light gray T-shirt tucked in that does nothing to hide his broad chest, bulging biceps, or the muscled forearms.

He takes my hand and pulls it to his lips. "You're quiet."

"It's exhausting," I say as I lean my head back.

He chuckles. "Shopping?"

"No, watching all of those women check you out." I sigh. "I don't like it."

"There were women in the stores?" he questions, looking over at me.

I roll my eyes. "Yes."

"All I saw was you." He smirks. "And underwear."

"Yes, I am aware that you saw underwear." I smirk, pointing behind us at all the bags filled with them.

"I can't wait to take them all off of you," he says in a throaty voice.

Going back to work is not something I want to do, but I love my job. I have to keep telling myself that, because deep down I know it's true, though I don't care right now.

Every day, I am faced with a new tragedy, the unexpected, looking into the eyes of someone who has just had their world rocked by the unforeseen. Every day, I feel their pain, and every day, I cannot wait to run back to Jason.

I stand in the nurses' lounge, gathering my things to head home. I smile at the thought and shake my head.

"Everything okay, Lorraine?" I jump when I hear Dr. Bennett behind me. "Did I scare you?"

I turn around and shake my head. "No, just startled me a bit. That's all."

"You seem detached, like you're not really all here," he says as he sits down.

"I'm fine. Truly, I am," I respond as I put on my coat and turn around. "How are you?"

"I'm worried about you." He looks up at me. "The man you're living with is violent, Lorraine. You can't feel good about that. It has to dredge up bad memories." He raises his eyebrows at me and lowers his voice. "I know he's the patient we treated who wouldn't give any information. I've known since he brought you in. He lives a dangerous life, Lorraine."

"I understand your concern, and I truly appreciate it, but he is a good man."

"And you believe this?" The flippant way he says it rubs me the wrong way. It confuses me, makes me feel defensive. Regardless, I know it's out of concern.

I set my bag down and sit, even though I know Jason is expecting me and I don't want him to worry.

"I feel safe with him, protected." I look down. "I have very strong feelings for him, feelings I have never had for anyone."

He looks at me, his expression unreadable. "He is unstable at best."

"I understand how you may feel that way, but he is the most stable thing I have had in years."

He shrugs. "Did we not help you enough? Did we fail you in some way?"

"I just need to move forward." As soon as the words escape my lips, the other Dr. Bennett walks in. Ryan.

"Move forward?" His voice shakes, and I fear his tone, his demeanor, will give away our secret.

I stand up and smile. "I'm very sorry if you feel put off by this. It's not my intention. Please excuse me. Jason is waiting for me." I walk away quickly and make my way out the door as fast as I can.

"Lorraine, wait!" I hear Ryan call me from behind. "Dammit, I need to talk to you."

I hear an engine roar and know without looking it's the black Chevy truck, the lights brightening the darkened parking lot.

I stop and turn around. Ryan is unaffected by the revving engine.

When he gets close enough, I hold up my hand. "Stop."

"Stop what, exactly?" Ryan sounds annoyed.

"Stop calling. Stop following me. Stop, Ryan, and move on. Heidi would want that."

He looks as though I have slapped him in the face. "So, that's it? She means nothing to you anymore? I mean nothing to you?"

I shake my head. "That's not true. I just think we need to focus on the future."

"And he is your future?" Ryan closes his eyes and looks down.

"Without a doubt," I answer. "Be happy for me, Ryan, and find happiness for you, too."

I turn and use the key fob to unlock my vehicle. I get in, start the car, and pull out of the parking lot, knowing I am safe and hopeful that this is the end to my confrontations with Ryan.

While I drive home, the lights behind me don't follow closely, but I see them.

Jason Stanley—Cobra, the abused boy, the man who made horrible mistakes—is changed. He is watching over me. He is making sure my past is lit up and I am no longer incapacitated because of it. He is my beacon, a light to follow. My future is no longer scary and alone.

Not everything is certain or uncomplicated, but my feelings for him are without a doubt.

Chapter Twenty - Four

My phone pings with a text from Brock. It's a location and time for a fight tonight. I've had my fighting on hold for healing and then to help Lo. She's been my release and my focus. I haven't needed to pound someone into the ground like before. My stomach tightens at the thought of leaving Lo at home. However, my own insecurities of losing my cool with her have me needing to release Cobra, at least for a few strikes tonight. I have spent so much time keeping myself in check, maybe now is the time to let loose and see if I really have found a way to overcome my own past.

Having an office job, even one I hate, has afforded me time and access. Lorraine's dad stumbled upon not only my father beating the shit out of me when I was younger, but he also uncovered numerous district redistributions of thousands in construction funds. Projects that council members voted on and approved were never completed. The trails move the money to multiple people, all of whom landed on Lorraine's suspect list, my father included.

Having all my documentation copied and saved, as well

as locked away for an insurance plan, I know the only person left who could have killed her family was Waters, possibly with the help of my father.

Inside, I'm twisted at the knowledge that the man who gave me life could have taken Lo's whole family from her. If I can prove he did this, I swear on everything I have ever done right or wrong, I will be the one to serve my own fucking justice for me, for Lo, for her mom, her dad, and for her twin sister. Corruption feeds corruption.

Waters, too. I will take every fucker who caused her this pain down one by one.

The king cobra inside me is ready to strike. I feel the agitation and the tension building in every fiber of my being. Whomever I fight tonight, they better bring their game, because I'm hell-bent on destroying someone or something today.

When my cell rings, I force my mind to steady.

"Yo," I answer without looking at the caller ID.

"I know what you've found, Jason. We need to meet," my father says in a low tone.

"No time."

"I need to explain. There are more people you will hurt with this information than me."

I laugh. "You don't need to do shit, Dad, except stay the fuck away from me and Lo."

"You owe me this."

Rage fills me. I don't hold back as I stand from my desk and shut my office door. "I don't owe you one motherfucking thing. You better pray to any god, or the devil himself, that I don't find the reason and opportunity to take you down. Steer clear of me and mine, Father, and I'll do the same."

"Don't you threaten me, boy!"

"I'm no boy, and it's no threat." I don't give him another minute of my time before I disconnect the call.

Immediately, my phone rings again, and again, I don't bother to look at the screen. Sliding my finger to accept the call, I want nothing more than to throw the fucking thing.

"Motherfucker, I told you to back the fuck off!"

"Jason," Lo says my name softly, and I can hear her concern.

"Lo, did my father call you? Or come see you?" I bark out as I grab my keys. If he has reached out to her in any way, I'm going to fuck him up right now.

"No, I was calling to see if you planned to go to the gym after work or go home." She starts to ramble. "I had a moment, and I, uh . . . I thought about dinner. I could bring it home after work, which would be your normal gym time. If you're going home right after, though, you would have to wait the few hours till my shift ends."

"I have a fight." I try to calm my breathing and steady my voice. I don't want her to be upset at work over some bullshit with my father. I also don't want to let her know I am suspicious of him until I have more proof.

I wasn't kidding. If I find he had anything—and I mean anything—to do with her family's deaths, I will kill him with my own two hands.

"Oh, um . . . what time?" She hesitates. "I could come to wherever you are—well, that is, if you want me to."

I'm so amped up. Maybe she does need to come and see me fight.

"Yeah, I'll get you the info. You really think you can handle this shit, Lo?"

She doesn't hesitate at all. "There is nothing I can't face, can't do, or can't see as long as I'm with you. Together?"

The beast inside me settles at her final word.

"Together," I whisper.

"All right, I'll see you there, then. Anything else I need to know?"

"Not right now, angel. I promise, when we have time, I will share with you, but this isn't the time."

"Okay. I'll see you tonight." She clicks off, and I am left in shock.

She said okay without missing a beat. She takes me as I am at every turn. I have never had someone who is with me through everything no matter what.

Regardless, fight night with my woman in my corner causes apprehension to hit me. The last woman I introduced to my world used it all against me time and time again. Lorraine isn't Missy, though. I finally have a woman in my life who doesn't get off on my pain.

The rest of my day passes with me amped up to beat the shit out of my opponent. Brock is picking up Lo so she doesn't have to drive or worry about getting in tonight. I want her to know she is safe with me, even if I'm not directly by her side. Shit gets real at these things, and it certainly isn't the place for just anyone.

This one, we get to fight in the basement of an old gym on the other side of Detroit. Walking in through the front door is an odd feeling, but somehow, it doesn't seem as dirty as what I'm used to.

For a moment, I let myself believe I'm doing something on the up and up.

I will never be a good man. I damn sure won't be a great man, but maybe with Lo, I can finally do something halfway right.

It starts tonight. She will see the worst side of me, no holding back. If, in the end, she can still stand by my side, then she damn sure can take all of me.

I make my way downstairs where the atmosphere

immediately changes from one of working out to the adrenaline-charged, backroom fight that it is. The concrete walls aren't painted down here like upstairs, and there are no posters or mirrors for motivation.

I go to the corner that is roped off for opponents, blowing out my breath long and hard. My lungs burn as I fight to inhale and exhale in the place. The air is damp from the lack of ventilation, and the stench of too many bodies in a small place permeates my nose.

The energy is high, the noise loud, and the space is full. The concrete is cold as I toss my shoes into my bag. I face the wall with my head covered by my hoodie, bouncing on the balls of my feet to get the blood flowing. I notice they have an octagon set up with a floor-to-ceiling cage and a proper mat under us.

I feel eyes on me and turn to the staircase to see her watching me. Her blond hair is once again shining like an angel as she descends the steps to the bottom. Her green and white top flows loosely around her with her jacket draped over her arm, and her jeans hug her hips. The knee-high black boots are sexy as fuck.

I have to stop myself from getting hard at the thought of what she has on under her clothes. I can only hope the fight amps her up, because we are going to bed when we get home, and it won't be to sleep.

Brock guides her to me, and I immediately pull her in for a sloppy kiss. I only pull away when I know I have kissed her hard enough to leave her lips plump and aching.

"This . . ." she says on a whisper. "This is . . ." She bites her bottom lip. "I don't know what it is, but it's hot."

Leaning down, I nip her earlobe. "You're hot, Lo." I run my hand down her back to squeeze her ass through her jeans.

"Are they usually this crowded?" she asks, looking around at all the spectators.

"Each one varies." I keep my arms tightly around her. I should be loosening up my body, but I can't avoid touching her when she is this close to me.

The announcer yells through a bullhorn, getting everyone's attention, "Fighting in the yellow shorts tonight, we have Alex 'Ripper' Long. Fighting in the green shorts tonight, we have Jason 'Cobra' Stanley. This should be a great matchup, as both men are great grapplers and have equal reach."

With a chaste kiss to Lo's lips, I pull away to toss off my hoodie before I climb into the cage. Alex meets my eyes and stares. He should know better than to taunt a cobra.

I smack the snake tattoo on the side of my neck as we dance around each other. A beep sounds, and then we lock onto each other.

I see Brock with Lo in my peripheral vision, and I can't help smiling. My girl, my fight—what a wonderful fucking life. The beast inside me is ready to let loose.

I dive low to take out his legs, but he moves to avoid my reach. I jab out at him as he ducks in and hits me with an uppercut. The contact feels good. The pain brings me to life. Then he goes to grab for me, and I jump back.

I see the dollar bills moving around between people outside of the cage.

I jab again and make contact under his eye. It immediately reddens and swells. With a quick left, I hit him again, breaking his nose. Blood pours out onto the mat as he shakes off the pain. He then throws a right hook at me, and I take the hit to my jaw. As he moves back, though, I take the space and hit him with a roundhouse kick.

KO. He crashes to the mat as people rush in.

The crowd is full of boos and cheers equally. I don't

give a shit. There is only one person here I need approval from, and when my green eyes lock onto her heavenly blue ones, I see pride, love, and I see happiness.

I push my way out of the cage and over to my woman. Dropping my head, I kiss her and don't hold back as my cock comes to life, tenting my shorts. When she grabs me as hard as I am grabbing her, I can feel her energy, and it feeds the beast inside me.

I break away and growl in her ear, "I need in."

She peeks up at me with hooded eyes. "Then what are you waiting for?"

I toss a finger up at Brock and nod my head for him to handle the payout. Then I take her by the hand, grab my bag and hoodie, and walk barefoot up the stairs and out the door of the gym.

People pat my shoulders as we pass by, but I don't stop. I don't slow down until we get to my truck, and I have to reach in my bag for the keys. Putting her between me and the car, I touch my lips to hers, separating them with my tongue. I invade her mouth, unable to get enough.

With her back to my car, I fight with the button on her jeans before I can finally get my hand down her pants. Instantly, my fingers are dipping into her wet heat. I need my cock in there more than I need in my car.

When I remove my hand, she whimpers as I turn her around. Then, taking her hands in mine, I place them on the window of my truck on either side of her head.

"Don't move them."

She nods her head as I slide her jeans and panties down over the globes of her ass.

Seeing her skin out in the cold, Detroit air, knowing anyone could walk up on us, only has me needing inside her more.

I bite her ass cheek, and she rocks back for more.

With her soft shirt against my sweaty chest, I spread her cheeks apart as I pull my cock from my shorts and slide into her.

"Jason," she says in a breathless whisper.

My name on her lips is all the encouragement I need as I slide in and out at a pace that leaves us both unable to catch our breaths.

A win in front of my woman and a win with my woman, this is everything I never thought I could have and more. Fuck yeah. I slide into her once again. Fuck yeah.

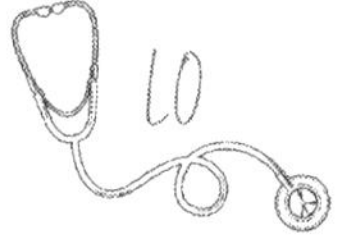

Chapter Twenty - Five

He is inside me as he groans, "This one's for the win. When we get home, it's for you, it's for me, and it's for—"

"Us," I say as I grind against him.

"Yes . . ." he hisses, thrusting harder into me.

I hold myself up against the cold metal, trying to open my legs that are trapped by my pants, as he rubs himself up and down my sensitive folds and thrusts in hard. I lose my breath momentarily, and then he pulls out.

As he rams inside me harshly, I feel my knees weaken. He senses it and wraps one arm around my waist, holding me steady as he plunges in and out of me.

"So hot, so wet . . . fuck," he growls.

I close my eyes, feeling his other hand glide down my tummy before he finds my clit and starts rubbing circles on it. I arch back toward him, and he kisses the side of my neck as he fucks me hard for the win.

His growls, his pants, the manly scent of him, the feeling of his cock and his hand set me off, and I come, fighting pleasure, fighting my cries, fighting to hold back so he can come with me.

"Let go, angel," he hisses.

"Come with me, Jason. Please!" I cry, unable to hold back anymore.

"Fuck yes," he groans, and his thick, hot cock twitches as he fills me with a growl. Then he pulls out quickly and just in time, as people start exiting the building. He pulls up my jeans and opens the door. "Get in."

We drive in silence. His body is still tense, even after his release. He thumps on the steering wheel with his thumb as his knee bounces impatiently. He is amped up from his win, and I'm fired up from seeing how quickly he took his opponent down.

Evidence of our lust on my panties is making me wet, making me want more. I can't get enough of this man.

We are twenty minutes from home, but with traffic, it may take longer.

I close my eyes and picture Jason in his boxing shorts, sweat drenched, and the way he bounced before the fight began. In one swift move, he dropped his opponent to the mat and then looked at me. His nose flared, and then he quickly looked away as his opponent jumped to his feet. Alex, the other man in the cage, hit him hard, and I almost looked away, almost. Something stopped me, though.

His chest expanded, his eyes looked more focused, and he appeared even more ready for the fight than he did before.

When Alex swung again at Jason, my heart was in my chest. I wanted to help him, and Brock had to hold me in place.

Jason hit him not once, but twice. I knew Alex was injured and thought he wouldn't recover. Then he swung at Jason, and Jason ducked right before his strong, muscular frame kicked up, connecting with the side of Alex's head and knocking him to the ground.

I feel the intensity of his stare as the truck stops at a light. I look over to see he is searching my face. He is looking for answers. He's worried.

"Tell me what you're thinking," he demands.

"It was quicker than I thought," I answer.

His face scrunches up. "Angel, I said I'd make it up to you. Have I ever lied to you?"

It takes a minute before I realize he is talking about sex, and I bite my lip to stop myself from laughing.

"You came," he says smugly, then looks away.

Now I laugh out loud, and he shakes his head as he hits the accelerator.

"Don't poke the snake, angel. I will make you sorry you did."

I laugh again. "I was talking about the fight, but if you want to make me sorry, I can pretend I was talking about what just happened between us. You know, the one for the win."

He smirks then shakes his head. I hear a low chuckle, and then he says, "Sorry, I'm a little off."

"If it's any consolation, champ, I think you were pretty right on. A knockout." I smile.

He laughs and grabs my hand, placing it on his shorts. "You do remember I can go more than one round, don't you?"

I grip him hard, and he groans.

"I'm counting on it."

"I need a fucking shower," he declares, pushing up off the bed. "You wanna join me?"

I cross my legs without thinking, and he laughs.

"I promise to leave you alone . . . for a little while, anyway." He grabs my hand and pulls me up.

My legs are shaking, almost rubber-like, and he notices.

He bends down and swoops me up. "Let's take a bath."

"Sounds perfect," I say, scratching my nails up his neck, causing him to shiver.

"You better not do that again," he grumbles.

I shriek when my ass hits the cold countertop he sets me on.

He chuckles. "Did you hear that sizzle?"

"Hear it? I felt it," I answer, allowing myself to sink into the coolness.

He starts the water then walks back over to me, looking over my shoulder into the mirror. He lifts his chin and rolls his eyes.

"He looked worse than you."

"Always do." He sighs.

"Not true."

He grabs me around the hips and spins around before setting me in the bathtub. "That night was an exception. But I would get my ass kicked again if it landed me at your feet once more," he says, stepping in the tub and settling in.

I can't stop the smile that spreads across my face. "You mean it?"

His eyes narrow as he looks me over. "Do you really have to ask?"

I shake my head.

A smile plays on his lips as he pulls me by my ankles toward him. "Good. Now I need to ask, was tonight awful? Is that side of me too ugly? Can you handle—"

I take his face and hold it between my hands as I pull myself onto his lap. "I have never felt happier or safer than I do when I'm with you, regardless of whether I am in this bath or in the basement of a building with a hundred people." I lean in and whisper, "It was incredibly hot, too."

The past week has been amazing with Jason. I told him that I am considering leaving the hospital, that both Dr. Bennetts make me think of the past, and I am ready to move forward. He sends me ads and links he finds for registered nurse positions elsewhere. All are weekends off, all are nine-to-five jobs, and all are in offices. All of them sound like a dream compared to what I am doing now.

I walk out of the lounge and see Ryan walking toward me. I look around and see his father watching us.

"You are really considering leaving here?" Ryan asks once he is within a foot of me.

"It's a good career move for me," I answer with a smile.

"It's him, isn't it?" He looks somber.

"No, I needed a change, and Jason is being very supportive," I reply, walking past him.

"Lorraine."

I stop and turn around.

"I want you to be happy."

"Thank you." I nod. "He makes me happy."

I wake up to find Jason is not in bed. I'm not afraid, though. I know he would never leave me without telling me he was stepping out.

I get up and walk out into the living room, where I find Jason with his hands clasped behind his neck as he stares at the laptop sitting on his legs.

"Fuck," he sputters, and my chest tightens. "There has to be something somewhere." He rolls his neck and sighs. "Come on; let me find a connection. Let me see it. Let me see you, motherfucker."

"Jason," I say as I walk up and put my hands on his shoulders.

He looks up. "You should be sleeping. You have to work tomorrow."

"So do you." I walk around and sit beside him. "Talk to me."

"I'm not getting any closer," he grumbles.

"You've narrowed it down," I say, trying to ease his angst. He looks down. "Jason, what if I was wrong this whole time? What if—"

"Then I'll make damn sure there is no doubt, and then I will push to reopen their case until we find out who did it. Fuck!" He stands up and sets his laptop on the coffee table. "I hate the cops."

I stand up, shut his laptop, and take his hand. "I want to go to bed in the arms of the man who makes me feel safe."

He falls asleep before I do, and I watch him.

It scares me to think I may never find out who killed my family, but it scares me more to think that, if I am wrong, I am pushing him too hard. But what terrifies me most is the thought I could push him completely away.

I can't do that.

I feel my phone vibrate in my pocket as I put back the medical chart. I pull it out of my pocket and sneak into the bathroom.

"Hey, there." I smile as I answer.

"You wanna turn up the heat tonight?" Jason asks.

"Do you really have to ask?" I whisper.

"It's fight night, angel." His voice is gravelly.

"Oh," I say, not knowing if he hears me.

"You sure you're up for it?" he questions.

"Yes." I close my eyes as soon as I realize how throaty I sound.

"You just made me hard," he whispers.

"The next four hours are going to be hell."

"You wet?"

"Jason," I scold lightly.

He laughs. "I'll take that as a yes."

"I can't wait."

The rest of the night is quiet, which makes the time go by even more slowly. I am nearly out of my mind in anticipation of fight night, taking one for the win, one for him, one for me, one for us. I should feel anxious, nervous, worried, but I'm not. I know he will win. I know he will fight hard to get to me. And I will be standing in his corner, just like he is in mine.

I walk out into the cool night air and look around for the black Chevy. I spot lights in the distance and almost run toward them.

Chapter Twenty - Six

"You're off your game tonight, Cobra," Chainz says as I take the hit to my gut.

Where the fuck is she? I keep looking around for Lo, but she's not here. Brock is waiting outside for her, so I have no one in my corner. My head isn't in the fight. For once, my need to beat the shit out of something, out of someone, is gone. My only concern is for her. Where the fuck is she?

"Guess my boys didn't need to step in last time," Chainz goads.

I need him to shut the hell up. I need this fight to be over so I can find Lo.

My insides twist and turn, knotting up as the adrenaline pumps through my system. My nostrils flare as I fight to breathe. My lungs burn as I take his hits.

Backing up, I get the space I need to see clearly. Waiting as I duck and dodge, I find my opening. With a left uppercut, I hit the sweet spot, and down he goes.

His crew rushes the cage, and I ready myself. I will beat the fuck out of every one of them to get to her if need be.

Thankfully, they are too concerned over Chainz's unconscious state to bother with me.

I bolt out and grab my bag. Once again, I don't bother to cover up or put on shoes. I find Brock right out front, still waiting.

"Handle the shit," I say, taking off to my car.

He can keep the money for all I care right now. I need to get to Lo. I need to feel her, touch her, hold her, and breathe her in. I need to know she's okay. She is everything right in my world of wrong.

I call, getting no answer repeatedly. Her voicemail driving me crazy, I drive straight to the hospital. I don't bother to look for her car. She has to be pulling a double shift. It happens in her line of work. Not often, but it does happen.

When I don't find her in the emergency department, I ask the receptionist, and she pages. No response.

She dials the nurses' station. The brown eyes of the woman meet my cold, green stare, and I fight inside to hold it together when she speaks.

"Lorraine is off for the evening, sir."

I slam my fist down on the countertop before taking off out the automatic doors, rushing back to my truck.

I drive absently, calling her over and over with no answer. My panic only rises.

I call the front desk of my complex. She hasn't been seen coming or going since she left for work this morning.

I keep driving and calling and driving. It's not until I stop in the driveway I realize where I have carried myself.

Home.

Well, that's what most people would call it when they come back to the place they grew up. The place my parents live should be home, but it's not, and I don't know that it ever has been.

I jump out of my car and rush to the front, where I pound on the door. My father answers, his surprise visible.

"Jason." He says my name calmly as he steps back to allow me to enter.

"What the fuck did you do with her?"

"Who?"

"Don't you fuck with me right now! I know what you and your council friends did. I know about the money you all filter around and split. I have proof and a backup, so do not fuck with me. Where the hell is she?" I roar, not caring who hears me.

"Jason, you watch your tone and your mouth. I'll ruin you personally if it comes to it, son or not."

I can't contain my fury. I can't hold back. I put my hands around his throat and squeeze.

"Your days of having any power over me are gone. I'll fucking kill you, and I won't lose one bit of sleep. Where the fuck is Lo?"

He slaps and pushes at my forearms, trying to relieve the pressure from his neck unsuccessfully. He fights to shake his head. He gasps for air, and I squeeze more firmly. He then kicks out, wasting precious energy.

I back him up to the wall and slam his head into it. "Where the fuck is Lo?" I yell again.

I let up enough for him to answer. He chokes at first before finally catching his breath somewhat.

"I don't know where she is. It's not my job to track your newest whore." He looks up at me, my own green eyes staring back at me. "I'll be happy to show her what a Stanley man is capable of when you're done with her, though. Missy sure was a lot of fun."

I swing, and my fist connects with his face.

He smiles at me sinisterly. "All those hours at the gym and that's all you've got?"

I swing and connect again.

He is off balance and stumbles.

"That one is for her sister." I hit him again from the other side, and he sways. "That one is for her mother."

He shakes his head. "What the fuck are you talking about?" he growls, gripping his now bloody nose and tipping his head back.

"You and your goons killed them all to protect your scheme."

He snaps his head to attention. His eyes meet mine once again. "Jason, I'm a lot of things, and none of them are good, but I did not have anything to do with those murders."

I grab him as I kick out behind his knees, taking him down before he can realize what's happening. As I straddle him, I am in control. For the first time in my life, I have the power over him.

"I didn't . . . I didn't," he stammers with his eyes as wide as saucers. "None of us had anything to do with the Bosch family murders. Yes, he knew what we had done, and he threatened to out us, but we didn't have him killed."

If he didn't . . . if they didn't . . .

My mind races.

I take his head in my hands and slam it into the tiled floor. It knocks him out, and I don't bother to care if I did damage or not. I have to find Lo.

Jumping off my unconscious father, I rush out of the house, not even bothering to shut the door behind me.

Driving home, I try to focus my mind. I try to call the Bennetts, getting no answer.

Where are you, Lorraine?

Once I get to the condo, I pace, trying to think of what to do now, only to find I am making the cats panic as they feed off my energy. I pet Boots as Socks keeps his distance, sitting on a box from Lo's house. I go over and pick up the cat.

"It's okay, buddy. I'm going to find your momma. I promise," I whisper to the fur ball.

The box gets my attention. I don't know why, but my gut says to look inside. The flaps of the box have separated some, and I can see a pale blue notebook at the top.

Putting Socks down, I sit on the couch, sliding the box over to me. Then I open it and find a sky-blue journal with a detailed peacock feather on the front. I trace the edge of the book before turning to the first page. The handwriting is fluffy, like a female's, but it's not Lorraine's. I have seen her scribble notes around the house, so I am familiar with her handwriting.

February 12, 2011

I sat, watching her sleep. I sat there and watched her. There isn't another person in this world I have ever wished to be except her. I would give anything to be able to be like her.

Things are not complicated. She keeps her life simple. She does what is expected and keeps to herself. Boys don't matter; status doesn't matter; clothes, makeup, hair color, friends—none of those things matter to her.

I watched her sleep, knowing she hasn't been burned, broken, or felt battered inside. I envy that.

I wanted to wake her, but I didn't. Instead, I walked across the hall, grabbed this diary, and decided to fill it with the story I want to tell her but won't, because she didn't go asking for this kind of pain. And although we are twins who have shared everything, I cannot share this, never this.

I love Ryan. I love him so much. He is generous, giving,

caring, and he loves me. He still says it through texts, but I don't say it back.

Last week was our one-year anniversary. One year of being the girlfriend of the boy everyone wanted and nobody could have: Ryan Bennett.

Ryan made plans for us to have a weekend at the river house. It was the first time we would have a weekend alone. No hiding, no need to hurry, a weekend to hold each other and make love without the threat of interruption.

I made up an elaborate story, and my overprotective parents bought it hook, line, and sinker.

When he called the day before and said he didn't think he could make it, I made plans with a friend to avoid arousing suspicion.

When he sent me a text telling me that he could meet me, I told my friend's parents I had to get home. I lied and said Lo was having boy problems and needed me.

When I got to the river house, I couldn't get out of my car fast enough. I nearly ran up the dimly lit walkway. Then, when I opened the door, I saw candlelight, and the fireplace was roaring. My heart swelled at the thought behind such a romantic setting.

When I took my coat off and placed it over the back of the couch, I saw him, and I saw a woman on the floor in front of the fire on the bearskin rug. She was naked, straddling him. The noises coming from her made me sick. The way his hands gripped her ass and guided her made my heart break. The things he said to her disgusted me.

"That's it. If you wanna fuck me, you little whore, then fuck me right. That's it, you little slut, you dirty, filthy little slut." He groaned.

I covered my mouth to strangle my cry, and then she looked over her shoulder.

I froze. I couldn't move. I couldn't scream. I couldn't

believe what I was seeing. She turned around and sat on him backward. I heard his hand hit her ass hard, and she looked up and saw me.

She didn't look surprised. She held his dick in her hands, her eyes glued to mine, and she sank down on him. My body trembled, and her eyebrow rose as she fucked him, crying out his name, all the while looking at me.

I turned and ran out of the house. I don't even remember driving home. I have no idea how I made it without getting into an accident.

I don't know what I am going to do. I don't know how something like this could happen. And I don't know how I couldn't have seen it all along.

I want to fall asleep, but when I close my eyes, I see her, I hear him, and I feel my heart breaking again.

My stomach tightens, and my fear heightens. That sick son of a bitch used his love for Hi to fuck Lo when he never loved Hi. No, Ryan Bennett loves his dick and nothing more.

I'm a fucked-up mess of a man, but this is beyond the realm of pain even I would inflict upon someone I claim to love.

I dial Ryan Bennett. No answer. I dial Dr. Bennett. No fucking answer. I dial Mrs. Bennett. I come up empty-handed.

I sit back with my phone in one hand and the diary in the other. As I turn the page, I fight inside not to completely lose my shit and take out every motherfucker who ever came into contact with the Bosch family.

February 19, 2011

It has been a week that I have ignored his calls, deleted his messages, and felt like I existed in a world where nothing was real. In a world where things that never should happen do happen. Things that are wrong, disgusting, and despicable. A world where Ryan and her sleep together.

He was outside today when I came out of school. He blocked me in and wouldn't let me out. He got in my car, and he cried. He cried and told me he didn't understand why I was avoiding him, that he was sorry he couldn't make it.

I slapped him across the face and told him I saw him. I saw them. I couldn't even say her name. I told him I hate him, that he was disgusting, and all six feet of him curled into himself and trembled, right before opening the door and throwing up.

I told him to get out, to go to hell, to never look at me or speak to me again.

He told me that, since it started with her, he has wanted to die. The guilt, the disgust, the shame, the lies ended that night. She promised him it would be the last time. She promised him all the photos, videos, everything she held over his head would be destroyed if he would just be with her one last time.

I told him I saw them. I told him I got a message from his phone telling me to meet him. I told him I heard him and that it was something I would never forget and never forgive.

He told me he loved me, and if it took him forever to make me forget, he would. He told me if it took him forever to make me forgive him, he would. He told me if he had to die trying, he would do that, too.

He wouldn't get out of the car. He looked like hell. He cried, and then he stopped.

"I was fifteen; she was eighteen. I am so sorry. Forgive me and tell my father I love him. Tell him I'm sorry."

He let go of my hand. I didn't let go of his.

I don't know if I can do this. I don't know, but like he

said, he was fifteen, and she was eighteen. I sure as hell am going to try, and I am going to make the bitch pay.

I fight my own need to vomit. Ryan Bennett, who the hell was the girl riding you that night?

Going on instinct alone, I drive to the Bennetts' home and wait. I have nothing else to go on. I have to find her. I know something isn't right. I feel it, and I'm not going anywhere until I have some fucking answers.

Answers for Lo, for Hi, for me, and for us. Everything is for us.

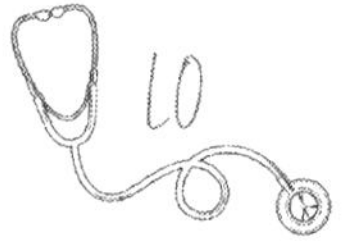

Chapter Twenty - Seven

I wake up, fighting to open my eyes. My body hurts, and I can't move.

I hear someone whistling.

I clear my throat. "Help," comes out weakly, and then I feel a cloth cover my mouth before my eyes are covered, too.

Jason will worry that I'm not there for the fight. He will think I ran. He will think I don't love him.

"Jason." My cry is muffled.

"Jason?" I hear a voice chide. "Jason or Ryan? Ryan or Jason? Oh, the choices you had. The fun, the games, the heroes, the villains."

"Please," I cry.

"Begging must be genetic." The voice is female. Rochelle. Oh, God. "Your mother begged for her life. Your sister didn't, shame on her. Your father, he cried like a little bitch as he watched me kill them."

"Why are you doing this?" I scream, unsure if she can hear me.

"I'm doing this because you deserve it." I feel a sharp blow to my head, and consciousness leaves me.

I wake sitting up, tied to a chair, and my head is pounding. I am facing a fireplace in a cabin.

I look up on the mantel and see pictures of Ryan and his family. I'm at the river cabin.

Why would Rochelle bring me here?

It's hot, so hot in here. My throat is dry, and I need a drink.

"Thirsty," I croak out, but no one answers. "Thirsty! I'm thirsty! Rochelle!" I yell. "I know it's you. The Bennetts have security! They'll know. They'll find me!"

I am going to fight. I want to fight. I am no longer afraid. I am going to fight for them, for vengeance. I finally have something to live for.

Jason.

"Stop hiding from me! Stop being a coward and face me!"

"Stupid, stupid, little whore." I hear her behind me. "Your paranoia makes this so much more fun."

I turn my head and hear a burst of laughter from the other side of me.

"I should be afraid of you, but I'm not. If you're going to kill me, do it! Kill me, you sick bitch!"

I hear the floorboard creak and look back, fighting the fear. I cannot be afraid.

"He loved her. Ryan loved her. He pretended you were her, made you wear a wig and all. How did it feel? How did it feel to fuck your sister's boyfriend? He never loved you," she taunts.

I cringe at someone knowing my dirty little secret, sex with Ryan as Heidi.

"Face me!"

"The ugly duckling. The sweet little girl whose family

was slaughtered," she sneers. "A whore! Nothing but a little whore!"

The back of the chair gets pulled, and tied to it, I crash to the ground. Pain sears through my body. I hold my mouth closed so I don't cry out.

I open my eyes and gasp. "Why! Why! Why!"

From the corner of my eyes, I see her boot coming closer and then feel it connect with the side of my head.

I wake up in pain. I'm cold, tied to a bed, and I am naked.

"Wakey, wakey." I see her standing beside the bed, holding a knife. "Oh, there she is. Do you have a headache, Lorraine?"

"Fuck you," I spit out, and the back of her hand immediately connects with the side of my face.

"Is that any way to talk to the woman hosting you tonight?"

"Why! Why are you doing this?"

"Oh, poor little Lorraine. Such the sweet and innocent little thing until you fucked Ryan!" She hits me again.

"I have no idea what you—"

Another blow and the metallic taste of blood fills my mouth.

"I saw you, whore. I saw you and him!"

"He's your brother!" I scream at her.

"No!" She grabs her own hair. "No, he's not! If we'd found each other before they did, he would have loved me! He would have loved me and not her!"

I try my best to keep calm. Rochelle is clearly insane, yet I don't care. I hate her. I hate him.

Did he know? Did he know she killed my family? Did Ryan know she killed the girl he said he loved? Oh, God. Oh, God, she killed them! She killed them all.

I feel tears coming. I feel my body tremble.

Jason. Oh, God, he thinks his father had something to do with my family's death. What have I done?

I need him to know. I need to tell him I'm sorry. I need to find a way to get out of this and back to him.

Tonight, he fights in a cage while I will fight just as hard for us.

"You're right!" I cry out. "He would have loved you."

"Don't patronize me!"

"I'm not!" I yell. I can't yell. I have to keep calm. "I've seen the way he looks at you. He cares for you."

"I know he does! He loves me." She covers her face. "He loves me, and if you and that man weren't nosing around, I would have left you alone. I would have, but now I can't. I can't, and it's your fault!"

"I want to help you. I want to get back to Jason. Then you can get back to Ryan. No one has to know."

She laughs maniacally. "I killed your family! Do you think I believe you?"

Biting back rage, I try to say whatever I can in order to make it out of here alive. "If they weren't gone, I would have never met Jason."

She looks at me curiously.

Oh, please forgive me, Heidi.

"Heidi wouldn't have let me be with a man like him."

Her eyes narrow.

"She would have hated him like she did anyone else I ever wanted to date."

Rochelle nods. "She threatened to tell. She threatened to tell my mother, Ryan's father."

"She didn't understand," I say as bile fills my mouth.

She shakes her head. "She needed to die."

I hold back a sob and close my eyes.

She grips my shoulders and shakes me. "She needed to die!"

"Okay!" I cry out. "Okay!"

I open my eyes, and they meet hers. Her eyes are as black as night, her pupils fully dilated. She is fucking gone.

"He knows," she whispers and smiles. "He knows I killed them. He hates that I killed them."

"I'm sure he hates the position it puts you in." I cringe inwardly.

"What position!" she spits, and her saliva hits my face.

"He loves you, right?"

"Of course he does!"

"That position. Putting someone he loves in the position that they"—I pause and try to remain calm through the lie—"kill for love."

"I did it for love. I did it all for love." She steps back and starts pacing. "I went to talk to her. After she threatened to expose us, I wanted to make sure she kept her mouth shut. Your parents came into the room and told me to leave. I hit him over the head with the barrel of my stepfather's gun. I made them tie him up. Then I made your sister tie your mom. She wouldn't stop screaming, so I cut your mother. I cut her up good."

I close my eyes and try to focus on something other than her voice as she continues to tell me how she slaughtered my family. I don't know how I manage, but I do.

"I didn't shoot them." She sits at the end of the bed. "It would have been easier, but then Ryan's father would have gone to jail. It was smart thinking on my part. It all was. No one suspected a twenty-two-year-old graduate student could pull that off."

"I need to use the bathroom," I tell her.

"No. No, because I haven't decided what I am going to do with you yet." She sneers, "I can't stand the sight of you."

"I understand," I lie. "Can I at least get a drink? My mouth is dry. And maybe a blanket? I'm very cold."

She stands up and walks out of the room. I pull on the ropes tied to my wrists, trying to break free, but the pain sears through my right wrist, and I know it's broken from the fall. I whimper and close my eyes tightly.

No, I tell myself. No crying. Be strong, be strong.

She leaves me alone for a long time. I don't know if I am in shock or if I am just unfeeling. I know my head, my wrists, my whole body hurts, but I don't let it take me.

I ready myself for a fight. I ready myself for vengeance. I ready myself for any opportunity given to unleash years of fury. And if all else fails, I ready myself for death.

She comes in and tells me to open my mouth as she holds a glass of water in her hand. I do as she asks. I open my mouth for more, and she shoves something in it and holds my mouth shut.

"Swallow!"

I fight as I feel the pill dissolve in my mouth, trying to push it to the side with my tongue so it doesn't go down my throat.

"Swallow the fucking pill. If you want to use the bathroom, swallow it!"

She is growing more and more irritated. I open my mouth and stick out my tongue.

"Not as stupid as you look," she sneers. "In twenty minutes, after the pill kicks in, you can use the bathroom."

"What did you give me?" I ask, trying to remain calm.

"Don't worry about it."

She leaves again, and when she comes back in the room, she looks at me. "I won't hesitate to shoot you in the fucking head if you try anything stupid."

She unties my wrists and then my feet. I look at my wrists, both swollen, one definitely broken.

I stand up from the bed, and she shoves me. I fall on the floor, and she laughs.

"Get the fuck up, whore."

I push myself up on my elbows, ignoring the pain. I know it's now or never.

I turn and lunge at her.

"You sick bitch! You sick fucking bitch!" I use what strength I have to try and wrestle the gun from her hands. It slips from her hands and slides across the floor.

She is bigger and unharmed. She pushes me off her and kicks me.

"No! Please no!"

I scramble toward the gun, and she kicks me again. I reach for it, grasping the cold metal.

"I don't want to kill you," I tell her, pushing past the pain to hold the gun in my hands like Jason taught me. "I don't want to, but I will."

I sit up, pointing the gun at her, and she laughs.

I click the safety off. "I will. Don't you move!"

"Fuck you!" she screams and lunges at me.

Chapter Twenty - Eight

Ryan and Dr. Bennett pull up in the same car. I don't even bother saying hello as I go directly to the passenger seat and yank Ryan out.

"You sick, sorry bastard! I know what you did to Heidi. Now you tell me where the fuck Lo is, and you tell me now, or so help me God, I'm going to rip you apart slowly and painfully like you did Heidi's heart."

His mouth opens and closes, but no words come out as Dr. Bennett rounds the front of their overpriced foreign car.

"Now, Jason, there must be some sort of misunderstanding. Our family loves Lorraine, and we loved Heidi as well. Ryan didn't do anything but fall in love as a teenager with a girl he planned a future with. It was ended all too soon and tragically, but he loved her, and then we took in Lorraine."

"What do you know?" Ryan finally croaks out.

I pull him back and slam him against the car. "What do I know? What the fuck do I know! I know you cheated on Hi. I know she wanted nothing more to do with you until you threatened to kill yourself. I know that after she died, you manipulated Lo into wearing a wig and fucking you, all so you could pretend you still had Hi. I know that you did all of this to Lo in this very house." I point to their home behind me.

"You wonder why she went back to her own mental prison." I look to Dr. Bennett. "Because living here, she wasn't Lorraine, not to your twisted-ass son. She was Heidi."

I turn my gaze back on Ryan. "And you were dead to Heidi long before she was dead to the earth. So tell me, pretty boy, who were you fucking?"

He hangs his head in shame.

"Dammit." I shake him and slam him into the car again. "I don't know where Lo is. I don't know who the fuck killed her family, but I do know it ties back to this family. So, Ryan, I'm going to ask you one more time, and if you ever loved Heidi one little bit or cared for Lorraine even the slightest, you will answer me. Who were you fucking?"

He looks at his dad.

"Let it be, Mr. Stanley," the doctor practically growls at me.

I turn to him, releasing Ryan, and hold my hands up. "You have no idea what these are capable of when someone I care about is in danger. Lo is a woman of her word. She said she was going to be somewhere, and she wasn't there. I can't find her, and I have a feeling you guys somehow might know where she is or who she's with. I don't want anything more than answers." I shake my head at him. "You've gotta know, Dr. Bennett, that I'll get those answers by any means necessary."

"She's missing?" Ryan asks from behind me.

"That's what the fuck I said and why the fuck I'm

here." I look over my shoulder at him. "Honestly, the past is the past. I don't care where you get your dick wet. I care about finding Lo and making her feel safe for now and forever."

"Rochelle," he whispers.

Dr. Bennett moves toward us. "Shut up, Ryan. Shut the hell up right now. You're under duress. Our lawyers will blame coercion. Shut your mouth, son."

I laugh. "You think I'm going to the cops? No, I know the system is fucked from the inside out, so no, this won't go beyond us." I look at Ryan. "Rochelle, as in your stepsister?"

He nods.

"Where the fuck is she, then?"

He looks at his dad then back at me before shrugging his shoulders.

I swing and connect with Dr. Bennett's jaw. He stumbles and falls backward onto the pavement of their driveway. I land on top of him and start pounding. The cobra inside me is ready to kill.

"Stop!" Ryan yells like the pussy he is. "The river house! Rochelle stays at the family house when she's in town, but she's not expected here this weekend."

I get off Dr. Bennett and grab Ryan, yanking him over to my car. Pushing him inside, I round the front and climb in.

Dr. Bennett is on the ground, holding his head. I don't give a shit if he calls the cops. Let them come to the river house. I have a feeling there is a much bigger story for them than my assault and battery charges on the doctor back there.

"Directions," I bark, and Ryan mumbles off where we need to go.

I peel out of the driveway and don't bother looking in the rearview mirror.

"Rochelle is sick. She's mentally ill," Ryan says, looking out the window.

"You're right; she is sick. As in sick and twisted. At eighteen, why would she want to fuck her fifteen-year-old stepbrother?" I raise my hand. "Never mind, I don't want to know. Just shut the fuck up and let me get to Lo."

"I hope she hasn't done it again," he says in a whisper I don't think he intended for me to hear.

I grab him by the hair and slam his head into the window of my door. "Talk, Bennett. What could she do again?"

"It's my fault," he cries out as tears stream down his face.

"Look here, fucker. I don't care if you piss your pants or cry a fucking river; the only thing that matters is Lo. Now you fucking talk and tell me everything you know."

"It's because of me. She killed them all because of me."

I slam my hand down on my steering wheel as I turn down the secluded road to their river house.

"She wasn't taking her meds. I told her Heidi was going to break up with me if I didn't end it with her. I loved Heidi. Rochelle promised no more—she promised. She went to the Boschs' house. She said it was just to talk to Heidi. Only, when she got home, she was covered in blood, wearing a sick smile."

I don't bother listening anymore. I throw the car in park and jump out. The river house is smaller than the Bennetts' home, but no less elaborate. The lights are all off, and there is no sign of life here. I don't care. This is the only lead I have, so I have to follow it.

At the front door, I turn the knob to find it locked. At

the back door, I find the same, so I bust the glass and reach in with my hand bleeding to get inside.

Immediately, I hear her voice arguing with Rochelle. Following the sounds, I storm into a bedroom, not thinking about what I may find on the other side of the door. Ryan barrels in behind me.

The sight in front of us kills me inside.

Lorraine's blond hair is a mess around her face. There are streaks of blood down her mouth and across her cheek like she tried to wipe it away. She stands with a gun pointed at Rochelle, but her right wrist is swollen and bruised and at an awkward angle. She isn't shaking; there is fury in her voice; and she has the gun in a firm grip, given all her injuries.

"Lo," I say on a whisper, and her eyes come to mine.

"She did it, Jason," Lo says with venom in her voice. "She killed them."

"She's sick," Ryan tries to defend.

I look over my shoulder at him and glare.

For the first time in my life, I am fighting the demons inside me to handle this. I want nothing more than to have Rochelle die by my hands, but there are guiltier parties than just her. Ryan and Dr. Bennett know what she is capable of, yet they still put Lo in danger.

"I'm sick and twisted," Rochelle cackles at Lorraine before spitting at her feet.

Reaching out, I put her in a sleeper hold.

Ryan steps toward me, and Lo moves the gun to him. "Don't, Ryan. I don't want to hurt you."

When Rochelle passes out, I drop her to the floor before grabbing the asshole beside me.

"She's sick. She's fine when she's on meds," Ryan continues to defend her.

I pull his arms painfully behind his back. He doesn't

fight me like I would expect; he just keeps his eyes on Rochelle.

"She's not right. Dad always told me I had to look out for her, even though I was younger. He said she was delayed, and I had to be her protector." He shakes his head and continues mumbling. "I didn't do my job. I didn't protect her from the pain of the world. It was my job to keep her safe, yet I'm the one who broke her heart. She's okay if she takes the pills." He looks at Lo. "I promise you, if she takes her medication, she can be controlled."

"I think you're all sick if you ask me, fucker. There is no controlling someone like her," I tell him as I take off my belt and tie him to the bed with it. "Put the gun down, angel. Don't have this on your conscience. We do this the right way. Everything with us will be right."

When Rochelle starts to come to, I scoop her up and lay her beside Ryan. She looks at me then at him and snuggles closer like he can somehow protect her. I watch as Ryan fights to keep himself from throwing up at her touch. I shake my head, not understanding their dynamic.

Reaching in my back pocket, I toss my phone to Lorraine. "You need to call the cops."

She grabs it and winces from the pain in her wrist.

I stand over Rochelle and Ryan, waiting for either of them to make a move.

Before Lo can get off the phone, I hear the sound of a car pulling up. I take Lo into my arms and hold her tight as I tuck the gun into my waistband.

Dr. Bennett rushes in and sees Ryan and Rochelle, but says nothing.

Lo looks at me, then at him, and I give her a squeeze.

"Why?" she asks him. "Why help her and then take me in?"

"We thought we could make it up to you," Dr. Bennett

says without meeting her eyes. He doesn't move into the room with us, just stands in the doorway as we hear the sirens getting closer.

I fight my need to make them all suffer. I fight the urge to drain their lives with my own hands. I will fight my demons to give her the good she gives to me. I will fight the demons to give her a new start.

Lorraine is my angel, and as much as I believe in an eye for an eye, she's had enough tragedy in her lifetime. I will not leave her with more dark memories.

With her securely against me, I place a kiss on top of her head. I will fight with everything I have to keep her safe with me until my very last breath.

"How?" She looks up at me. "How did you know?"

"I didn't. Heidi wrote it in her journal. Heidi gave you to me."

"She always looked out for me." There is sadness in her tone.

"She loved you, Lo."

She leans against me. "She was my Hi."

"Always, baby."

She breathes heavily against me. "All I wanted was to get back to you."

I tip her chin up so she looks at me. "I'd move heaven and earth to find you, angel." I pause to give her the words I have never meant more in my entire life than I do now . . . with her. "I love you."

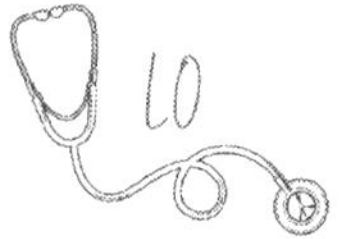

Chapter Twenty - Nine

After the detectives took my statement in the hospital, I hated myself for asking what would happen to the Bennetts.

"Dr. Bennett was good to me," I whisper, hoping like a child hopes when their eyes are closed that no one will see them. I need to be honest with the police officer, even if it hurts or makes me feel less than sane.

Jason's chest rumbles as he sits on the hospital bed, kicks his boots off, and pulls me into a protective hug, which is exactly what I need right now.

"He and his son are facing some pretty stiff charges. Both will lose their medical licenses. As for Rochelle, she is going away for a very long time. You have nothing to worry about anymore, Miss Bosch." The cop looks at Jason, and I assume he told them how I lived in fear for so many years.

I hear a knock on the hospital door, but the medication the doctor gave me or the drugs in my system from Rochelle make it impossible to open my eyes. Still, I feel Jason tense up. I can't manage to say anything coherent, but he gives me a gentle squeeze and a kiss on the top of my head, and I know without a doubt that things will be all right.

"What?" Jason asks harshly to who I'm not sure.

It's a fog in my mind as I think I hear his father speak. "Just got off the phone with the press. It seems my son's a hero." I hear shoes against the tile floor as Jason's dad steps closer. "You going to drop your little investigation?"

"You can turn right around and leave." Jason's chest rumbles as he speaks.

"I see," his father says calmly. "I will let you know, the house your little—"

"My girlfriend," Jason interrupts, and the words bring me a new kind of peace.

"Yes, of course. Well, it sold."

"No, thank you. I don't want to owe you shit," Jason says in a low whisper. Clearly he wants nothing to do with his father; I can't blame him for not accepting his help.

"It wasn't me. I had nothing to do with it. Although, I did call to put an offer in to make this all"—he pauses—"go away. But if you insist on pushing forward with your witch hunt against me, I can promise charges against her will be brought—"

"Shit-can the threats, Father. She wanted her family's killer brought to justice. It happened. This is over."

"Do I have your word?"

"You self-important, arrogant ass," Jason grumbles. "Just leave. She needs her rest, and honestly, so do I."

"I've made sure you've been approved for an extended leave at the office," Mayor Stanley says, but Jason doesn't respond. "If you need anything . . ." He leaves it hanging, and then I hear him walk out the door.

"Jason," I whisper.

"Sleep, angel," he whispers back.

. . .

It has been two weeks since I left the hospital. Jason has been amazing. He has been patient with me, kind and nurturing. With two broken wrists and casts, he has taken on all my personal hygiene . . . all of it.

At first, I was completely devastated. I even cried, but he didn't bat an eye. It was like a job to him, and he reminded me that being a nurse, I should be accepting of his help.

I nodded, and he smiled in a very gentle, caring way. Then he told me that he loved me and that there was nothing he wouldn't do for me. I believe him with all my heart, and I feel the same way.

I hang up the phone, thinking I am alone in the room, and I let my emotions overtake me.

When I look up, he is walking in the bedroom, wiping his hand on a towel.

"Talk to me, Lo."

"My grandparents are coming in for the pretrial. They wanted to stay with me—us. I can't tell them no." I have no idea how he can understand what I'm saying since I am a blubbering mess.

He sits down next to me and rubs my legs. "This is your home. Of course they can stay."

"That's not it." I wipe my eyes and flop back on the bed. "They'll know everything. They'll know how awful I am, how—"

"If they say that, I'll be hard-pressed to keep my mouth shut. Where the fuck were they?" He flops down beside me.

"I pushed them away, Jason. I chose to stay. I listened to him. I thought, What's a couple months? I never expected—"

"Of course you didn't. No one would have." He rolls to his side and kisses my tears. "Look at me. There is not one thing we can't get through. We've more than proved that."

"You promise?"

"I don't need to promise, Lo. A promise given is one begging to be broken. My word is mine: good, bad, or ugly."

He spends the entire day cleaning and moving things out of his guest room for my grandparents, stacking everything into the master closet and leaving some boxes by the entryway.

Brock comes to help, though Jason didn't ask him to. He just showed up and took boxes away.

"Same place?" Brock asks.

"Yeah, that Nest place, I don't like the Caldwells, but Morrison and his woman did set up something nice for the community. I'll do my part in support of Tatiana and the family she has found with them," he grumbles.

Brock gives me a sympathetic glance and a nod before leaving.

"We need to do some shopping," Jason tells me as he leans against the doorjamb, looking into the bedroom. "How does that online shit work?"

"We can go out, Jason." Apparently, I'm not as convincing as I thought I was.

"Show me," he instructs as he walks over and grabs his laptop.

He walks out of the bathroom, wearing khaki pants and a button-down shirt, looking nervous.

I look down at myself in a navy blue dress that hits just below my knees and a matching jacket.

"They're meeting us at the courthouse. Their plane was delayed," I tell him.

"I know. You told me, remember?" he says as he walks toward me.

"Right. I forgot." I shake my head.

"Understandable." He hesitantly leans in and gives me a peck on the cheek.

When I reach out and grab his hand like it's a lifeline; he sighs.

"Jason, something's changed," I say quietly.

"Everything has changed," he agrees.

"Will it always be this way?"

"I hope so." His eyes narrow. "Are we okay?"

"Yes." I sigh, realizing I'm being ridiculous and knowing I am trying to redirect this nervous energy.

"Talk to me." He grips my elbow. "Look at me when you do."

"I miss you." I keep my eyes closed, but I raise my chin.

"I need the words, Lo."

I shake my head.

"Lo. Talk. To. Me," he says in a voice I have missed, one that makes my body come to life. "I'm not a mind reader here."

I open my eyes and stare into his, heat against heat.

He steps toward me and raises my arms, resting them on his shoulders. "You need this now?"

"I always do," I say with my lip quivering. "But if you don't—"

His lips crash into mine, and I open my mouth to his. His tongue caresses mine, and he grips my hips, pulling me snugly against him. I feel his erection against my stomach as he devours my mouth.

He pulls back and hikes my dress up slowly as he looks down at me. "You think I haven't craved this?"

I shrug.

"Angel, it's been hell lying next to you every night. I have been giving you time, space—"

"I didn't want it. I wanted you."

He lifts me up, and I wrap my legs around him while he unbuttons his pants, pushes my panties to the side, and rubs himself against my opening.

"It's gonna be fast."

"Please." I push against him.

He thrusts upward, and I cry out.

"Fuck," he groans, pivoting his hips as he pushes in farther, walking us toward the kitchen island.

As soon as my ass hits the granite, he thrusts in and out of me, holding nothing back, not being cautious or going easy. He is giving me exactly what I need, and I quickly fall apart, connected to him.

When we walk into our home with my grandparents, he watches them as they appraise his home—our home. He carries their bags to the spare bedroom, and I look at my grandmother, whose arm has been wrapped around my waist since we got out of the car.

"So, this boy . . . ?"

"Jason." I nod and look at her.

"Do you love this Jason?"

"I do, and he loves me, too." I smile.

"And he's the one . . ." She pauses.

"He saved me." My voice cracks, and I clear my throat. "He loves me. I feel safe with him."

"Then we love him, too." She smiles. "Very much."

I look up and see him stop dead in his tracks when he hears her. He takes in a deep breath and swallows hard.

"Jason," my grandfather says, extending his hand. "I don't know how we can ever repay you."

"No need." He nods. "I would do anything for her."

My grandmother sobs into her hands. "We should have been here."

"I should have come with you. I should have left—"

Jason is at my side, holding my head against his chest. "No, you were both where you were supposed to be, and the assholes responsible are behind fucking bars."

"Come home with us now," my grandmother cries, and Jason tenses. "Come home with us."

"My home is with Jason. But I promise I won't hide from you or push you away anymore." I reach out and hug her.

"And we promise, if you try, we won't let you. I wasn't strong enough then," my grandmother says, wrapping her arms around Jason and me. "I am so sorry, Lorraine."

As we lie in bed that night after quietly making love, Jason asks me, "What ties do you have to this place?"

"You," I answer honestly.

"I'm ready for a change if you are." He looks down at me. "Nothing is holding me here. If you wanna leave this hellhole, I'm with you every step of the way. I love you, Lo. I love you so much."

Epilogue

Three months later

She is on her back in the entryway with her dress bunched up around her waist. Her panties are on the floor beside us. I carried her across the threshold to our new home in Ormond Beach, Florida, before laying her down and breaking our home in right.

Lifting her legs onto my shoulders, I drop my head to her pussy and lick her outer lips before parting them and rolling my tongue over her nub as I tease her opening. She rocks her hips, wanting more. When she cries out my name, I lean back and release my cock, sliding into her.

"Couldn't make it any farther, huh?" she says breathlessly while I'm not holding back.

"Fuck no," I say with a smile before crashing my mouth onto hers. I taste the mint she ate earlier, and her pussy juices mix with the taste in the most delicious way. I break away and growl against her ear. "Angel, I'm just getting started."

She laughs, and I swear I have died and gone to heaven. I'm balls deep inside her in our home we recently purchased while she is carefree. Yeah, it doesn't get any better.

The hold of the past was left in Detroit. The cycle of abuse ends there. We both agreed we would start fresh with each other and not let the past define our future.

I used my paid leave from the city to put my condo on the market. I declined the first offer since I'm pretty sure my father was behind it. When multiple offers started coming in, the place actually got into a bidding war that earned me ten thousand over my asking price.

Since Lorraine and I have no ties to Detroit anymore, and she wanted a chance with her grandparents, we made the move to Florida. They live in Deltona, which isn't too far away. Using the money from the sale of my place, we put a nice down payment on our new construction, four-bedroom, three-bathroom house with a pool. We had been staying in a studio apartment until we could get into this place. Home sweet fucking home.

I scored a job with the contractor who built the home. There is nothing more satisfying for me than to see something come together from the ground up by my hands. It's rewarding. I have never been afraid of hard work. With Lo by my side, I'm even more determined to make it my way this time.

Lorraine had to have her nursing license approved from Detroit to Florida, which took some time and a test, but she is certified here now. She also found a job at a pediatric doctor's office, so no more night shifts, twelve-hour shifts, or weekend work.

We both leave early in the morning and come home to

have our dinner together before going to bed and repeating the same thing the next day. There is calmness in having a routine. More than that, there is calmness in knowing Lo is with me through everything.

I slide into her as I find my release. "You are home, Lo."

She looks up at me, her angel blue eyes finding their way to lock onto my green ones. She wraps her arms around me tightly and says, "As long as I'm with you, I'm always home."

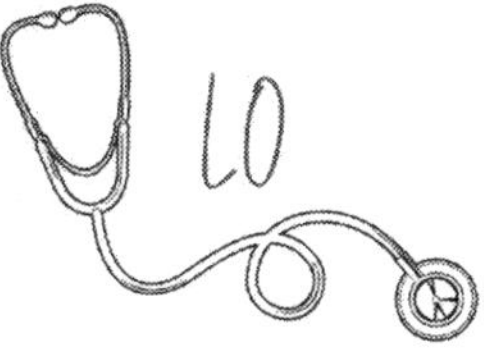

Home.

How could a word with only four letters mean more than anything one could ever have imagined? It's more than a house, more than four walls, more than a place to hang your hat.

Home.

If you asked me four years ago what home was, I would have shuddered at the thought of it. My home—the place I was raised, loved, nurtured, belonged—became my hell. Not only did I accept it, but I embraced it. I didn't want to be there. I didn't want to be in a world that my family was not. I couldn't be anywhere else, either. Not until I brought their killer to justice.

Hate and fear overtook my heart. The only time I felt

like it was still beating was while at work, because I felt needed. I felt like I could do something that mattered. I felt like I could save people.

I am graced with Jason's laugh, with his dimple, his love, and his touch every day. I give it back to him without question.

Jason, the man who told me he was bad, is far from it. He is my hero, my savior, my love, and now my home.

In his arms, I am safe. His past is just that. He is no monster—not in the dark, not in the light. He was raised in a way that it would be expected, but he was stronger than his past. He broke those chains. No, he shattered them, and then he helped me. No, he forced me to do the same.

We were both damaged. We are no more. We have scars and memories that will fade in time and the light. No more hiding in the darkness.

No more.

We now live.

I stand in the bathroom at the pediatric office where I now work in always sunny Florida. Jason suggested I work somewhere where death is not inevitable but where life surrounds me.

There is a knock on the bathroom door. "You okay in there?" It is Dr. Laura.

I open the door and smile as I walk out. "I am great, actually."

"You sure? Sometimes, news like this can be overwhelming." She gives me a shoulder hug as we walk past reception, and I realize everyone has gone for the day.

"I'm sorry I held you up," I tell her, grabbing my coat and purse.

"No hold up at all." She hands me a paper bag as we walk toward the door leading outside. "Have a great weekend."

I pull into the garage where Jason is pacing. I know he worries when I am even a few minutes late, even if he doesn't want to. It's not going to change anytime soon, especially now.

I sit back and look at him. His hair is less spiky now, it's wavier and softer. His after-shower look is incredibly sexy.

He tilts his head to the side, and his beautiful green eyes narrow a bit. Then he juts his head forward as his palms turn up. He has no idea what I am doing, and for some reason, that makes me laugh.

He walks over and opens the door to the car. "Lo, you're late."

I can't help laughing harder.

"I sure am."

He sighs and squats down. "You're home now."

The concern in his expression somehow begs me to calm down. I don't want him to think I'm regressing, because I'm not.

"We're home," I say, taking his face in my hands and kissing him.

"Mm . . ." he moans, leaning in and taking control of the kiss just like I need, want, and desire.

After a few moments, I pull back and rub my thumb up his jaw. "I am late. Very, very, very late, and until today, I didn't realize just how late."

He looks at me curiously, and I smile and nod.

"I threw up—"

He immediately brings his hand to my forehead. "You should be resting."

"I threw up, and then realized how late I am."

He shakes his head, clearly not understanding what I'm saying.

I take his hand and hold it to my stomach. "I am late."

"Let's get you inside. I'll make you some soup and—"

"No, Jason." I reach over and grab the bag sitting in the seat next to me then hand it to him. "A gift . . . of sorts."

He opens it immediately, needing answers. My love is not all that patient. That is surely about to change.

He pulls out the long, narrow, rectangular plastic stick and looks at it. "Is this . . . ?"

"Yes." I wrap my arms around him and hug him.

"Lo," he sighs. "We're going to have—"

"A baby." I pull back, wanting to see his reaction.

His face is blank before he swallows hard. For a moment, I second-guess myself. He may need more time to get used to the idea.

When he closes his eyes tightly, a tear falls then another and another. I kiss them away.

He pulls me out of the car and holds me securely against him.

"You're happy," I tell him. "You're going to be such a good father, Jason."

My feet leave the ground as he spins me in a circle, laughing like I was minutes ago.

My feet hit the ground, and he grabs each side of my face.

"Angel." He gets choked up again and kisses me gently, softly, lovingly, and then sighs. "I'm going to be the best father in the universe."

"I know you are."

"I—" He clears his throat and smiles. "I want a dozen."

I smile back. "Let's start with one."

"I'm serious, Lo. We're going to have so many kids. We're gonna show them what home is, what love is."

I nod. "Yes, we are."

"Nobody loves like we do, Lo. Nobody."

"I love our love."

"There's no deeper out there."

I lean in to kiss him, but he leans back. "Is there a chance two may be in there?" He puts his hand on my belly and kneels down in front of me, inching my scrub top up.

I giggle as he looks at my stomach, no doubt wishing he had X-ray vision.

"There is a possibility, but—"

"I think I see two," he says before kissing my tummy, making me squirm. "Hold still." He leans back on his heels and shakes his head. "Hey, it's your father. I don't know you yet, but I love you so damn much." A tear falls as he leans his head against my tummy. "Your mom and I have broken free of the chains that held us. We are stronger than ever because we stand together, so strong. I am the man I have always wanted to be because of her. I am going to be an even better man for you."

Tears fall freely down my face as he looks up. "We're their home, angel."

I nod as he stands and hugs me. "I love you so much, Jason."

"I know, Lo. I love you as much." He holds me tight, and I know without a doubt that our life will continue getting better and better every day.

The End

Something Special
BONUS SCENE

The Longest Fight

Hair damp and sticking to her blotchy skin, she's finally resting.

My Lo, is a beautiful mess.

She fought so damn hard, harder than I ever have in my life. Harder than I ever did in the ring, on the streets, against my father or against my own demons.

Looking down at her long eye lashes fanning across her face, I still —after all this time— see an angel who's circumstance caused her to fight demons who did not overcome her. Instead, of letting them do so, she

Cupping the back of our boys head —a surprise, we didn't want to find out, and were sure was going to be a girl — and holding him tight to my chest, I lean over and push her hair away from her face before kissing her cheek rosy cheeks softly, not wanting to wake her.

Lo, fought so fucking hard the past twenty-four hours to do this the way she wanted to, *all natural and unassisted.*

Only had to tell her three times that asking for help to deliver our nine-pound baby wasn't a sign of weakness.

She hissed at me through a contraction and then cried as she told me, "I'm a nurse Jason, I know that. But." And then she stopped talking.

The inability to protect her from that pain, nearly shattered me, I knew damn well she saw it.

And she did.

Through her own pain, she saw mine. She's the only person who has been able to see that in me. *The only person I have never felt I didn't have to defend myself against. The only person who hasn't wanted something from me, to hurt me, or to take something away from me.*

My angel.

I hold her hand as I sit back and look down at our son who half an hour ago was pulled from her stomach, bloody and crying, now clean, pink, beautiful, and resting contently.

Pride swells in my chest, but love overtakes it's venom. "I promise never to look over or past you to get to something, because nothing is more important to me than you and your mother, and never will be. I promise you are not an object. I promise no one will ever strike out against you. I promise you'll be loved by an angel, protected by a lion. I love you son. I don't know if I deserve you, but I'll make sure that every day. You and your mother are my gifts, my salvation, and I will remember that every day."

I hear Lo sigh and look over as her eyes flutter open, and she smiles softly at me… us.

"Angel sleep," I plead softly. "You need to rest."

Clearing her throat, she turns to me as I lift her hand to my lips and brush them across her knuckles. I then stand and lay him on her chest. "He's beautiful. Perfect. Just like you."

She kisses the top of his head and wraps her arm around him protectively. "He's big and strong. He looks like you. He's perfect."

I smile down. "He opened his eyes. There all you. He needs a name."

"You just named him."

I cock my head to the side, confused and wondering just how much the pain meds are affecting her.

She squeezes my hand as she presses her lips to his head and whispers. "Isaiah." Still looking curiously at her she smiles and explains. "It means God's salvation."

Salvation is something I never imagined having. The road to redemption is not a smooth ride. My road to redemption is something I'll never let go of, these two are my rainbow after the storm. My woman and my son, present in this room with me. Everything I never thought I would ever have I hold so close.

My son. My reason to breathe. My saving grace. Once I was lost, but now I am found. I am the man I want to be today because my Lo had the strength to stand by me when many would have walked, no ran, away.

I'm not a perfect man. I have made more mistakes than most. Some of them are truly unforgivable. The woman beside me, the woman I vow to give my best to, my all to, thank God she sees the good in me that I struggle to find for myself. Thankfully she loves me beyond the broken.

My Lo has given me my Isaiah.

In this I find peace. I have love, I have happiness. More than anything I've broken the cycle of pain.

Next on Redemption Road

READY FOR ANOTHER ANTI-HERO?

One Click Use Me Now!

Read Chapter One

USE ME

Chapter One

Legacy Gym

Present day

I look around the gym. The walls are black and mirrored, the floor is black cement covered in red mats. The back wall, where all our daily equipment is stored, is covered floor to ceiling in black lockers. Hand wraps, gloves, medicine balls, headgear, nut cups, first-aid equipment, and clothing that have our logo on them.

Our logo. I am a part of something. There was a time in the not so distant past when I wasn't sure I would ever be anything. There are still days I couldn't give a shit less if I do.

To the left are sparring mats and a few pieces of cardio equipment. To the right are free weights, a few high-end weight training machines, five heavy bags, seven speed bags, and five timing bags. In the middle is where I prefer to spend my time and energy. The cage.

I look at the large clock hanging above the doorway to

our office. Nine-thirty at night. That means I have been here for thirteen and a half hours.

Eight hours would send a normal man my age running home to his family, to a hot meal, or to a bar where he could have a drink and relax with his friends. I am not a normal man.

Normal men don't have blood on their hands, and if they do, they have it with remorse in their hearts, or the blood came from fighting a greater cause. The blood on my hands came from an anger that took control, from the rage within me, a rage that still controls me.

"Put one foot in front of the other. Stand tall and proud. Make the decision that you are both of those things and never let them think any differently. You are a good man, a good kid. Your past doesn't define you; your present and future do." Shaw, my father's oldest and closest friend, words ring inside my head as I look at the picture of him, Jagger, and I hanging on the wall, illuminated by bright white up-lighting.

If only putting one foot in front of the other wasn't so hard. The weight of the world is heavy on my neck, making holding my head high almost impossible.

Shaw believed in me when I didn't believe in myself. Now Shaw is gone.

After killing the lights and locking the doors, I let out a breath and walk toward the door in the back left-hand corner of the gym that leads to my apartment upstairs.

I stand in the apartment above Legacy, a gym that Jagger Caldwell and I inherited. A gym that trains people like me. It was willed to us when Shaw's fight with cancer ended.

I suppose he did it to make sure his promise to his best friend, my father, was kept. He made sure I had something, an income, a place to live—a piece of something tangible while I served out my parole sentence for a crime I committed eight years ago.

Honestly, it feels more like a curse, a cage, a confined space, than a new beginning.

My body aches. It's bruised and sore, all feelings I not only accept, but embrace. The harder I push myself, the more men I get in the cage with to train, the more hits I take, the closer I get to controlling the fury that simmers just beneath a boiling point inside my soul.

I walk to the bathroom and stand in front of the distressed mirror above the small sink that is rust-stained from the constant drip of a faucet that I keep telling myself I will fix, but I have no intention or desire to do so.

I strip off my sweat-drenched clothes and turn toward the shower to start the water. It takes a good five minutes for it to heat enough for my liking, and while I wait, I brush my teeth and open the cabinet.

I stare at the last bottle of pain meds prescribed to Shaw. I pocketed them after he died when the rage became worse. It is a battle of wills to tame the beast inside me. Waking up and looking in the mirror, knowing what I did and why I did it.

I twist off the childproof cap and count as I dump the pills out into my hand. Twelve. I have twelve nights left to sleep, and then the nightmares will ensue. I make a mental note to space the pills out to every third day. I can do without sleep for that long, no more.

I let them fall one by one back into the bottle, except one, as I feel my exhausted body become tense again. Anxiety is starting to creep in, so I take the last pill in my hand, toss it in my mouth, and swallow it down.

Before the pill's effects kick in, I get in the small shower and bend so the water falls over my head instead of hitting the middle of my shoulders. When the water starts to run cold and I feel a bit drowsy, I step out, towel my hair lightly, and then drop it to the floor, allowing my body to air dry. Then I look up at my reflection and see a man who looks much older than his twenty-five years.

My eyes, once bright green and alive, are now dead and unreflective of feeling. My hair, once cut close to my scalp by my father's own hand, is now well past my shoulders and a mess of brown waves. It's only down after a shower or bedtime; otherwise, it is always tied up in a knot on the back of my head. I don't have any damn desire to go to the barber. That would mean I would have to talk to someone. I'm functioning just fine here without making those types of connections, and there is no appeal in changing that up.

I run my hand over my beard. It's been three days since I last groomed. I shave every fourth or fifth day, but never down to the skin.

I am six-foot, five-inches of intimidation. I weigh in at two hundred and forty-eight pounds of muscle, and my skin is covered in black prison ink. I have no desire for anyone to look at me and become confused as to who I am. No desire to have someone look at me and want to know more about me. I have no desire for anything but the occasional release I can get anywhere. All I have to do is force a smile and say a word or two in order to get that need met.

My appearance is intimidating. It keeps people away. I'm not trying to give off the illusion that I'm unapproachable. Illusion would imply it wasn't real.

It is real.

I am Michelangelo Mazzini. I was once called a saint by my peers, my teachers, and anyone who knew me.

Not anymore.

Now I am known as Kid.

I lay on the king-sized mattress that sits in the middle

of the floor and stare at the ceiling, waiting, waiting, waiting for sleep to take me. The numbness that is my life isn't holding me back. Rather, it's my mind that won't turn off, waiting for the next move.

I try not to close my eyes on my own. I wait for exhaustion and the drugs to do the work for me. Otherwise, I will be fighting a losing battle.

***

One Click Use Me Now!

Chelsea Camaron

USA Today and *Wall Street Journal* bestselling author Chelsea Camaron is a small-town Carolina girl with a big imagination. She's a wife and mom, chasing her dreams. She writes contemporary romance, romantic suspense, and romance thrillers. She loves to write about blue-collar men who have real problems with a fictional twist. From mechanics, bikers, oil riggers, smokejumpers, bar owners, and beyond she loves a strong hero who works hard and plays harder.

Check Out Chelsea's Website

Email Chelsea

Join Chelsea's reader group here

Sign Up For Chelsea's Newsletter

Check Out Chelsea's Social Media sites below

MJ Fields

MJ Fields is a USA Today bestselling author of contemporary and new adult romance novels. She lives in New York with her daughter and fur babies — a smoochie faced Newfie, Theo and diva / hell raiser Eleanor. When she's not locked away in the cave, she enjoys spending time with her family, listening to live music, watching theatre, attending sporting events, traveling, singing off key, dancing to her own beat, listening to audio books, and reading— of course.

Forever Steel!

Join MJ's mailing list:

MJ Fields
USA Today Bestselling Author
REAL. RAW. ROMANCE

Visit MJ's website here:

Follow MJ on social media

Other works by MJ Fields

MJ FIELDS

More From MJ & Chelsea
Caldwell Brothers Series:

Recommended Reading Order

Hendrix

Morrison

Jagger

Redemption Road:

Recommended Reading Order

Break Me

Use Me

The following books are available from all retailers and the first in each is ***FREE.***

The Norfolk Series
(Military Alpha Male Romance)

Irons 1

Irons 2

Irons 3

Shadows

Titan

* * *

Timeless Love series
(Billionaire /Age Gap Romance)
Unraveled
Deserving Me
Hearts So Big
Couture Love

Standalone Sports Romance
Offensive Rebound

THE BLUE VALLEY LEGACY SERIES
FAMILY OF BOOKS
(Recommended reading order)

The Blue Valley series
Tessa Ross
Blue Love
New Love
Sad Love
True Love
Or get the Box Set
Blue Valley

The Brody Hines series
(Emma Fields & Brody Hines)
Wrapped In Silk
Wrapped In Armor
Wrapped In Us
Or get the Box Set
The Brody Hines series

The Burning Souls series

(Maddox & Harper)

Stained

Forged

Merged

Or get the Box Set

The Burning Souls series

LYA leads to more second generation books

Love You Anyway

More from the Ross Family?

The Way We Fell

(Kendalls story)

Coming in Winter 2023

The Way We Met

(Phoebe's Story)

The Way We Love

(Jade's Story)

The Truth About Love duet

(Ava Links)

27 truths

27 Lies

Or get the Box Set

The Truth About Love

The Firsts series

(London Fields)

Her First Kiss

His First Crush

Their First fall

27 Truths About Their First Goodbye

Their First Time

Or get the Box Set
The First Series

* * *

THE STEEL WORLDS
(Recommended reading order)
The Men of Steel Series
Jase
Cyrus
Zandor
Xavier
Forever Family
Raising Steel
Or get the
Men Of Steel complete box set

The Ties of Steel Series
Abe
Dominic
Eroe
Sabato
Or get the
Ties of Steel complete box set

The Rockers of Steel Series
Memphis Black
Finn Beckett
River James
Billy Jeffers
Or get the
Rockers of Steel complete box set

The Match Duet

Match This!
ImPerfectly Matched!
Or get the
complete duet

The Steel Country Series
Hammered
Destroyed
Wasted
Or get the
Steel Country complete box set

Tied in Steel series
Valentina
Paige
Gia
Or get the
Tied in Steel complete box set

Steel Crew
(Men of Steel generation 2)
Tagged Steel
Branded Steel
Laced Steel
Justified Steel
Tricked Steel
Busted Steel
Smashed Steel
Marked Steel
Maxed Steel

West Side
(Ties of Steel generation 2)
No Mercy

Other Works By Chelsea Camaron

Love and Repair Series:

Crash and Burn

Restore My Heart

Salvaged

Full Throttle

Beyond Repair

Stalled

Box Set Available

Hellions Ride Series:

One Ride

Forever Ride

Merciless Ride

Eternal Ride

Innocent Ride

Simple Ride

Heated Ride

Ride with Me (Hellions MC and Ravage MC Duel with Ryan Michele)

Originals Ride

Final Ride

Hellions Ride On Series:

Hellions Ride On Prequel

Born to It

Bastard in It

Bleed for It

Beauty in It

Breathe for It

Bold from It

Blue Collar Bad Boys Series:

Maverick

Heath

Lance

Wendol

Reese

Devil's Due MC Series:

Serving My Soldier

Crossover

In The Red

Below The Line

Close The Tab

Day of Reckoning

Paid in Full

Bottom Line

Almanza Crime Family Duet

Cartel Bitch

Cartel Queen

Romantic Thriller Series:

Stay

Seeking Solace: Angelina's Restoration

Reclaiming Me: Fallyn's Revenge

Bad Boys of the Road Series:

Mother Trucker

Panty Snatcher

Azzhat

Santa, Bring Me a Biker!

Santa, Bring Me a Baby!

Stand Alone Reads:

Romance – Moments in Time Anthology

Shenanigans (Currently found in the Beer Goggles Anthology

She is …

The following series are co-written

The Fire Inside Series:

(co-written by Theresa Marguerite Hewitt)

Kale

Regulators MC Series:

(co-written by Jessie Lane)

Ice

Hammer

Coal

Summer of Sin Series:

(co-written with Ripp Baker, Daryl Banner, Angelica Chase, MJ Fields, MX King)

Original Sin

Caldwell Brothers Series:

(co-written by USA Today Bestselling Author MJ Fields)

Hendrix

Morrison

Jagger

Stand Alone Romance:

(co-written with USA Today Bestselling Author MJ Fields)

Break Me

Use Me

Ruthless Rebels MC Series:

(co-written with Ryan Michele)

Shamed

Scorned

Scarred

Schooled

Box Set Available

Power Chain Series:

(co-written with Ryan Michele)

Power Chain FREE eBook

PowerHouse

Power Player

Powerless

Made in the USA
Columbia, SC
20 December 2024

50222123R00178